Highlander Sworn

Courageous Highland Hearts
Book Four

JAYNE CASTEL

WINTER MIST PRESS

Highlander Sworn, by Jayne Castel

Published by Winter Mist Press

ISBN: 978-1-99-117471-0 (paperback)

Edited by Tim Burton
Cover design by Winter Mist Press
Cover photography courtesy of www.shutterstock.com
Dagger vector image courtesy of www.pixabay.com

Visit Jayne's website: www.jaynecastel.com

Letting her instincts rule could mean her ruin. A prisoner, a clan-chief's daughter, and an impossible love.

Beautiful yet flighty, Eilidh Munro has caught a chieftain's eye—but it's not him she wants. Instead, she longs for the enigmatic Gunn hostage, who works the fields by day and is locked away in the dungeons beneath her keep at night.

Will Gunn has never understood the influence women wield over men: he lives on his terms, and no one else's. And right now, he's focused on gaining his freedom and returning home to his kin.

Yet Will finds himself distracted by visits from the lovely Eilidh. The raw, fierce connection between them can't be denied.

When the shadow of war falls across the Highlands, and the Mackay clan-chief sets Will free, Eilidh is elated. Finally, they could have a future together.

But how much does she really know about the man she's fallen for?

HIGHLANDER SWORN is Book Four of the Courageous Highland Hearts series. This steamy and emotional follow-up to Jayne Castel's bestselling Stolen Highland Hearts series follows the lives of four battle-hardened Highland warriors and the courageous sisters who capture their hearts.

Historical Romances by Jayne Castel

DARK AGES BRITAIN

The Kingdom of the East Angles series
Night Shadows (prequel novella)
Dark Under the Cover of Night (Book One)
Nightfall till Daybreak (Book Two)
The Deepening Night (Book Three)
The Kingdom of the East Angles: The Complete Series

The Kingdom of Mercia series
The Breaking Dawn (Book One)
Darkest before Dawn (Book Two)
Dawn of Wolves (Book Three)
The Kingdom of Mercia: The Complete Series

The Kingdom of Northumbria series
The Whispering Wind (Book One)
Wind Song (Book Two)
Lord of the North Wind (Book Three)
The Kingdom of Northumbria: The Complete Series

DARK AGES SCOTLAND

The Warrior Brothers of Skye series
Blood Feud (Book One)
Barbarian Slave (Book Two)
Battle Eagle (Book Three)
The Warrior Brothers of Skye: The Complete Series

The Pict Wars series
Warrior's Heart (Book One)
Warrior's Secret (Book Two)
Warrior's Wrath (Book Three)
The Pict Wars: The Complete Series

On the Empire's Edge Duet
Taming the Eagle

Novellas
Winter's Promise

MEDIEVAL SCOTLAND

The Brides of Skye series
The Beast's Bride (Book One)
The Outlaw's Bride (Book Two)
The Rogue's Bride (Book Three)
The Brides of Skye: The Complete Series

The Sisters of Kilbride series
Unforgotten (Book One)
Awoken (Book Two)
Fallen (Book Three)
Claimed (Epilogue novella)
The Sisters of Kilbride: The Complete Series

The Immortal Highland Centurions series
Maximus (Book One)
Cassian (Book Two)
Draco (Book Three)
The Laird's Return (Epilogue festive novella)
The Immortal Highland Centurions: The Complete Series

Stolen Highland Hearts series
Highlander Deceived (Book One)
Highlander Entangled (Book Two)
Highlander Forbidden (Book Three)
Highlander Pledged (Book Four)

Guardians of Alba series
Nessa's Seduction (Book One)
Fyfa's Sacrifice (Book Two)
Breanna's Surrender (Book Three)

Courageous Highland Hearts series
Highlander Defied (Book One)
Highlander Tempted (Book Two)
Highlander Healed (Book Three)
Highlander Sworn (Book Four)

Epic Fantasy Romances by Jayne Castel

Light and Darkness series
Ruled by Shadows (Book One)
The Lost Swallow (Book Two)
Path of the Dark (Book Three)
Light and Darkness: The Complete Series

***

For my readers—your love of these stories means so much to me.

And for my wonderful husband, Tim, whose tireless support and enthusiasm just add to the joy of being a storyteller.

***

Pronunciation note

The heroine of this novel is called **Eilidh**.
Her name is pronounced *Ay-lee*

A huge thank you to Mary Alderson, who provided the
name for the youngest Munro sister!

"What's yours will find you."
—*Unknown*

1

LIKE A MOTH TO A BLAZING FLAME

Castle Varrich
Strathnaver, Scotland

Mid-August, 1439

EILIDH MUNRO WAS returning home from a ride when she spied him.

It was a bonnie evening, for the wind had died to a whisper, and the lowering sun cast a golden veil over the rolling hills beneath Castle Varrich. Warm light also gilded the rugged walls of the fortress and made the distant slopes of Ben Loyal and Ben Hope stand out in sharp relief against the lilac sky.

Nonetheless, Eilidh found it difficult to focus on her surroundings. Instead, butterflies fluttered in her belly as she surveyed the fields.

These days—whenever she ventured out of the keep, usually to walk into nearby Tongue village or exercise her pony—she looked for the prisoner.

This evening was no exception.

She longed for a glimpse of him—the man who'd taken up too much space in her head of late.

And there he was.

The cottars were finishing work for the day, hoisting their tools over their shoulders and trudging home for a well-earned meal and rest. However, William Gunn didn't join the farmers as they headed back to Tongue.

Instead, he turned and crossed the fields, making his way toward the dungeon at the base of the rocky promontory where Castle Varrich perched.

Eilidh's gaze tracked him, and her breathing grew shallow.

Why did he fascinate her so? The man was unkempt, filthy. She shouldn't find him attractive, and yet her pulse raced every time she saw him.

William Gunn was far removed from the comfortable, safe world she inhabited.

Ever since Neave and Jean—who'd once been her constant companions—had left Varrich, Eilidh had become more solitary, going out for rides alone and getting lost in her own thoughts for hours on end. The youngest of four daughters, she'd always been dependent on her sisters, but these days, she felt rudderless, lonely. Who was she without them? Aye, she still had Beth, yet they'd started to clash recently. Her eldest sister seemed intent on clipping her wings.

But Gunn represented freedom and risk. He had an edge to him that made excitement quicken within her. Eilidh was tired of safety. She wanted to taste a little danger.

Despite that Gunn had been outdoors for most of the day—weeding, planting, and preparing the soil—he walked tall. Yet his gait was slow, thanks to the heavy shackles he wore around his ankles. The clank of iron drifted toward Eilidh, and she slowed her pony's pace.

Gunn's route took him across the stony path and directly in front of her—and as he drew near, the prisoner's gaze settled upon her.

Holding his eye, Eilidh drew up Gypsie, and for a long moment, she and Gunn merely stared at each other.

The intensity of the moment reminded her of the only other time their paths had crossed. Three months earlier, the wind had ripped a shawl from Eilidh's shoulders during a walk into Tongue. She'd chased the shawl across the fields, but it had blown straight into William Gunn's arms. And then, just as now, she'd been drawn into his gaze, captivated by its smoky depths. Gunn had eyes the color of a stormy sky, grey with a hint of purple. Eilidh was entranced.

During their last meeting, Eilidh's sister Jean had interrupted her reverie, but Jean now resided at Melness Broch with her husband, Robin Mackay. Today Eilidh was alone—and so was he. It surprised her the dungeon guards didn't go out to the fields to retrieve him. Gunn had been a Mackay prisoner for two years now, and he and his guards had clearly gotten into a routine of sorts.

"It's Eilidh, isn't it?" Gunn broke the silence between them, his mouth lifting at the corners in the slightest of smiles.

Eilidh's breathing hitched.

Ay lee—she liked the way he drew out her name in a soft, sensual roll.

He remembers my name.

Favoring him with a shy smile, Eilidh nodded.

"It's a fine evening for a ride," he continued. His voice was low and smooth, beguiling.

"Aye," she replied, finding her tongue. "It seemed a pity to stay indoors." She gestured behind her. "The kyle is lovely with the tide in." In fact, the waters of the wide sound were glassy, reflecting the surrounding mountains and sky. But the only thing she could focus on was him.

Gunn's mouth curved, his eyes crinkling at the corners. Indeed, he was a wild-looking individual with his ragged, sweat-stained lèine and braies; long, tangled dark hair; and equally wild beard. All the same, there was something about this man that drew Eilidh to him like a moth to a blazing flame.

"Ye are one of the Munro sisters, are ye not?" he asked after a moment.

"Aye ... I'm the youngest," she admitted. Once again, a wave of nervousness swept over her. She was keenly aware of him, despite that they stood a few yards apart. She shouldn't be talking to the prisoner—should dig her heels into Gypsie's flanks and ride past him—but Eilidh did no such thing. Instead, she drank William Gunn in.

"I hear the clan-chief has taken to visiting ye regularly?" she asked when it became clear he was comfortable with the yawning silence between them. She didn't really know what to say and was suddenly self-conscious. Her kirtle was dusty, and her hair knotted into a messy bun. She resisted the urge to reach up and tidy her hair. Such a move would look vain and a trifle foolish.

Gunn was a prisoner after all. She shouldn't care what he thought of her.

His storm-grey eyes glinted. "Aye ... he brings an Ard-ri board with him sometimes too."

Eilidh smiled, pleased to hear that Niel Mackay made such an effort with his prisoner. Time was when the clan-chief would have run the youngest of the Gunn brothers through with his claidheamh-mòr rather than exchange two words with him. Willingly spending time with a Gunn was once unthinkable.

But Niel had changed—and his wife was largely responsible. The connection Niel and Beth shared was powerful indeed—so powerful that Eilidh sometimes felt a little envious of her.

All three of her sisters were wives to men who adored them. All eyes were on her now, for only *she* remained unwed. Over the past months, Beth had pestered her to choose someone, although her insistence had just made Eilidh dig her heels in.

She'd not be rushed into the most important decision of her life.

"And who wins most of the games?" she asked.

William Gunn pulled a face. "He does ... although that'll change soon enough. I'm out of practice, that's all."

"Gunn!" An irritated male voice rumbled across the road. "Stop flapping yer tongue at the lady and get in here."

Tensing, Eilidh glanced right at where a hauberk-clad guard stood at the entrance to the dungeons.

"Keep yer hide on, Craig," Gunn drawled. His lips twisted into a harsh grin. "Missing me, are ye?"

"Shut yer mouth," the guard muttered. "Or ye shall get a kicking."

They were strong words, yet there was little force to Craig's voice. It seemed to Eilidh that the pair were merely bantering.

Favoring Eilidh with a nod, Gunn crossed the road. "A good eve to ye, Lady Eilidh," he murmured.

Eilidh's gaze tracked his departure. "Goodbye," she breathed.

William Gunn entered the dark recesses of the dungeon, and Eilidh roused herself, nudging Gypsie into a swift trot.

Anxiety fluttered through her, quickening her pulse.

God's blood, it was just as well Jean hadn't witnessed that exchange too. The last time Eilidh and Gunn had crossed paths, Jean had told her off for staring at the prisoner so brazenly. She'd warned her that nothing good could come of such behavior.

Aye, her sister would have been vexed to see Eilidh meet William Gunn's eye so boldly and engage the prisoner in conversation.

Mouth compressing, Eilidh turned her garron right, onto the path that wound up the promontory to where the castle perched.

As much as she missed Jean, she didn't need her censure. She didn't need any of her elder sisters telling her what to do.

If I wish to talk to him, I shall.

Gypsie doggedly made her way up the steep track, and Eilidh leaned forward to ease the pony's way.

She'd stayed out later than she'd realized, and the sky was beginning to dim, streamers of purple and pink arching overhead. Breathing in the grass-scented air, Eilidh smiled. She was indeed glad she'd taken a ride this evening.

Clip-clopping into the bailey, she reined in her pony in front of the stables. Swinging down from the saddle, she was about to lead Gypsie indoors, when a male voice hailed her. "There ye are, Lady Eilidh."

Stiffening, Eilidh glanced over her shoulder, her gaze alighting on the tall, broad-shouldered man approaching. Her breathing grew shallow, not from excitement as when she'd spied William Gunn, but alarm.

Iver Mackay was oblivious to her reaction. He was smiling, his dark-blue eyes warm.

The chieftain of Dun Ugadale was attractive; there was no denying it. His mane of white-blond hair and height made him stand out in a crowd. Iver was young, around her age, yet he ruled the southern branch of the Mackays—a branch of the clan that resided upon the Kintyre peninsula farther south.

Over the last year, Iver had started to show an increasing interest in Eilidh whenever he visited Castle Varrich. At present, he was attending a clan meeting. Two or three times a year, Niel called all his chieftains to him, and they were currently discussing their deteriorating relationship with the Sutherlands.

When Iver wasn't involved in discussions with the other chieftains, he sought Eilidh out, ensuring he sat next to her at mealtimes. This eve, she'd deliberately taken her supper in the women's solar to avoid him.

"Good eve, Iver," she replied with a polite smile.

Why was she avoiding him?

Iver was most women's dream. She was a clan-chief's daughter and he a chieftain: it would be a fine match for them both.

However, as handsome as the young laird of Dun Ugadale was, it wasn't *his* face that Eilidh thought of as she lay abed at night. It wasn't *his* voice that rumbled in her ears. Instead of dark-blue eyes, she dreamed of storm-grey ones.

She wasn't sure how old William Gunn was, around thirty perhaps. It was difficult to tell with his unkempt hair and beard—but he held the authority and confidence that men only gained with age.

Despite his imposing build, Iver seemed an eager pup in contrast.

Drawing near, Iver halted. "Would ye like me to stable yer pony for ye?"

"That's kind of ye," Eilidh replied, still smiling, "but I like seeing to Gypsie." It was true—she enjoyed rubbing down the garron's sleek chestnut summer coat and murmuring endearments to her as she worked. Her father had given each of his daughters a sturdy pony years earlier. Gypsie had been with Eilidh a while now, and she spent a lot of time with her. She wasn't a skilled horsewoman like Beth and Neave, yet her rides out brought her much joy.

Iver nodded, although his smile dimmed, just a little. "Very well." His gaze roamed over Eilidh's face. "I'm surprised ye ride out alone … surely, it would be wise to bring an escort with ye?"

Irritation spiked through Eilidh. She'd already had this discussion with Niel. She hated riding out shadowed by guards. Although she often felt a little lonely these days, it was difficult to relax with an escort dogging her steps. He hadn't been pleased by her insistence yet had relented in the end.

"I stay close to the keep," she explained, her tone cooling. "And the clan-chief allows it."

Iver's smile faded. "Sorry if I offended ye … I was just showing concern for yer well-being."

"And that's appreciated," Eilidh replied quickly. "But ye needn't worry."

Iver nodded. He hesitated then, clearing his throat, and she realized he was nervous. Iver was usually confident to the point of arrogance—yet this evening, she had him on the back foot. "Would ye take a cup of wine with me … after ye have seen to yer pony?" he asked after a pause.

Eilidh's first instinct was to refuse. She didn't usually drink wine this late in the day—and didn't wish to encourage Iver in his wooing.

But the boyish hope in his eyes made the words turn to ashes on her tongue.

No, Iver wasn't the man she daydreamed about, wasn't the man she'd just crossed paths with, yet that wasn't his fault. She couldn't crush his hopes under the heel of her boot.

A cup of wine wouldn't hurt.

"Of course," she murmured. "I shall join ye in the great hall shortly."

Iver flashed her another smile, his confidence restored. Stepping back, he allowed her to lead Gypsie away toward the stables. "I shall await ye there, Lady Eilidh."

2

A GAME OF STRATEGY

"YER MOVE."

WILLIAM Gunn glanced up from where he'd been studying the board before him and cocked an eyebrow. "I'm aware of that."

The Mackay clan-chief held his gaze. "Good to hear … I was beginning to think ye'd gone to sleep."

Will snorted. "I was thinking."

Niel leaned back and folded his arms across his chest. "Well, hurry up, man … I'm getting a numb arse sitting here."

Will shrugged, shifting his attention once more to the wooden board. A grid had been carved into the polished oak, and several counters—some black, others white—lay scattered across it.

The two men—clan-chief and prisoner—sat inside Will's cramped, damp cell. A lantern burned upon the wall above them, illuminating their game of Ard-ri— High King. If someone had told Will a year ago that Niel Mackay would end up visiting him every couple of days to sit and play Ard-ri with him, he'd have laughed in their face.

But here he was, deliberating over his next move while nursing a tankard of ale. The Mackay always brought down clean tankards and a skin of ale, mead, or wine for them to share while they played.

It was funny how life could surprise one.

The first time Niel had appeared in the passage outside his cell, Will had longed to be able to slam his fist through the bars and flatten his patrician nose to a pulp.

The hatred between the Mackays and the Gunns was longstanding, and it ran deep on both sides. The last battle had ended in a crushing defeat for the Gunns. Will should have died in that skirmish before the ruins of an ancient fort upon the beach, but the Mackays had taken him prisoner instead.

He'd lost track of time here, although his work in the fields allowed him to mark the passing of the seasons, at least. His days were drudgery, a back-breaking repetition of the same tasks.

And yet he still allowed the Mackay into his cell—and these days, he actually looked forward to their games of Ard-ri.

Nonetheless, he never lost sight of who they both were. A Mackay and a Gunn, sparring.

Leaning forward, Will moved one of his counters. As usual, after a tense exchange, the game had shifted in Niel's favor. However, this time, it had taken Niel much longer to gain the advantage.

Will's strategy was improving. One day, he'd beat the bastard.

But not today. Will had stared at that infernal board, his gaze circling over each of his counters, looking for a way to prevent Niel from making a winning move. Yet there was none; he'd just have to concede defeat.

The clan-chief flashed Will a smug grin. "Victory is mine." With that, he moved his king to the edge of the board, signaling that he'd won the game. He'd played defender, while Will had been leading the attack with the aim of building a blockade around Niel's king.

Will snorted before lifting his tankard to his lips and draining the dregs. "One of these days, I'll vanquish ye," he muttered. "And when I do, I shall enjoy wiping that smirk off yer face."

Niel's smile widened. "I, too, look forward to that day … although ye might be grey-haired by then."

Will tensed. He then set down his tankard, his gaze settling upon the clan-chief. They often traded insults. It was under the guise of banter, yet some of the things they said to each other held a sting—as this one just had.

"If I continue to rot in this dungeon, I won't live to grow grey hairs."

Niel pulled a face. "Aye," he admitted. "Ye won't."

They both knew this life would wear him out. If his body didn't give out from overuse, sickness would end him one winter.

The moment drew out before Will met Niel's eye. "So … is this a life sentence, Mackay?"

It wasn't the first time he'd asked the question over the past months. What prisoner didn't want to know if he'd eventually die in his squalid cell? Bitterness filled Will's mouth every time he imagined his future.

Summer was almost over, and soon they'd begin the steady slide into autumn and then the bitter months. The thought of a third winter in this dungeon filled Will with dread. He considered himself brave—he was a Gunn, and their father had beaten any softness out of his sons—but the cold that drilled into the marrow of his bones was cruel indeed.

Niel's expression veiled. "I don't know," he replied after a pause. "It depends."

"On what?" Heat ignited in the pit of Will's stomach as his anger quickened. God's teeth, he hated being at this man's mercy.

"Yer brother."

Will's mouth pursed. "Has Tavish been stirring up trouble?"

"No." Reaching out, Niel cleared the counters off the board, depositing them into a pouch. "But that doesn't mean he won't."

"It's been a while now, Mackay," Will growled, striving, and failing, not to let his burgeoning anger show. "How much more proof do ye need that he'll keep the peace?"

The clan-chief didn't reply. He merely rose to his feet and picked up the Ard-ri board, the empty skin of ale, and the two tankards. A moment later, he moved to the locked, iron-barred gate. "I'm ready," he called out.

Will glared at him. Niel took a risk every time he visited him here. Aye, Will's ankles were shackled, but his hands were free.

Yet the Mackay didn't show the slightest fear of him—and his supreme self-confidence warned Will against trying to attack him.

It was a move he could only make once.

The heavy thud of booted feet approached, and one of the guards appeared, a ring of iron keys rattling upon his belt. As the guard unlocked the gate, Niel swung back, his gaze fixing upon Will. "I know what it's like," he said softly. His expression was still inscrutable, yet the shadow in his eyes gave him away. "Those ten years at Bass Rock nearly broke me ... the monotony ... the cold." He paused then, his mouth lifting at the corners. "Just be grateful we let ye outdoors every day ... the only sky I saw for a decade was a tiny strip outside a high window."

Will stared back at him. Of course, he knew of Niel's history, of the years he'd spent locked away in the island prison of Bass Rock at the king's behest. His father had betrayed him—offered Niel up to save his own neck. When Niel finally escaped, he'd been looking for vengeance, and he'd taken it against his enemies. The Gunns.

Will was surprised the man hadn't been eaten up by hate and bitterness, but over the past months, he'd noted that the clan-chief appeared at ease, happy.

"Is that why ye visit me here then?" Will asked, his tone deliberately goading. "Ye miss the squalor of prison life?"

Niel flashed him a wolfish smile. "Perhaps ... or maybe I just want to beat ye at Ard-ri." He nodded to Will then before stepping through the gate. Iron clanged as the guard slammed it shut, the key grating in the lock.

3

HONEY CAKES

STILL SEATED UPON the stool before the low table, where they'd been playing the board game, Will watched as the clan-chief and guard departed, swallowed up by the gloom inside the passageway.

A short while later, he was alone with only the whisper of his breathing and the steady drip of water in the corner of his cell for company.

Muttering a curse, Will rose to his feet, shackles rattling, and moved to the gate. Reaching out, he fastened his fingers around the cold bars. Even though it was late summer, the heat didn't reach in here, deep inside the tunnels and cells under Castle Varrich. The air was heavy with damp and the musty odor of mildew.

At least, as soon as the sun rose, the guards would fetch him and take him out to the fields to work alongside the cottars. It was back-breaking toil, and the heavy shackles around his ankles hampered movement. Nonetheless, it was infinitely preferable to remaining in this foul hole.

Will closed his eyes, his grip upon the bars tightening as a crushing wave of desperation crashed over him. He needed to escape this place, to return to his clan—to his kin.

Aye, his situation could have been much worse. He'd nearly died during his first winter—of a lung sickness—and would have perished already if his living conditions hadn't improved. Now, the guards brought him roast meat, cheese, and bread to eat alongside his porridge.

They also ensured he had clean, comfortable blankets upon his sleeping pallet.

But whenever Will thought of the freedom the Mackays had stolen from him, his throat clenched.

Memories of Castle Gunn—his clan stronghold—flitted across his mind then: the view from the keep's rooftop terrace out to sea on a clear day; the barking of the Highland collies as they rounded up sheep on the rolling green hills west of the castle; and the sight of Robina's goshawks circling above the keep, scanning for prey.

Robina was his brother Tavish's wife. When she'd come to live at Castle Gunn, she'd brought her hawks with her. Robina and Tavish often went hawking together. The couple had four sons now, so there were no concerns about succession.

And then there was Allison.

The fine memories of his home shattered like ice under a heavy mallet.

Will's eyes snapped open, and he grimaced.

Aye, as much as he longed for home, life at Castle Gunn wasn't idyllic.

But then, it never had been.

He looked down at his chafed, calloused hands then. They didn't look like the hands of a clan-chief's son. Life had indeed dragged him low, yet there were some things about Varrich that brought rays of much-needed sunshine into his life.

Will's expression softened, his mouth curving.

Eilidh Munro was one of them.

He'd marked her over a year earlier, walking with her sisters into the nearby village—it was impossible not to, with her gamine beauty. However, they'd met properly for the first time earlier in the summer when a gust of wind had torn Eilidh's shawl from her shoulders—and brought it straight to him. Close up, the lass was even more beguiling. Both her hair and large eyes were the same color—of burnished oak—and her voice was soft and musical.

Will had plenty of time on his own in the evenings, and at night, when he'd lie upon his pallet and think. Often his thoughts led him to dark places, to regrets and resentments, but after meeting Eilidh, he found himself thinking about her.

And this evening, she lingered in his thoughts as well.

He'd seen her again the eve before when he'd been crossing the road back to the dungeon. She'd reined in her pony, those soulful brown eyes resting upon him with breathtaking frankness.

The lass was a contradiction: both guileless and knowing, playful and shy. He guessed her to be nearly a decade his junior. They were as different as two people could be—her pure with an almost ethereal beauty, and him disgraced, filthy, and in chains—but they had two things in common. Both their fathers were clan-chiefs, and they were both the youngest sibling in their families.

Breathing a curse, Will released his death-grip on the bars and moved across to his pallet, lowering himself onto it. He then dragged a hand down his face.

Instead of letting his thoughts drift to Eilidh Munro, like a moonstruck fool, he needed to use his wits to come up with an argument that would persuade Niel to release him.

The clan-chief literally held the key to his freedom.

They weren't friends—but as long as Niel continued to visit him, he had a chance of convincing him that holding Will prisoner no longer served his needs.

The Mackay was sharp and mercurial, not that different to Will himself in character. He wouldn't respond to trickery or manipulation. If he was to free Will, it would only be because it served him.

Just like Ard-ri, Will was playing a game of strategy. Unfortunately, he'd learned over the past months that Niel Mackay was a difficult man to beat.

"Thank ye for the cakes, Lorna." Eilidh picked up the basket, inhaling the buttery aroma of the baking wafting from it. "The poor of Tongue will indeed be grateful."

The older woman flashed her a distracted smile. "Ye are welcome, Lady Eilidh." Lorna then turned back to the stew she was tending. Around her, cooks and scullery maids hurried about, shouting at each other. The noon meal was about to be served.

Clutching the basket tightly, Eilidh backed away.

Time to leave, before someone enlists my help.

It had been a busy morning, and she'd worried she wouldn't get away. After making the request for honey cakes to Lorna first thing, Eilidh had attacked the pile of mending in the women's solar before hurrying down to pick up the baking.

She slipped out the kitchen door and into the bailey. Around her, warriors were making their way indoors to take their place at the long trestle tables inside the great hall.

Some of them greeted her, and Eilidh waved back as she made for the gates.

Her pulse started to race then. She should be inside, pouring wine for the clan-chief and his kin, before taking her place upon the dais. However, she was skipping the noon meal today.

Eilidh glanced around nervously, half expecting Beth to appear and call her back to the keep. She didn't like sneaking around, yet she'd found herself growing increasingly secretive of late. In keeping part of herself private, she was carving herself out a little independence from her sister.

With just the two of them left at Varrich, Beth had become even bossier than usual. Aye, she was chatelaine here, and Eilidh's eldest sister, but she wasn't her mistress.

Hugging the basket against her hip, Eilidh quickened her pace, hurrying down the winding path below the fortress. The basket was heavy, and she'd indeed take it to the village.

But first, she'd take a detour through the fields.

She wanted to walk through them while Will Gunn was taking a rest. That way, she could talk to him for a little longer than she had on the previous occasions their paths had crossed.

There were few folk about at this hour too—for most of the residents of Castle Varrich, and indeed Tongue village, were indoors eating their main meal of the day.

Eilidh surveyed the fields, and there, seated alone on the ground—for the cottars had all returned to the village for an hour or two—was Will Gunn.

Her heart leaped, nerves fluttering afresh.

All she'd been able to think about, since encountering Will on the road two evenings previous, was how to organize another meeting. In the meantime, the Mackay chieftains had all departed Varrich. Hopefully, Niel wouldn't be hosting another meeting for a while.

Iver had returned to his holding far to the south.

Guilt stabbed through Eilidh then. Beth had told her that the young chieftain had gone looking for her on the morning of his departure. But she'd deliberately hidden away in the chapel to avoid him.

It might have appeared cruel, yet it was for the best.

She didn't want Iver, and it would be wrong to encourage him.

Wiping damp palms on her skirts, Eilidh crossed the field toward the prisoner.

Glancing up from his food, Gunn spied her. An instant later, he stilled, his lean frame tensing.

Eilidh's step faltered.

It occurred to her then, how little she knew about men. Her three elder sisters were wedded and had known carnal intimacy. She felt silly and sheltered in their presence. Beth, Neave, and Jean all carried a worldly air about them now.

What if Gunn thought her a goose-witted chit? Eilidh knew she could come across as flighty at times. Perhaps she had misread the interest in his eyes two days earlier. What did she know about men anyway?

Forcing herself on, she closed the distance between them, taking the narrow path between rows of cabbages and kale. As she approached, Will put aside the bread and cheese he'd been eating and rose to his feet, chains clanking.

"Lady Eilidh," he greeted her, his mouth curving. "Greetings."

Bolstered by his warmth, Eilidh quickened her step and flashed him a smile. "Fine day to be outdoors, is it not?"

A brisk wind raced in from the kyle, although the sun was warm on Eilidh's face. The air out here was heavy with the scent of rich earth and growing things.

"It is," he replied, inclining his head. "Where are ye off to?"

"I have some honey cakes to deliver to the poor," she replied, halting before him. "But I thought I might share one with ye." She gestured to the meal he'd just abandoned. "Please … don't let me interrupt ye."

Will nodded, sinking to the ground with surprising grace, for the shackles didn't ease his movement.

Without hesitation, Eilidh followed suit, arranging her skirts around her.

When she glanced up at Will, she saw he wore a bemused expression. "Won't ye dirty that pretty kirtle?" he asked.

Warmth spread across Eilidh's chest. She'd taken great care when dressing that morning. She and her maid, Clara, had spread a selection of kirtles out on the bed before she'd eventually settled on a jade-green one.

"The ground is dry," she replied. "A little bit of dust won't matter."

Reaching forward, she removed the cloth one of the cooks had placed atop the basket of honey cakes. The sweet, heady aroma of baking drifted out, enveloping them.

Still smiling, Eilidh reached out and took a cake. "Help yerself."

She boldly held Will's gaze for a moment before taking a dainty bite.

An instant later, he grinned. The expression was both boyish and roguish. His teeth flashed white against the darkness of his beard.

Eilidh's belly flip-flopped. Although the cake was delicious, she suddenly lost her appetite for it. Despite her smiles and feigned confidence, she was all a jitter in this man's company.

Will finished his last bite of bread and cheese and reached for a cake.

Eilidh nibbled at her own while he wolfed his down. The man worked hard from dawn until dusk. She wasn't surprised that he had an appetite. She'd heard that Niel had instructed the prisoner to be brought heartier food, to ensure he didn't sicken. However, she imagined no one ever brought him honey cakes.

She was right, for a look of rapture suffused his face as he ate. When Will took his last mouthful, a sigh of pleasure gusted out of him. "That was good."

Pleasure glowed within Eilidh at his comment. "The recipe is my sister Beth's," she explained. "She's always been a talented cook ... although when she arrived at Varrich, she had a lot of work on her hands ... the food coming out of the kitchen wasn't the best." Her voice died away then, heat rising to her cheeks. Lord, she was babbling. This man made her nervous.

Will Gunn's gaze held hers. "And what of ye, Eilidh?" he asked, still smiling. "Are ye an able baker too?"

"I'm afraid not ... I can cook simple things, but whenever I try pastry, it turns out like leather. Beth says I 'overhandle' the dough." Eilidh broke off once more, silently cursing her nervous chatter. And when Will snorted a laugh, her cheeks started to burn. The man's grey eyes now glinted with mirth.

"What?" she demanded, slightly affronted.

"I don't think I've ever met anyone like ye, Eilidh Munro," he replied. His expression sobered then, although humor still shone in his gaze. "Even if the sun wasn't out today, ye'd bring brightness to the world ... ye shine like a candle, lass."

4

OUR SECRET

EILIDH'S BREATHING CAUGHT. She hadn't expected such an answer. Indeed, no one had ever said anything of the like to her. Aye, men had flirted with her over the years—a few months ago, Iver had even serenaded her in the great hall, much to the delight of everyone except her—but none had ever looked her in the eye as Will Gunn was now and spoken with such sincerity or frankness.

"Thank ye," she murmured, glancing down at the half-eaten cake she still held. She was sure her face now glowed red like the setting sun.

"I wasn't trying to flatter ye, Eilidh," he said softly. "It's the truth."

Mastering her embarrassment, Eilidh raised her chin, meeting his eye once more. "There are plenty of cakes," she said softly. "Would ye like another?"

His mouth quirked. "Of course, I would."

They ate in companionable silence for a short while, although Will inhaled his second cake as fast as he had the first. Observing his face, Eilidh noted that he wasn't looking as emaciated as he once had. Hard work and more substantial meals had filled out the gaunt angles on his face. However, his dark hair and beard were as untamed as ever, and his clothing was filthy and worn. And sitting a few feet back from him, Eilidh could smell him.

The man was in desperate need of a bath.

She should have been repelled by him—for she'd rarely ever seen such a wild-looking man—but whenever she looked into his eyes, whenever she marked the curve of his mouth, something tightened under her ribcage.

He was the sort of man her sisters would all counsel her to run from. One of the hated Gunns—forbidden yet fascinating.

"Lammas approaches," Eilidh said after a long pause, overcome with sudden shyness. "Will ye have a day off work?"

He shrugged before reaching for the bladder next to him, unstoppering it, and taking a gulp. "I hope not ... I'd prefer to be out here in the open air than back in that cell."

Eilidh tensed. She'd never been inside the dungeon, yet she'd heard it was a dank, awful place.

"The cooks will be baking a selection of breads to be placed before the alter in Varrich's chapel and at the kirk in Tongue," she said, gathering her courage. "My favorite is the braided loaf with boiled eggs in it ... I can bring ye one, if ye like?"

Will inclined his head. "That's generous of ye, lass." He paused then. "However, ye might get yerself into trouble ... I don't think the cooks wish their hard work to go to a prisoner ... or a *Gunn*."

"Aye, well, they need not know." Eilidh then favored him with a coy smile. "It shall be our secret."

Will's expression altered, losing its teasing edge. His grey eyes darkened. They stared at each other for a long moment before he finally answered. "Ye are kind to me, lass ... although I can't understand why."

Eilidh swallowed, discomfort filtering over her. Out of her depth, she tried to think of a clever reply. She didn't want to admit her fascination for him—and yet she didn't want to say anything daft either. She wanted Will to think her a woman to be reckoned with, not a silly lass. She wished she didn't blush so easily around him.

"I'm not a Mackay ... I'm a Munro ... and my clan has no quarrel with yers," she replied, dropping her gaze. "I wish to be yer friend, William Gunn ... will ye allow it?" She started to sweat then. Mother Mary, she'd been too bold.

But when she glanced up, she noted that Will's gaze was warm. And then a wide, genuine smile creased his face. "A man in my position doesn't have many friends," he murmured. "I'd be a fool to refuse such a generous offer."

Will eyed the basket of cakes. He'd liked to have asked for another, yet he didn't want to take advantage of her generosity. Raising his gaze, his attention rested upon Eilidh's sweet face. She was a delicate beauty, with eyes as wide as a fawn's. He found it hard not to drown in their oaken depths.

Eilidh bestowed him with a gentle smile then. "I imagine ye miss yer home ... and yer family ... greatly?"

Will nodded, his mouth curving. "My brothers and I have always gotten twitchy whenever we stray beyond Caithness."

Her head inclined. "Ye have a few brothers?"

"Aye, I'm the youngest of six."

"One lives among the Mackays, doesn't he?"

"Aye ... Alexander, the eldest."

Eilidh's lips quirked. "There are few folk in the Highlands who haven't heard that tale ... of how he won Jaimee Mackay's heart." She halted then, a soft sigh escaping her. "It's so romantic."

Will bit back a cynical comment. Eilidh was lovely, yet she was clearly sheltered. There was nothing romantic in Alex's actions. He'd been selfish and disloyal. Yet his behavior over the years hadn't been as bad as Roy's. The third-born Gunn brother was a blight on their clan name.

As if reading his thoughts, Eilidh's expression sobered. "I met another of yer brothers when he worked as the blacksmith in Tongue." Her gaze narrowed then. "Roy tried to rape my sister."

"I heard about that incident ... and the other ones too," Will replied, deliberately keeping his expression shuttered. He dropped his gaze then and plucked a blade of grass from beside him, tearing it in half. "Roy was always a bad seed." His mouth twisted as bitter memories swirled up. "Even as a bairn, he was a vicious bully."

Eilidh's brow furrowed. "Is that why Tavish exiled him?"

Will glanced up, his gaze spearing hers once more. "Roy hated the fact he wasn't the Gunn firstborn. He tried to kill Tavish ... so he cast him out." He pulled a face. "That was a mistake ... Tav should have strung him up from the walls."

A brittle silence fell, and Eilidh's frown deepened. "Ye hate Roy, don't ye?"

"Aye," he replied roughly. "A few days before he tried to seize the clan-chief's seat for himself, the bastard nearly beat me to death."

Eilidh went rigid, her eyes snapping wide. "What?"

"Tav had to intervene ... although I didn't wake for two days afterward."

Eilidh's face shadowed; a shiver then rippled over her slender shoulders. "God's blood ... what a brute."

"Aye, and it's a pity he keeps slipping the Mackays' net," Will replied. "Kin or not, Roy deserves to die."

He tensed then. Talking about Roy brought out his blood-thirsty side, yet he didn't want to shock her.

But to his surprise, Eilidh merely nodded, her jaw tensing. After a pause, she favored him with another smile, although this one was veiled. "It's not always easy being the youngest sibling, is it?"

Will snorted. "No ... I grew up the most aggressive of all my brothers, I'd wager. I don't remember a time when I didn't have to defend myself against their fists ... or my father's."

Eilidh's heart-shaped face went taut once more, and Will wondered why he was being so candid with her. The lass was so easy to talk to—and he'd spent too much time alone since his incarceration. He could have remained here with her all afternoon; however, the guards would start shouting at him soon.

"It's not like that between sisters ... at least, not between mine." Eilidh paused then, pulling a face.

"Although, I'll admit my eldest sister, Beth, gets bossier by the day."

Eilidh wore a wide grin as she walked into Tongue a while later.

I did it!

She'd summoned her courage and approached Will Gunn—and he'd welcomed her. Aye, she'd been a bit nervous, but he hadn't minded.

His smile. Her belly fluttered. *His eyes.* Even now, her breathing quickened at the memory of their stormy depths and the intensity of his gaze.

Their conversation had ended up being far more frank than she'd expected too, for they'd talked of their families. She'd learned much about the man she'd watched from afar.

Oblivious to her surroundings now, Eilidh floated through the outskirts of the village, making her way to the first of the cottages, where she handed out honey cakes to an elderly couple. She chatted with them for a short while, although it was difficult to concentrate with her thoughts elsewhere.

Wishing the couple a good day, Eilidh delivered the rest of the cakes. Then, basket empty, she continued toward the heart of Tongue. She emerged from her happy daze, to remember Beth had lamented that the apples they'd picked from the trees in the walled garden just outside the castle walls were pithy. Eilidh had some coin in the purse at her waist and a basket in need of filling. The market would soon be packing up for the day, but she'd be in time to buy some apples first.

Humming a tune, Eilidh drifted into the market square. As she'd predicted, some of the vendors were starting to pack up their wares. Yet Bram, an elderly man who sold the sweetest of apples, was still there.

She was filling up her basket—while the rumble of William Gunn's voice echoed through her mind—when coarse male laughter intruded.

"How many fingers am I holding up then?"

"Three of course," a softer, female voice answered.

"Wrong, lass … that was two!"

More snorts of mirth followed.

Eilidh frowned, irritated by the heckling. Smiling at Bram, she handed him over a penny for the apples. However, the villagers weren't yet done with their loud exchange.

"Well, it looked like three … ye have fat fingers, Rab Scobie," the lass replied.

"Is that so." There was a jeer to the man's tone now. "Let's give ye another test, shall we?"

A female cry carried across the square, and this time Eilidh scowled. Placing her last apple in her basket, she turned. Her gaze alighted on a big, broad-shouldered young man with a shock of yellow hair, holding a basket just out of reach of a tall, thin lass. Cheeks flushed, she kept making grabs for it, yet he jerked it just out of reach.

"Come on, Ava Bain!" he jeered. "Can't ye see it?"

"Aye!" Her voice was low and held a tremble, as if she might burst into tears at any moment. "Give it to me!"

"It's right here … God's blood, ye really are blind, aren't ye? No wonder ye can't find a man!"

The youth then smirked at his friends, two heavyset young men who looked like twins, earning more laughter.

Heat flared like a pitch torch under Eilidh's ribs. These lads were enjoying tormenting the lass. It was cruel.

"I'm not blind!" Ava's blue eyes sparkled with tears. "I see the world a little blurry, that's all."

"Aye … and that'll be why ye can't grab this." Rab dangled the basket just in front of her before yanking it away as Ava made another lunge for it.

Yet more laughter rang across the square.

Glancing around her, Eilidh noted that none of the husky-looking farmers appeared to be coming to the lass's aid; indeed, they all seemed to be focusing elsewhere.

Jaw clenched, Eilidh decided she'd have to do it herself.

Without another moment of hesitation, she marched up to the bully, ripped the basket from his hands, and thrust it at Ava. And then, as Rab's lips parted to snarl, what was likely an insult, Eilidh cut him off.

"I'd be careful what ye say to me if I were ye—I'm Lady Eilidh Munro, daughter-by-marriage to Niel Mackay." She paused then, letting her introduction ring out across the now silent square. "And when I tell him ye torment those weaker than ye ... he will have ye put in the stocks."

Rab's mouth snapped shut, although his blond brows crashed together, and spots of high color rose upon his cheeks.

Eilidh met his eye boldly, even if her pulse now hammered in her ears. She didn't enjoy confrontation, yet she couldn't let this continue.

Long moments passed before Rab was the first to break the stare. Muttering a curse under his breath, he turned and stomped off. His friends, who weren't looking quite so cocky now, followed like faithful hounds at his heels.

5

YER ACTIONS HAVE CONSEQUENCES

AVA STARED AT Eilidh, her blue eyes narrowing while she tried to make out her features. She held the basket, which was full of shopping, tightly against her chest—as if she feared someone else might try and wrest it from her grip.

She then stepped close and peered at her rescuer, her lips parting in surprise when she realized the woman who'd come to her aid was about the same age as her, and around six inches shorter. "That was brave," she whispered.

Eilidh harrumphed, even though her heart was still racing. "Not really ... those lads are clodheads ... but smart enough to fear Niel Mackay." She paused then, flashing the lass a smile. "I don't think they'll harass ye again today, but just in case, I shall escort ye home."

Ava smiled, tension ebbing out of her thin shoulders. "That's kind ... although, I live at the mill outside the village. My father is the miller. Ye don't mind walking that far?"

Eilidh shook her head. "That's not far at all. Come on." With that, she linked her arm through Ava's, steering her through the crowd. As soon as Rab and his cronies had departed, everyone lost interest in the two young women.

"I thought he was going to drop my basket," Ava admitted, casting a concerned look down at her shopping. "I have a dozen eggs in there."

Eilidh gave her a side-long look. "Has Rab always tormented ye?"

"Not always, no." A blush rose to Ava's cheeks. "He liked me once … I used to live in hope that he'd woo me … but after my sight got bad, he started mocking me."

"Then he's not worth a moment of yer consideration," Eilidh replied, squeezing her arm. The lass was wiry, with the lean muscle of someone who worked hard. She would toil all day alongside her father at the mill. "If I were a man, I'd have given him a sound beating."

Ava grinned and gave her arm a light squeeze in return. They'd left the last of the houses behind now, crossing behind the kirk toward the lazy flow of the river. The mill hove into view in the distance before them: a tall wooden structure built upon the riverbank, its water wheel slowly turning.

A few yards from the mill, Ava extricated her arm from Eilidh's and halted, turning to her. "I'd better get inside … Da will be wondering where I've gotten to." Her mouth quirked then. "I can't thank ye enough, Lady Eilidh … ye have a stout heart indeed to come to my rescue as ye did."

Eilidh grinned back at her. "Ye're welcome … and just call me Eilidh." She paused then, shyness stealing upon her. Having grown up always in her sisters' company, she wasn't used to making new friends. "Shall I call upon ye sometimes? I could bring some treats next time … and we can sit and chat on the riverbank."

Ava's lean face split into a radiant smile, her blue eyes shining. "What a bonnie idea … I'd love that."

Niel Mackay threw down the missive he'd been reading. "Maggot-spawn!"

Eilidh halted, in the midst of pouring cream onto her porridge, while across from her husband, Beth stiffened.

Wee Angus perched on her lap, chubby hands clenched around the piece of bannock he was attempting to stuff in his mouth.

"Niel?" Beth murmured, her brow furrowing. "What's wrong?"

"John's got more problems with the Sutherlands," her husband ground out. "They've started pushing into the Lochnaver. They raided one of the villages four days ago."

Eilidh put down the jug of cream, frowning. "Lochnaver ... isn't that the area ye gifted John?"

Niel nodded, his jaw bunched. "Aye, my great-grandfather claimed the loch and the surrounding lands ... I gave it to John in thanks for his loyalty while I was locked up at Bass Rock ... but the Sutherlands have always insisted the land is theirs." His dark brows crashed together. "It isn't."

"They grow increasingly bold, Niel," Beth said, her gaze still upon her husband.

The clan-chief scowled. "Aye ... our patrols don't seem to be doing any good. Robert Sutherland is spoiling for a fight."

"Are ye going to give him one?" Beth's voice was calm. However, Eilidh noted the lines of tension around her mouth and nose. She'd almost lost Niel once to battle—she was understandably afraid of going through that again.

"Aye," Niel grunted. "If it comes to it."

"He's deliberately goading ye, love." Beth's gaze never wavered from her husband's face.

The clan-chief and his wife stared at each other. Long moments drew out, and Eilidh shifted uncomfortably on her chair.

Niel and Beth always insisted she break her fast with them in the mornings. They sat at the large oaken table in the clan-chief's solar. Outdoors, the sky was the color of smoke, and it was drizzling. The warm summer weather had ended abruptly a week earlier, bringing with it days of heavy rain. Yet—thanks to the glass windows

Niel had bought, at great expense too—the weather didn't intrude into the chamber.

"I'm aware of the game he's playing, mo chridhe," Niel said, breaking the silence. His tone had softened now as he marked Beth's upset. "But I must defend my territory. Our people inhabit those lands, and he's terrorizing them." Niel pushed back his chair and moved to the desk by the window. Pulling up a chair, he settled down into it and reached for a sheet of parchment. "Robin Mackay will aid me to keep the Lochnaver secure," he announced. "He and his men should be here in a couple of days if I send a rider out to him this morning. I shall let John know we're coming."

"Stir the batter harder," Beth instructed. "It's got lumps in it ... look."

Brow furrowing, Eilidh glanced down at the cake batter she'd been preparing under her elder sister's instruction. As always, it wasn't going well. "I *am* stirring hard," she insisted. "My arm feels like it's about to drop off." She cast Beth an arch look then. "Ye're always telling me off for over-mixing the batter."

Beth snorted. "Aye ... but ye can't leave great lumps of flour in it." Her sister then reached out, giving Eilidh's upper arm an experimental squeeze. "Ye need to build up yer muscles, lass ... yer arms are like bird wings."

Eilidh stopped stirring. "They are not!"

She thought then of Ava. The lass had arm muscles like cords of rope. She supposed she was puny in comparison.

"A couple of mornings a week kneading bread in here should remedy that," Beth continued, ignoring her protest. "Keep stirring!"

Jaw clenched, Eilidh did as bid. God's teeth, Beth was even more domineering than usual this afternoon. Her discussion with Niel in the clan-chief's solar at dawn had put her in an ill mood, likely for the rest of the day.

"That's better," Beth said with a nod as Eilidh took her frustration out on the hapless bowl of batter before her. The pair of them stood at a large, scrubbed table in

Castle Varrich's kitchen. Around them, cooks and scullery maids were hard at work, preparing the supper. The thud of knives on chopping boards and the clatter of iron pots rang through the bustling, smoky space, giving the two sisters relative privacy, even amongst the chaos.

"Can I add the apple now?" Eilidh asked.

"Go on then."

Relieved that she could finally give her aching arm a rest, Eilidh poured in the bowl of chopped apple.

Folding the fruit into the batter, she cast her sister a veiled look. "Are ye worried we'll go to war with the Sutherlands?"

Beth's full lips thinned before she nodded. "It's been building for a while." She heaved a deep sigh then. "After Ruaig-Shansaid, I thought the Mackays were done fighting their neighbors … but it never ends, does it?"

Eilidh pulled a face. "At least, we aren't at war with the Gunns anymore."

"Aye … but it's a fragile peace, Eilidh."

"Has Niel said anything to ye … about releasing his prisoner?" Despite her light tone, Eilidh's pulse fluttered. William Gunn was never far from her thoughts these days. Ever since she'd taken him cakes a week earlier, she'd been looking for another excuse to visit him. But the rain had prevented her. The bad weather had come at a poor time too, for the folk of Tongue were bringing in their harvest. The oats and barley the locals reaped needed to see them through a long and bitter winter. They couldn't afford to lose any of it.

"No," Beth replied. Eilidh glanced her way to see that her sister was watching her, a line etched between her brows.

Eilidh's heart kicked against her ribs.

Mother Mary, she knows!

"I heard ye visited him in the fields," Beth said then, confirming Eilidh's fears. Her hazel gaze was unwavering. "Why would ye do that?"

Eilidh inhaled slowly, carefully considering her response. Part of her wished to be honest with Beth about the fact that the Gunn prisoner dominated her thoughts.

But another part whispered a warning. Jean had reacted badly to her behavior toward Will—and it was likely Beth would do the same. Her sisters took too much interest in her affairs. If her feelings for Will remained a secret, Beth couldn't crush them.

"I was on my way into Tongue with those honey cakes, and I saw him sitting there, alone," she replied, favoring her sister with a blithe smile. "I felt sorry for the man ... so I approached him and offered him a cake."

"According to the guards, ye did more than that," Beth replied, her gaze narrowing further. "Ye sat down and chattered away to him like a magpie for a while."

Heat blossomed across Eilidh's chest. She hadn't exaggerated when she'd spoken to Will about her relationship with her sisters. Beth meant well, yet she sometimes spoke to Eilidh as if she were her mother.

"We conversed for a spell, aye," she confirmed, her smile fading. "What's wrong with that?"

Beth's mouth thinned. Wordlessly, she picked up a buttered iron tin and handed it to Eilidh, making it clear she wasn't to forget about her cake. "Be careful, lass."

Ire simmering in her belly, Eilidh snatched the tin, thumped it down on the table, and poured the batter into it. "I don't need ye to warn me, Beth," she said, her tone sharpening. "I wasn't doing anything wrong."

"William Gunn is Niel's prisoner," Beth pointed out, unnecessarily. Her gaze shadowed then. "I don't want ye to get yer heart broken."

Eilidh gave an unladylike snort. "God's blood ... all I did was talk to him. Ye are making far too much of it."

However, Beth wasn't put off. Folding her arms across her impressive bosom, she continued to regard Eilidh with an all too familiar look. Despite Eilidh's best efforts, she hadn't fooled her. "Ever since ye were a wee bairn, we've done our best to shelter ye," Beth said after a heavy pause, "but I think Neave, Jean, and I might have gone too far."

Eilidh slammed the now empty bowl onto the table. She wasn't enjoying the direction this conversation was heading in. She wasn't one given to fits of temper, but she could feel her anger rising like a spring tide. "What do ye mean?"

Beth sighed before reaching up and pushing a lock of walnut-brown hair that had escaped from the loose bun she wore out of her eyes. "Ye behave as if none of yer actions have consequences," she said, her tone grave now. "I'm sorry to have to remind ye of this … but they do."

Eilidh stormed up the stairs leading to the top floor of the keep. Muttering a curse under her breath, she stomped along the narrow corridor and into the women's solar. "*Yer actions have consequences*," she grumbled, mimicking her sister's stern tone. "Does everyone think I'm a goose-wit?"

The solar was empty this morning. Half-finished sewing projects lay scattered over the various chairs, and balls of wool sat upon the floor. The chamber had grown increasingly untidy of late, for Eilidh wasn't the neatest of the sisters. Jean used to complain loudly about her messy ways.

Walking to the window, Eilidh halted before her loom. She was weaving a tapestry. It was a landscape of rolling hills edged by a wide kyle, with a castle perched atop a rocky outcrop overlooking it all: Castle Varrich and its environs. The tapestry was the most detailed one she'd ever embarked on, although it was progressing well.

She usually spent a few hours each afternoon at her loom, but today she was too agitated to pick up her shuttle and resume work.

Moving away from the tapestry, she threw open the shutters, letting in the grey morning and damp, misty air. It was still drizzling, although lighter than earlier. Heavy clouds hung over the surrounding hills, blocking the view.

Restlessness churned within Eilidh.

She'd spent most of the past week cooped up inside, pacing the confines of this solar, and after her argument with Beth, she longed to expend some energy. The weather was clearing now. Finally, she'd be able to make it into Tongue. She'd visited Ava once before the rains arrived but hadn't seen her since.

It was time to remedy that. Her new friend wouldn't criticize her the way Beth did.

Decision made, Eilidh turned from the window and hurried out of the solar, heading toward her chamber, where she'd fetch her woolen cloak.

Maybe, if fortune shone upon her, she'd even catch a glimpse of Will Gunn on her way to the mill.

6

AFTER THE RAINS

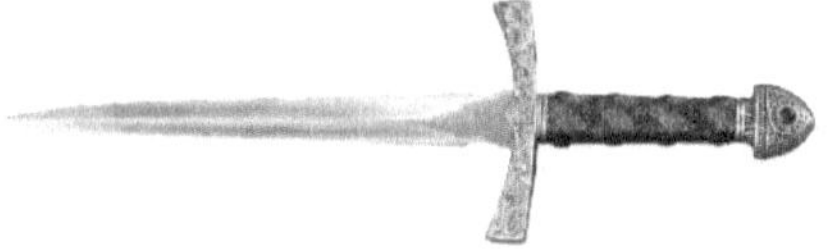

"THE FIELDS HAVE all flooded … I was worried the mill would have suffered from the rains too." Standing on the northern side of the Rhian Burn, Eilidh scanned the waterlogged land to the south, where cottars worked hard, ankle-deep in water and mud, to salvage a crop of kale and turnips.

"Aye … we're fortunate indeed that the northern banks of the Rhian are higher," Ava replied, nibbling an oatcake. Eilidh had brought a basket of food—left over from the day before—from the kitchens down with her. "Da says the mill has never flooded."

Eilidh tore her attention from the fields to focus on the mill. Indeed, the great wheel was turning this afternoon. The rasp of a man's coughing filtered out from the wooden structure. "That's a relief," she replied. "I wouldn't want ye to lose yer livelihood."

"The mill is all we have," Ava agreed. "My uncle used to work it with Da … but they fell out two winters ago … now Da toils alone." She paused then, her brow crinkling. "He finds it difficult these days though … he gets out of breath and isn't as strong as he used to be."

Eilidh frowned, her chest tightening. "Then it's just as well he has ye."

Ava pulled a face. "I could be of more assistance if I could see properly."

Eilidh glanced back at the flooded southern fields. Of course, Ava was frustrated that she couldn't see as well as other folk. Eilidh took her clear sight for granted most of the time, yet she didn't this afternoon. Pale sunlight glittered on the flooded ground, and the purple outlines of Ben Hope and Ben Loyal formed a backdrop to Castle Varrich's bulk.

Eilidh's attention drifted back to the fields then, as she searched for a familiar face.

On the way into Tongue, she'd spied Will Gunn among the cottars. He hadn't seen her at first, for he was too busy yanking kale plants out of the boggy ground and depositing them into the wicker basket he wore slung over his back. But, as Eilidh approached, he'd looked up, his gaze traveling to her. He was some yards distant, yet Eilidh caught his smile.

Warmth flowered across Eilidh's chest at the memory.

"Ye are all flushed ... why's that?"

Jerking out of her reverie, Eilidh turned to see Ava had stepped close, peering into her face.

Eilidh's hands flew up to her cheeks, to find them hot. "Am I?"

"Aye ... yer cheeks are glowing like embers."

"I'm just warm from the ride."

"Ye keep staring out at the cottars." Ava favored her with an arch look before folding her arms across her chest. "Are ye looking for someone?"

Eilidh swallowed. The miller's daughter's vision might be flawed, but her wits weren't.

"Perhaps," she replied lightly.

"Who then?" Ava wasn't giving up.

Eilidh hesitated. After her argument with Beth earlier, she was wary to discuss the Mackay's hostage. However, Ava wasn't her sister. She wasn't likely to stand in judgment of her. Eilidh grew weary of keeping her feelings locked inside and longed to confide in someone. Surely, it couldn't hurt if she told Ava?

Inhaling deeply, she then replied, "William Gunn."

A pause followed. Ava inclined her head, taking this admission in. The miller's daughter then gestured to the patchwork of kale, cabbages, and turnips on the southern side of the river. "I've heard the prisoner works the fields opposite." She paused then, her mouth quirking. "What does he look like, this William Gunn?"

"Tall, dark … and brooding," Eilidh replied with a smile.

"And handsome?"

"Aye … despite the rags he wears, and his long hair and beard."

Ava snorted. "He sounds frightening."

"To some, maybe, but not me." Eilidh heaved a sigh then. "My sister suspects I like him though … she's not happy with me."

Ava nodded, her expression sobering. Eilidh didn't need to explain why a liaison between the clan-chief's sister-by-marriage and his prisoner wasn't something Beth would welcome.

Silence stretched between them while Ava continued nibbling at her oatcake. After a spell, Eilidh cleared her throat. She didn't know Ava that well and felt a trifle foolish at being so open with her. "It's best ye don't tell anyone I carry a torch for Gunn," she murmured.

Ava dusted oatcake crumbs off her bodice before flashing Eilidh a conspirator's smile. "Fear not … yer secret is safe with me."

The shadows were lengthening when Eilidh set off home.

She'd lingered with Ava longer than she'd intended, chatting to her while the lass resumed her chores, and even helping her sweep up the interior of the mill. Ava had protested, yet Eilidh insisted. She'd already kept the lass away from her work for long enough and didn't want her to get behind.

The miller had thanked Eilidh when she eventually took her leave. Short and heavily muscled, with a high-colored face, Cormac Bain appeared a gruff, yet kind-hearted man.

As Eilidh had left, Ava was fussing over him, pouring her father a cup of ale and rushing off to prepare his supper. The lass clearly adored her Da.

Riding past the kirkyard, Eilidh found herself thinking of her own father. Tightness constricted her chest then. She hadn't seen George Munro in many months and missed him.

Gypsie's feathered hooves squelched on the wet ground as she approached the bridge spanning Rhian Burn. Drawing nearer, she roused herself from thoughts of her father and looked once more for Will.

She spied him working with a group of men to the right of the road leading toward Varrich. However, he hadn't seen her.

Disappointment arrowed through her. His smile earlier had illuminated the dull day and given her hope for the future.

Hope for what, exactly?

Curse it, it was as if Beth's voice now whispered in her ear, urging caution. *He's a Gunn and ye are now under the protection of Niel Mackay. Even if he released Will tomorrow, he'd never agree to let the pair of ye wed.*

Eilidh's pulse quickened. Mother Mary, she was getting ahead of herself. The pair of them were barely friends, and already she was thinking about marriage. Next, she'd be imagining how many bairns they'd have, and whether they'd favor him or her.

Confiding in Ava about her interest in the man had made her reckless. She needed to rein in such impulsive thoughts.

Maybe Beth was right about her.

Silently cursing her foolish daydreaming, she dug her heels into Gypsie's sides. The garron sprang into a jolting trot, splashing through puddles and clattering onto the slippery wooden bridge. Rhian Burn was swollen after the rains, the usually gentle flow transformed into a mud-brown, turbid torrent.

Pony and rider were halfway across the bridge when a deep groan cut through the damp air—the noise of wood splintering.

Eilidh glanced around her, surprise sliding into alarm when the bridge listed sideways.

Gasping an oath, she urged Gypsie on. The far side of the bridge was just a few yards away, yet it suddenly seemed a great distance. With a panicked squeal, the mare scrambled to reach firm ground.

However, she never made it.

Time slowed.

The bridge continued moving right, causing the horizon to tilt. For an instant, it hovered there, as if trying to steady itself, before a final plunge. The bridge disintegrated around them—and Eilidh pitched sideways.

She hit the cold water and went under. Panic surged, and she kicked up, breaking through the surface and gasping a lungful of air. However, the strong current had her in its grip. Rhian Burn widened as it flowed out into the kyle. If she didn't manage to get to the bank, she'd be lost. Like her sisters, Eilidh had learned to swim as a bairn—yet she wasn't confident in the water, and her heavy skirts and cloak were dragging her down. Nearby, she could hear Gypsie's frightened neighing as the pony thrashed about—but Eilidh had no time to focus on the garron, for the water sucked her under once more.

She broke the surface, spluttering. Blind panic seized her, and she started to thrash against the river. At the back of her mind, she remembered her father warning her about trying to fight the current, yet terror overwhelmed her, dousing good sense.

Going under again, she clawed at the water as if it were her nemesis—and when she resurfaced, dragging air into her lungs, she heard someone shout her name.

A few yards away, a ragged figure scrambled down the bank downriver. William Gunn stumbled and slid, hampered by the chains around his ankles, yet his face was set. In one hand, he held a long hoe. "Grab the end!" he shouted.

Gasping and choking, Eilidh had only moments to comply. The river's flow had her in its grasp—and within a heartbeat, she'd be past him. Tamping down the terror boiling inside her, she lunged toward the bank, kicking out hard with her booted feet. The current fought against her, yet she used it to carry her close to where Gunn now held out the hoe.

Flinging out her hands, Eilidh caught the metal end of the implement. Iron dug into her fingers, but she didn't care. A sob choked from her as she clung on, kicking hard once more.

Will shuffled backward, hauling her with him.

He then lost his footing and fell. But he didn't release his hold on the hoe. Inch by inch, he pulled her to shore.

And when Eilidh's fingers dug into the soft soil on the muddy bank, another sob broke free and her knees buckled.

An instant later, strong hands grasped her, pulling her free of the river's hold.

Eilidh collapsed on top of her savior.

Cheers erupted around them.

Panting, as she tried to recover her breath, Eilidh raised her head to see cottars surrounding them. Other men had followed Will down the bank, yet he'd reached her first.

"Well done, Gunn!" One of the cottars—a hulking man with a bald pate—gave a gap-toothed grin. "Ye saved the lass's life!"

"Aye ... who knew ye could move so fast?" another cottar added. "And with yer ankles shackled too!"

They helped Will and Eilidh to their feet. However, Eilidh was shaking too much to stand unassisted. Wordlessly, Will wrapped his arm around her shoulders, holding her steady. Eilidh leaned into the hard strength of him, her gaze flicking back to the river. "My pony," she rasped. "Gypsie ... where is—"

Relief gusted out of her then when she spied the bedraggled Garron standing on the southern bank. The pony looked as traumatized as its rider: head hung low, sides pumping like forge bellows. But at least they were both safe.

Eilidh's vision swam as she shifted her attention to the man who still held her firmly against him. Their gazes met and held fast.

"Thank ye," she whispered. "If ye hadn't been there, I'd have been swept out into the kyle."

Will's jaw tightened. "Aye," he said roughly. "The river current is vicious after the heavy rain."

"Look at the bridge," one of the other cottars called out. "It's completely washed out!"

Heart still racing, Eilidh shifted her attention from her savior and looked back at where the wooden bridge had once spanned Rhian Burn. Indeed, the structure had completely collapsed. Most of it was traveling downriver and would end up in the kyle, while some of the heavier parts of the structure protruded from the mud-colored water.

"I thought the bridge was sturdy," Eilidh murmured.

"Aye, we all did, lass." The bald cottar said, his rough voice laced with exasperation.

"The bridge itself wasn't the problem," Will pointed out. "The rain must have eroded the supports."

"How will we get back into Tongue?" someone else asked. "That's the only bridge across the river."

"Inchverry Burn lies upstream ... we'll be able to ford it easily enough," the bald cottar replied, focusing on a skinny lad hovering a few yards away. "Lyle ... catch Lady Eilidh's pony and accompany them both up to the castle ... and let the laird know the bridge has washed out. The rest of ye, get back to work."

Eilidh realized he was likely the foreman, and he took charge now that the peril had passed. "The laird is away at present," she said. "He's taken men to the Lochnaver to aid John Mackay ... but my sister will organize the repairs."

The foreman nodded, although she spied disappointment flash across his eyes. He clearly thought Beth wasn't suited to this task. But Eilidh knew differently; there were few folk—men or women—who were as capable as her sister.

"Someone else will have to help ye up the bank, Lady Eilidh," Will said with a half-smile, releasing her arm. "I'm slow with these irons, and if I fall over, I'll take ye with me."

Eilidh favored him with a shaky smile. "They didn't seem to hinder ye on the way down the bank?"

His answering grin made her breathing hitch. "Aye, well … I virtually rolled down, didn't I?"

His comment caused snorts and laughter from the surrounding cottars.

A moment later, Lyle approached her, his cheeks pink from shyness. "Ye can take my arm if ye wish, Lady Eilidh?"

7

SANS PEUR

"GOD'S BLOOD, YE could have drowned!"

"Aye, but I didn't."

"I shouldn't let ye ride out alone!"

Eilidh drew in a deep breath, attempting to quash her rising irritation. "How would that have altered things, Beth? Instead of Gypsie and me ending up in the river, my escort would have as well." She paused then before reaching out and placing a hand over her sister's. "Stop fashing. Thanks to William Gunn, I'm alive and well."

Beth nodded, although her face was pale and strained. The two of them stood in the women's solar. Lyle had brought Eilidh back up to the keep, and she'd found her sister at her needlework, Angus playing on the rug before the hearth. Outside, the light was starting to fade. They would go down to the great hall shortly for supper. "Thank the Lord he was close by." Heaving in a deep, steadying breath, Beth then pulled herself together. "All the same, ye shouldn't have ridden into Tongue this afternoon ... not after such heavy rains."

Eilidh snorted. "Enough. There's nothing ye could have done."

Her sister meant well enough, although Eilidh was now clenching her hands at her sides as frustration boiled within her. She didn't need coddling.

"That accident could have happened to any of us," she added, unable to tamp down her annoyance now.

Beth frowned, her dark, winged brows drawing together. She clearly didn't appreciate her sister's tone.

However, Eilidh didn't care. She wasn't in the mood to be harangued over this.

She just wanted to be left alone to conduct her life as she wished.

"Well, yer near drowning hasn't dented yer willfulness," Beth muttered, casting aside her sewing. "We shall continue this conversation later. First, I must go down to talk to Captain Reay before supper … we must see about building a new bridge as soon as possible. He'll need to talk to the carpenters and builders in Tongue first thing tomorrow."

"When will Niel be back?" Eilidh asked, relieved that the conversation had shifted from her—for the moment at least.

Beth's full lips compressed, her hazel eyes shadowing. "I don't know," she murmured. "He was furious when he set off … I hope he won't do anything rash."

Marking the worry that gnawed at her sister, Eilidh forgot her irritation at her overprotectiveness. Of course, concern for Niel had made Beth prickly of late. Eilidh needed to remind herself of that before she let her sister vex her too deeply.

Taking Beth's hand, Eilidh gave it a gentle squeeze. "Fear not, he has a large company of men with him … and Robin will temper his recklessness." It was true, Jean had married a brave, loyal man who was a steadying influence on his clan-chief. Eilidh was glad Robin was at Niel's side.

Beth managed a tight smile, although her gaze remained shadowed. "I know … and he's also got John with him … he'll give Niel wise counsel." She paused then. "It just feels as if I have a stone in my belly whenever I think about the Sutherlands these days."

Roy Gunn pushed his horse hard along the shore of the firth. Sweat slicked the beast's sides, and foam flew from its mouth, spraying back in its rider's face as he bent low over its neck—but Roy paid it no mind. Frustration surged inside him like a king tide.

Reaching the far end of Dornoch Firth, he eventually reined in the courser.

The horse halted, sides heaving, head lowering. He'd driven it to the brink and cursed himself now. A broken-winded nag wasn't any use to him. Fortunately, he still had the horse that he'd stolen from a hapless traveler the past winter. He'd knocked the man off the gelding's back and slit his throat, before emptying his pockets of coin, and taking his food and horse.

A few months earlier, he'd been an outlaw, living wild—until a chance meeting with Kieran Sutherland, the clan-chief's nephew. That spring, Roy had been camping out on the windswept Strathnaver, a hunted man, when a party of Sutherlands had found him. He'd thought himself a dead man—but instead of sticking him with his dirk and stealing his courser, Kieran had invited Roy to join them.

And so, rather than remain on the fringes of Mackay territory, while nursing a grievance he was powerless to act upon, Roy had taken Kieran's advice and ridden south to Dunrobin Castle, where he'd pledged his loyalty to a man who hated the Mackays as much as he did.

Straightening up in the saddle, Roy wiped the sweat off his forehead with the back of his forearm. Days of rain had departed, leaving heavy clouds behind. Dornoch Firth was a bonnie spot. Emerald hills and thick woodland-filled vales rolled out around the thriving village of Golspie, while high, rounded hills cradled the wide firth.

Roy had been living at Dunrobin a few months now, had joined Robert Sutherland's guard—but things were moving far too slowly for his liking.

He clenched his jaw then, the rage that had driven him to push his horse into a gallop along the shoreline bubbling up once more. *We should have hit the Mackays hard by now*, he fumed silently. *Sutherland's dancing around them, giving them a chance to rally men. This can't go on!*

Twisting in the saddle, Roy turned his attention back to Dunrobin Castle. The fort perched above the firth. It nestled amongst trees with a patchwork of arable fields and the village beneath it. The cottages of Golspie clung to the shore of the firth; it was a bucolic scene, the kind of place a man could settle down.

Perhaps he should find himself a wife here. Roy had already noticed that the miller had three comely, unwed daughters. In the years after leaving Castle Gunn, he'd supported himself as a blacksmith, although he hadn't since his arrival at Dunrobin. But one day, he'd like to have his own forge again. Aye, he could grow old and fat in a village like Golspie.

However, he couldn't let his comfortable surroundings distract him. Before he settled down, he had vengeance to wreak—on both his kin and the Mackays.

Hate twisted his belly, and Roy growled a curse. "Enough tiptoeing around," he muttered. "I must talk to Sutherland … today."

Turning his horse, he headed back to Dunrobin.

Roy rode up the incline toward the castle. Towering curtain walls over six feet thick surrounded a square keep. Aye, it was a mighty fort, but in his opinion, none of the Highland castles he'd visited over the years compared to Castle Gunn, where he'd been born and raised.

It had been years since he'd seen the Gunn fortress, but when he closed his eyes, he could still recall how it perched upon a finger of land on a rocky promontory, looking out to sea. Waves boiled around the base, and seabirds wheeled overhead. It was a wild, brutal setting—and even over a decade after his banishment, he still missed it.

Pushing away thoughts of the home he'd never see again, Roy urged his horse through the arched gateway, clattering into the outer ward. He dismounted outside the stables and threw the reins to a waiting stable lad. "Rub him down well," he instructed tersely.

"Aye," the lad replied, eyeing the horse's sweat-slicked coat. Roy noted the judgment in the young man's eyes, at his treatment of the beast, yet he wisely held his tongue. Most of the men here had learned to mind Roy Gunn.

Striding across the cobbled outer ward, he passed under another archway into an inner courtyard, circuiting a walled garden where the clan-chief's wife was working with her sister, and entered the keep.

He found Robert, the sixth Earl of Sutherland, in his solar, writing a missive at his desk by the window.

Halting in the open doorway, Roy waited for the clan-chief to notice him. He was in an aggressive mood today, but he minded Robert, all the same. The past months had taught him that the Sutherland wasn't a man to be trifled with. A calm demeanor hid a blistering temper when roused.

Long moments passed before, feeling someone's gaze upon him, the clan-chief glanced up from writing. His gaze narrowed as it settled upon Roy. "What is it, Gunn?"

"Apologies for the intrusion, Sutherland," Roy greeted him, stepping into the solar. Although it was still summer, today was grey and damp. As such, a log smoldered in the hearth. The clan-chief's solar was a wide space with an unusually large window, paned with expensive glass. The Sutherland coat of arms—three golden stars upon a red shield—hung above the fireplace, while a heavy claidheamh-mòr had been mounted upon the pitted stone wall opposite. "But it's been nearly a fortnight since we raided the Lochnaver … what's our next move?"

Robert stared at him. Tall and lean, with pale-blue eyes and greying hair shorn close to his scalp, he was in his mid-forties, yet still as hale as a man twenty years his junior.

After a pause, Sutherland's thin mouth quirked. "Getting impatient, are ye, Gunn?"

"No," Roy lied, "although I do worry ye will soon lose whatever advantage ye have recently gained."

The clan-chief's smile faded. "What do ye mean?"

Roy folded his brawny arms—heavily muscled from years of wielding a blacksmith's hammer—across his chest. "Ye should have razed the Lochnaver."

The Sutherland placed his quill in its pot and leaned back in his chair. "Really?"

"Aye … those lands are yers, but ye won't get them back by 'hit and run' raids." Roy paused there, letting his words sink in. His loutish appearance often fooled folk. He had a sharp, cunning mind. Hadn't he convinced Niel Mackay to take back Dounreay? The lands that had once belonged to his clan but had been held by the Gunns for two generations. As expected, the act had enraged Roy's brother Tavish—who ruled the Gunns—and had culminated in a bloody battle upon Sandside beach. Roy knew how men in power thought; he understood their arrogance, but also their insecurities.

He'd been working hard on Robert ever since his arrival yet had been forced to prove his loyalty so the man would actually listen to him.

He was close now. All the same, he still had to choose his words with care.

"Ye need to strike hard … this is the time to make a stand."

The clan-chief pulled a face. "I fully intend to reclaim the Lochnaver," he replied, his voice low and hard. "In the spring."

"Why wait? Niel Mackay will sense something's coming. The Sinclairs will join ye, as will the Murrays. Take back the Lochnaver … before yer enemy has time to rally support." Roy paused there and sucked in a deep breath. "*Sans Peur*, Sutherland."

Silence fell in the solar.

Sans Peur—Without Fear—was the Sutherland motto.

The clan-chief's lean face tightened, his pale eyes narrowing. He didn't like Roy repeating the words he held so dear back to him. It was like sticking the man in the arse with a dirk, and Roy had taken a risk in being so bold.

Yet frustration boiled in his gut, like a slack tub in his forge when he plunged a glowing blade into it. He'd had enough of waiting.

When Sutherland finally spoke, his voice was rough. "This must be handled carefully, *Gunn*." He emphasized Roy's clan name, making it clear that he didn't appreciate his use of the Sutherland motto. "Courage is all well and good ... but last time I went to war against the Mackays, we suffered a defeat that took a great toll ... on my clan and my family."

Roy's mouth thinned. Indeed, the Battle of Drumnacoub, around five years earlier, hadn't ended well for the Sutherlands. Robert had promised his two daughters to the Nielson Mackays once they'd toppled Angus from power and taken Varrich for themselves— but his allies all died in the battle. Roy had heard that, in the aftermath, both daughters had enraged their father by wedding men far beneath their rank.

A victory against the Mackays was well overdue.

"Ye underestimated them last time," Roy said, deliberately softening his voice. Even across the room, he could sense the tension rippling out from the clan-chief's lean body. "But ye've spent the last year building yer strength, readying yerself for this day. Yer relationship with the Sinclairs has never been stronger. Promise them lands, if ye must, to buy yerself an army that will have the Mackays pissing their braies."

The Sutherland's gaze glinted. "Aye?" His voice still held a hard edge, yet Roy could tell the man was listening to him. Now was the time to press his advantage.

"Ye have to take control of the situation," he advised. "Be the one to set the terms … not react." A smile tugged at his mouth as an idea took root in his mind. "Pen a missive to Niel Mackay … and state yer ownership of the Lochnaver. It was stolen from yer clan by his great-grandfather, and ye will have it returned to ye. Tell him that if the lands are not handed over by the eve of Samhuinn, ye will raze the Lochnaver and kill any Mackay who still dwells there."

The clan-chief cocked his head. "Ye want me to draw them into open battle?"

"Aye … but don't send the missive until the last moment. Don't let Mackay know open warfare is coming until it's too late for him to gather support. In the meantime, stop harrying the Lochnaver with raids … and instead focus on amassing an army that will crush yer enemy with a hammer blow." Roy's skin prickled as he spoke.

Aye, this was the way forward.

He stalked into the solar then, and the clan-chief rose from his chair to meet him. A smile tugged at the corner of the Sutherland's mouth, and victory tightened Roy's chest.

He had him.

"That's a sound plan, Gunn," the clan-chief murmured. "Kieran did well to send ye to me." Sutherland's gaze guttered then. He'd sent his nephew into Mackay lands over the last winter and spring, to harry the outlying villages and rustle sheep and cattle. Unfortunately, Robin Mackay of Melness had caught them. Word had eventually reached Dunrobin that the chieftain had struck off Kieran's head with his battle axe. He'd then sent the other Sutherlands to Castle Varrich, where they'd been whipped before being allowed to return home.

Roy stepped closer to the clan-chief, and the two men clasped arms.

"Do this for him then," he replied. "And for every Sutherland who has died on a Mackay blade."

8

VISITORS

"I HEAR YE are a hero."

Will opened his eyes and glanced right, to see a familiar figure standing outside the gate to his cell. He'd been dozing on his pallet after yet another exhausting day. They'd managed to salvage more of the crops than expected though—something the folk of Tongue were rejoicing about. And despite that Will wasn't a local, and had no allegiance to these people, he'd smiled at their relief.

The cottars he toiled with shoulder-to-shoulder most days were decent men. They'd been wary of him at first, but many months of working together had broken down their reserve. These days, they enjoyed bantering with the sharp-tongued prisoner.

Niel stepped inside the cell, a teasing grin upon his swarthy face. "I came home from patrolling the Lochnaver to find everyone in my keep talking about how my prisoner saved Eilidh Munro from drowning."

Will sat up, while Niel lowered himself onto a stool and placed the Ard-ri board down.

The two men's gazes met and held for a moment, and then Niel's expression sobered. "Thank ye."

Will shrugged. "I couldn't let the lass be swept away, could I?"

"No ... yer quick actions saved her life."

An awkward silence fell in the cell. In truth, Will hadn't expected Niel's gratitude and didn't know how to respond to it. The Mackay was usually guarded with him, and Will was comfortable with that. Nonetheless, he might be able to use the clan-chief's softening attitude toward him to his advantage.

Getting to his feet, Will moved over to the table, chains clanking, and sat down on the low stool opposite Niel.

Meanwhile, the Mackay busied himself with setting up the board. He then produced two cups from a bag he'd brought with him and unstoppered a skin of drink. "This calls for some mead," he announced.

The sweet scent of fermented honey filled the cell, and a wry smile tugged at Will's mouth. The Mackay knew he had a fondness for mead. Taking the cup Niel handed him, he held it up in a toast. "To Eilidh Munro's health," he murmured.

"Aye," Niel replied, arching an eyebrow. "The lass won't stop talking about ye."

A strange warmth ignited under Will's ribs at this news. Shoving the discomforting sensation aside, he raised the cup to his lips and took a large gulp of mead. He then gave a sigh of pleasure. "This is good."

Niel fixed him with a level stare. "It's the least I could do." He paused then, his expression impossible to read. "Is there anything else ye want? A cup of mead isn't much recompense for saving my sister-by-marriage's life."

Will inclined his head, holding the clan-chief's eye. "Ye could give me my freedom? Allow me to return to my kin?"

Niel snorted. "Nice try, Gunn ... ask for something else."

Irritation spiked through Will.

Bastard.

What would it take for Niel to grant him his freedom?

Will took another pull of mead, forcing down the urge to bite back. Instead, he considered the clan-chief's offer. He was disappointed, but he wouldn't throw it back in the man's face. "I want a hot bath ... and a change of clothes ... once a week."

Niel's gaze snapped wide at this request. "A bath?"

"Aye ... I get sick of smelling my own stench."

Niel pulled a face. "Ye might have a point ... ye do reek a bit."

"So ye agree?"

Their gazes met once more, and then the clan-chief huffed a laugh. "So be it." He then gestured to the board between them. "What will ye be, this eve, Gunn ... attacker or defender."

Will glanced down at the board. He often took the position of attacker—it suited his aggressive nature—but today he wished to take a different approach.

After a pause he glanced up, his lips curving. "I'll protect the king," he replied.

As far as days went, this wasn't a bad one. Will had won his first game of Ard-ri against Niel, and he'd had a bath.

The clan-chief had taken his defeat with surprising grace, although it took a lot of self-control not to rub his victory in the man's face. Like all his brothers, Will was highly competitive. He loved to win.

The bath, his first proper one since his imprisonment, was an experience he'd remember until his dying day. Sinking into the steaming water, he let out a long groan of pleasure. Steam wafted up, enveloping him.

Niel had kept his word.

The guards had grumbled, for they'd had to haul down an iron tub from the keep and then heat pots of hot water over a firepit outside the dungeon. But the clan-chief was to be obeyed, and so they'd carried in the tub, as well as a clean set of clothes. They'd even given Will a cake of soap and a knife to shave with.

Picking up the soap, Will sniffed. Lavender.

The scent reminded him of Eilidh. Even the muddy odor of river water hadn't been able to mask the perfume of lavender he'd smelt in her hair. She'd clung to him after he'd saved her, and he'd been loath to let her go. The feel of her lithe body pressed up against his had been both a distraction and a pleasure.

Feeling his groin stiffen at the memory, Will muttered an oath under his breath and began to wash vigorously under his arms.

"Stop it, Gunn," he muttered. Best he didn't let his thoughts travel in that direction.

The sweet, herby scent of lavender drifted around him. Soon, a layer of scum floated on the surface of the water as he washed away ingrained grime. Will then washed his hair before soaping up his beard. Working by feel, he cut the beard short before scraping the blade over his cheeks and jaw to remove the stubble.

Afterward, he sank down up to his chin in the water and let the warmth soak through his limbs.

It was heaven. It was incredible what some warm water and soap could do. He almost felt himself again—the man he'd been before he'd been shackled in irons and carted back to Castle Varrich.

Will's jaw tensed then. Niel had denied yet another request for freedom. However, he wouldn't give up. While the man continued to visit him, he'd ask again. And again. Until Mackay granted him his freedom.

He was still in the bath, deep in thought, a while later, when the guards appeared.

"Out ye get, Gunn."

"Aye, ye shall turn into an eel if ye soak in there any longer."

Will snorted before heaving himself out of the cold water. It was a blessed relief to move around without the heavy shackles hampering his movements, although the reprieve would end soon.

"Push the knife under the gate, there's a good lad," one of the guards said, folding his arms across his chest.

Flashing his jailers a wolfish smile, Will scooped up the knife and did as bid.

Even after all this time, his guards were wary of him.

He was a Gunn, after all.

Will turned and walked over to his sleeping pallet, where he donned the clean clothes. The feel of freshly laundered cloth against his clean skin was wonderful. He almost didn't mind when the guards entered the cell and refastened the irons around his ankles.

Almost.

"What a brave deed!" Ava stared at Eilidh, clutching at her damp apron in alarm as her friend finished her tale. "It's just as well Gunn acted so quickly."

Eilidh smiled, her pulse fluttering at the sound of the man's name. She couldn't stop thinking about Will these days. "He *was* brave," she replied. "And I'm certainly grateful."

The two women stood outside the mill, next to where Ava had just paused from washing clothes. She'd been kneeling on the riverbank when Eilidh arrived, pummeling wet, soapy clothing with a laundry bat. The rhythmic 'thwack' of her bat had blended with the rumble of the millstones that crushed the grain within the mill itself. The sweet scent of oats laced the damp morning air.

Eilidh had walked down from Castle Varrich and crossed Rhian Burn upon the makeshift rope bridge the villagers had erected. In the meantime, work had started on a sturdy bridge of stone to replace the wooden one they'd lost.

Returning to her washing, Ava knelt, grabbed the pair of braies she'd been beating, and plunged them into the river, washing them free of suds. The lass then flashed Eilidh a coy look. "Have ye spoken to him since?"

Eilidh shook her head. "I thanked Gunn at the time." She paused then, grimacing. "But as I told ye ... my sister has warned me about consorting with him."

Ava's brow furrowed before she returned to her task. "I can't see the harm in ye *talking* to Gunn," she replied. "After all ... the man saved ye from drowning."

"I don't see the harm either," Eilidh agreed.

She watched Ava wring out the clothing, noting how work-worn the lass's finely boned hands were. Guilt darted under Eilidh's ribcage. The miller's daughter always appeared pleased to see her, but she knew that her visits put Ava behind with her chores. With her father's health declining, the lass always seemed to have a mountain of tasks to complete before sunset.

"Can I help?" Eilidh asked then, approaching the riverbank.

Ava glanced her way, her eyebrows drawing together. "Ye are kind … yet there's no need."

"But ye have so much to do … I only wish to make things easier for ye."

Ava's mouth curved. "Yer company is all I require … after Ma died, I've missed the companionship of other women." She paused then. "But let us return to William Gunn … what are ye going to do about him?"

Eilidh sighed. "Nothing … at present."

Ava made an impatient sound in the back of her throat. "Perhaps the clan-chief will release him one day … if this peace between the Mackays and the Gunns lasts. There's no reason why, once he's free, that ye can't be together."

Eilidh grew still. Ava made it all sound so simple—but what if it was?

"So ye think there is hope for us?" she asked, her voice catching at the thought that one day, she might be Will's wife.

Ava smiled. "There's always hope, Eilidh … but it's up to ye to find a way."

It's up to me to find a way, Eilidh repeated the words to herself as she drew Gypsie up before the entrance to the dungeons. However, it was hard to concentrate over the thunder of her heart. After her visit to Ava earlier in the day, she'd returned to the castle with determination burning inside her—yet now her courage was faltering.

Pretending not to notice the bemused looks the guards were giving her, she swung down from the garron's back.

"Lady Eilidh," one of the men greeted her. "What brings ye down here?"

She flashed him a smile. "A bonnie evening, is it not, Craig?"

"Aye," the guard agreed warily.

Indeed, it was. The depressing low cloud had finally lifted, and they'd had a warm, sunny day. It was growing late; supper had come and gone, yet the gloaming was only just starting to settle. The evenings weren't quite as long as they'd been in mid-summer—a sign autumn was approaching—but there was enough time for Eilidh to take an evening ride.

"Beth sent me down with some apple cakes for William Gunn," she said, moving to her saddlebag and removing a cloth-covered parcel.

"That's kind of the laird's wife," Craig replied. However, the man's expression was incredulous. Beth wasn't in the habit of sending food down to the dungeon.

"What about us?" His companion muttered under his breath. "Gunn gets treated like royalty these days."

Eilidh favored the grumbling guard with her brightest of smiles. "Would ye like a cake, Tate?" She paused then. "I made them myself." She had, although anyone who knew about her poor culinary skills would likely have been put off by the statement.

Tate's expression lightened. "Aye, lass … that would be appreciated."

Craig stepped forward from his post next to the doorway. He then reached for the parcel. "I'll see Gunn gets these."

Eilidh moved out of reach, clutching the food to her breast. "I shall take them to him."

Craig halted, his brow furrowing. "I don't think that's a good idea … a dungeon is no place for a lady."

Eilidh arched an eyebrow. "Fear not ... I can manage it." She paused then. "I haven't thanked Gunn properly yet for saving my life."

Craig and Tate exchanged looks before the former heaved a sigh and stepped aside. "Take care, Lady Eilidh," he murmured. "Don't stand too close to the bars."

"I won't," she assured him. Eilidh then unwrapped the parcel, extracted two cakes, and handed them to the guards. "Enjoy ... I won't be long."

Craig eyed her, clearly still not that happy about her entering the dungeons. "One of us should accompany ye."

Eilidh made a frustrated noise in the back of her throat. "Och, Craig ... don't be such an old woman. Fear not, I shall be wary." In truth, she wasn't the least bit afraid of Will. She wouldn't visit him otherwise.

"Take the left passage, lass," Tate instructed her finally. "He's in the fourth cell on the right."

Eilidh nodded. "Thank ye."

Pulse fluttering in the hollow of her neck—for she'd half-expected the guards to refuse her—Eilidh strode into the dungeon.

Torches hung on chains inside, illuminating the damp stone walls and low ceiling. The air was heavy and stale. It smelled as if no sunlight ever entered this place.

No wonder he got sick in here, she thought, taking the left passage. *And no wonder he prefers toiling in the fields.*

Indeed, it felt as if the weight of the promontory above pressed down on her as she ventured further into the tunnel. The squeaking and scurrying of rats made her skin crawl, yet she pressed on.

Counting the cells she passed, Eilidh came to a halt before the fourth on the right. A flickering torch on the wall behind her cast a dim light into the alcove that had been chiseled out of the rock. Legend had it that the ancient folk who'd first come to live upon the shores of the kyle had made their homes in these tunnels, although she couldn't understand why.

Her breathing quickened then, not in anticipation of seeing Will though, but in anxiety. It felt as if the walls were closing in on her. She really wasn't enjoying being inside the belly of the rock.

Maybe this wasn't a wise idea.

Shoving the sensation aside, Eilidh focused instead on the cell and the lean figure stretched out on the bed. She then cleared her throat. "Will."

9

RECKLESS

THE PRISONER ROLLED over, eyes flickering open.

Eilidh inhaled sharply. "Will?" she repeated, her pulse quickening once more. "Is that ye?"

The man smiled, revealing a deep dimple on his left cheek. "Aye."

Eilidh stared at him, stunned. "Ye look … different," she said, feeling foolish. She barely recognized him.

Even under all that hair and dirt, she'd found him compelling, but shaven and clean, and dressed in worn yet unsoiled lèine and braies, the sight of him took her breath away.

Tongue-tied, she merely gawked at him for a few moments.

She shouldn't be here, but she didn't care. Seeing him was worth it.

Still smiling, Will rolled to his feet. And then, chains rattling, he shuffled over to the gate. "This is a surprise … I can't believe the Mackay let ye down here."

"He didn't," Eilidh replied with a smile. "I told the guards my sister had given me permission to bring ye some cakes." She held out the package to him. "I'll likely get in trouble later … but it will have been worth it."

Will's expression sobered. "Ye shouldn't stick yer neck out for the likes of me, lass."

His words surprised her, and Eilidh's confidence ebbed. What if he didn't welcome her visit as she'd hoped?

"But I wish to," she replied, her voice lowering. "Ye saved my life … and I wanted to thank ye properly." She paused then, forcing herself to hold his gaze. "I hope ye like the cakes." Her cheeks warmed then. "They're apple … I baked them myself."

Will approached the bars. He reached a hand through them and took the cloth-wrapped parcel. "If they were made by yer fair hand, I'm sure I'll enjoy them," he said softly.

In the hallowed torchlight, his grey eyes were dark, almost black.

Eilidh cleared her throat. "Aye, well, I did warn ye I don't have the skill Beth does … I think she sometimes despairs of me ever becoming a decent cook. I do try though."

Will's mouth—sensual and well-molded, she noted—quirked. "It's good to see ye," he murmured.

Their gazes held, and Eilidh's pulse kicked up yet another notch. A blend of anticipation and nerves was making her lightheaded. His voice was low and warm, and it did strange things to her breathing. They stood barely two feet apart now, with the iron gate between them. She was keenly aware of his nearness, and the faint scent of lavender mixed with the smell of clean male.

Her belly somersaulted.

It was no good. She was well and truly infatuated with this man. It seemed the harder she tried to put him out of her mind, the more he took residence there. The rational part of her knew that to pursue this was folly, yet the instinct to seek him out was stronger. Whenever she saw him, she felt free.

"The keep and Tongue village have been alive with talk of yer valor," she said after a pause. "I was hoping Niel would release ye out of gratitude … I did ask him to."

Will huffed a humorless laugh. "I did the same … but he refused." He reached up then and rubbed his shaven chin. "However, he did agree to let me bathe and have a change of clothes once a week." His expression turned rueful then. "I'd prefer my freedom though."

"And ye shall get it, one day," Eilidh assured him. "I won't stop asking Niel … reminding him that I wouldn't be alive if it weren't for ye." She reached through the bars then, her fingers closing over the hand that grasped the parcel of cakes. "The clan-chief can be stubborn … but he isn't unreasonable. He will come around in the end."

It was a bold move, to reach out and touch him like this—and the guards had warned her to keep her distance from the prisoner.

But the instinct to connect with him was too strong.

Will stilled under her touch, and for a moment, Eilidh feared she'd overstepped. But he then lifted his free hand and placed it over hers. "Ye have a pure heart, lass," he murmured. "I don't deserve yer kindness … but I thank ye for it, all the same."

Eilidh inclined her head. "Why wouldn't ye deserve it?" Will was a political prisoner, a hostage, kept here to ensure the Gunn clan-chief didn't stir up any more trouble. He wasn't dangerous. "Ye haven't committed any crime, other than being born to the wrong clan."

The corners of his mouth kicked up into a wry smile. "I wish I was as good a man as ye believe, Eilidh … but I'm no saint."

Eilidh frowned. She didn't believe the man to be so, yet something in his tone warned her from pressing the matter.

An awkward silence fell, and then Will squeezed her hand; his grip was firm, strong, and warm. "All I'm saying is I've made a few mistakes in my time." Letting go of her hand, he stepped back from the bars. "Thank ye for the cakes, Eilidh … but I think it's best ye don't try to visit me here again."

Eilidh tensed, the warm glow that had wrapped itself around her during their conversation shattering. Embarrassment prickled over her, and her cheeks warmed. "Don't ye wish to see me?"

"It's not that," he replied, his face unreadable now. "But these visits can't lead anywhere. And if ye persist, ye risk tarnishing yer marriage prospects."

Heat ignited under Eilidh's ribs, and she lifted her chin. "Let me worry about that."

"But ye don't, do ye?" Will's voice roughened, his dark brows drawing together. "Visiting me is reckless ... and if word gets around, tongues will wag. I'll not be responsible for yer ruin."

"That's ridiculous," Eilidh replied, cursing the sudden wobble in her voice. "How would me showing ye some kindness ruin me?" The truth was, she didn't care if everyone on Mackay lands learned of her feelings for Will Gunn.

It was him she wanted. No one else.

The realization robbed her of breath. However, once again, his shuttered expression cautioned her from admitting such a thing.

Will was warning her off—and although she was impulsive by nature, she wasn't witless. As much as she yearned to be near him, she wouldn't push herself upon someone who didn't want her.

"I thought ye enjoyed my company," she said, stepping back from the bars and swallowing hard in an effort to loosen her aching throat. "I apologize for intruding where I'm not wanted."

Muttering a curse under his breath, Will raked a hand through his wild dark hair. "It's not that ... but nothing good can come from these visits. Surely, ye know this?"

Eilidh blinked rapidly. God's blood, she was on the verge of dissolving into tears. His rejection stung.

Will stared back at her, his expression thawing just a little. And for an instant, she glimpsed something—need, sadness—flicker across his face. But then it was gone. "Look to yer future, lass," he said finally, his voice barely above a whisper now. "Forget about me."

Eilidh fled then, turning on her heel and taking off down the tunnel. Daylight loomed ahead, and the urge to sprint toward it rushed through her. Yet some fragment of good sense remained, and she slowed her gait to a walk. If she bolted out of the dungeon like a frightened hind, the guards would assume Will had done something to alarm her.

Despite that he'd just sent her away, and warned her to keep her distance in future, she wouldn't risk him getting into trouble.

It hit her then, just where her impetuous behavior could lead.

Beth had warned her that she lived as if there were no consequences to her actions—but for the first time, she understood. She was naïve, unprepared for the harsh realities of life.

All it would take would be for someone to believe the prisoner had taken liberties or harmed her in any way, and he'd never see daylight again. In coming here, she'd taken a gamble with his future, not her own.

Plastering a serene expression onto her face, even if her heart now pounded like a smith's hammer against her ribs, Eilidh straightened her shoulders and emerged from the dungeon.

The guards had finished their cakes and looked visibly relieved to see her.

"All is well, Lady Eilidh?" Craig asked, his gaze roaming her face.

"Aye, thank ye," she replied brightly. "The prisoner appreciated the gift." She then smiled at him and Tate. "Did ye enjoy yer cakes?"

"Aye," Craig replied, a little too quickly she thought.

"Delicious," Tate chimed in.

They were both lying but were too polite to do otherwise.

Eilidh's throat constricted, the back of her eyes prickling dangerously. She had to get away from these two before she embarrassed herself.

Wonderful ... I put Will in danger and brought him inedible cakes.

"Good eve, then," she said, moving over to where one of the guards had tethered Gypsie to a tree for her.

"Good evening, Lady Eilidh," Craig called after her.

She couldn't get away from the dungeon fast enough. Dusk was settling, the last rays of sun painting the sky with ribbons of violet, gold, and dusky pink. It was the bonniest sunset that had graced Varrich in a long while, yet Eilidh didn't see it—for tears blinded her as she rode away.

10

THE MISSIVE

Two months later ...

"IVER MACKAY IS here."

Eilidh froze in the midst of weaving her shuttle through the weft of her tapestry. Mastering her reaction, she glanced over her shoulder at where Beth stood in the doorway, Angus perched on her hip.

"Is he?" she said lightly. "I didn't realize Niel had called his chieftains to him for another meeting."

"He hasn't," her sister replied, arching her eyebrows. "Iver's traveled from Dun Ugadale to see ye."

Eilidh's fingers clenched around the wooden shuttle. *Mother Mary, no!*

Drawing in a deep, steadying breath, she turned from her tapestry. As was her habit most afternoons, she'd retreated to the women's solar to weave. She'd been working hard on the tapestry of late, and it was turning out even better than she'd anticipated. She'd been lost in the repetitive rhythm of weaving, a process that calmed her, until Beth's arrival.

Now, her stomach clenched.

"Where is he?"

"In Niel's solar, catching up ... Iver brought a large company of warriors with him this time ... most of them will remain at Varrich after he departs."

"That's generous of him," Eilidh murmured, even as her palms turned slippery. "Niel will appreciate the gesture ... especially with the Sutherlands baying at his heels."

Indeed, ever since Niel had returned from the Lochnaver, the clan-chief had been on edge. After harrying the area for months, the Sutherlands had gone to ground—but Niel didn't trust their silence. Iver's gift would help the clan-chief protect his lands, but it would also smooth the young laird of Dun Ugadale's way to a proposal.

Moving into the solar, Beth studied Eilidh's face. "Try to look happy about his visit, lass," she said, her smile fading. "Iver would make ye a fine husband."

"I'm sure he would," Eilidh replied, throwing her shuttle into the basket of wool at her feet. "If I wanted to become his wife."

Beth folded her arms across her chest, her mouth tightening. "God's troth, ye aren't still pining for Gunn, are ye?"

Heat washed over Eilidh.

If only Beth knew.

These days, it felt as if a stone had taken up residence in her belly. Her appetite had waned, and her sleep had turned fitful.

Ever since she'd visited the dungeon, Eilidh had done as he'd asked—and stayed away. His rejection had stung, like vinegar on a graze. All the same, her feelings hadn't changed.

Not one bit.

Thoughts of Will dogged her steps all day.

In the meantime, Eilidh tried to keep busy. She hurried through her morning chores and had taken to visiting Ava daily. The bridge into Tongue had been rebuilt, stronger than ever. Often, they went to Tongue market together. She'd confided in her friend about what had happened with Gunn, and Ava had been sympathetic. But with the passing of the weeks, Eilidh took care not to mention him.

Recalling their conversation in the dungeons still made her burn with humiliation. And yet, longing for him stole upon her many times each day. She tried to focus on other things—yet whenever she let her mind wander, her thoughts always returned to Will.

Aye, she'd seen him from afar numerous times. And when she crossed the fields, her gaze always sought Will out: a tall, dark-haired figure in the distance. But unlike instances in the past, when Will would halt his work and look her way and sometimes wave, these days, he didn't look up.

Eilidh understood why, yet it didn't stop disappointment from knifing her breast each time.

He's trying to protect ye, she'd remind herself when the pain crushed her. *He doesn't want to see ye ruined.*

The reminder helped, yet it only made her miss him even more. *Why does everyone think I need protecting?*

"It doesn't matter what my thoughts are regarding Gunn," Eilidh finally ground out. "I can't make myself want someone I don't."

Beth frowned. "Will ye refuse to see Iver then?"

Eilidh huffed out a frustrated breath. "Of course not. I'm not cruel."

"But ye shall turn him down?"

"Aye … as gently as I can."

Helping herself to a slice of roast venison, Eilidh listened to the conversation between the men at the table. As she'd expected, Niel and Iver were discussing the Sutherland situation. Thankfully, the laird of Dun Ugadale hadn't yet asked to see her alone—but he would soon enough.

"They seem to have disappeared like wraiths, at present," the Mackay clan-chief muttered, swirling his pewter goblet of wine, his brow furrowed. "We camped out on the Lochnaver for weeks but saw no sign of the bastards."

"Ye clearly frightened them off," Iver replied. The chieftain regarded Niel, his handsome face serious. "Ye know how Robert Sutherland behaves … he likes to provoke, but not follow through. Maybe he's done for the time being."

Niel growled a curse under his breath. "Autumn is usually a busy time for raids and rustling. They like to do as much damage as possible before winter keeps them close to their hearths." The clan-chief paused then, his frown easing as he focused on the chieftain of Dun Ugadale. "Fortunately, thanks to yer generosity, I will be able to leave a permanent presence in the Lochnaver."

Iver flashed Niel a grin—an expression that was boyish and tinged with cockiness—before he shifted his attention across the table.

His gaze settled upon Eilidh, and his smile softened.

Eilidh favored him with a polite smile in return before looking down at her trencher. She usually loved roast venison and braised kale, but her stomach had closed. That look, and the earnest hope she spied in his dark-blue eyes, made guilt constrict her chest.

She didn't want to disappoint him, to hurt him.

But how could she agree to marry Iver when her heart belonged elsewhere?

And it did. She'd fallen in love with Will Gunn.

Ava knew how she felt, yet if she was to admit such to Beth, she'd think her foolish.

How can ye love someone ye barely know?

Aye, they'd spent little time together over the past months, and yet enough for her to know she wanted no other but him.

She was heartsick and miserable at the thought of never speaking to him again, never listening to the rough lilt of his voice, or witnessing the teasing edge to his smile as they conversed.

"Mackay!"

Ewan Reay's gruff voice splintered Eilidh's brooding, and she glanced up to see the Captain of the Varrich Guard approaching, his long legs carrying him swiftly across the great hall. Warriors seated at the long trestle tables glanced up in surprise, their gazes tracking their captain.

"A missive has come for ye … from Dunrobin Castle," Reay announced.

Silence fell across the table. The captain's announcement also caused the rumble of conversation in the hall itself to die away.

Eilidh tensed.

The Sutherlands.

Stepping up onto the dais, Reay handed the clan-chief a tightly furled scroll. It was sealed with wax, although from where she sat, Eilidh couldn't see the crest that would be stamped upon it. If it came from the Sutherlands, there would be a wildcat sitting upright, claws extended.

Niel Mackay set down his goblet and took the scroll. His mouth thinned as he broke the seal without preamble, unfurled the missive, and began to read.

Moments passed, and everyone's gaze remained on the clan-chief.

Niel's expression slowly darkened, deep grooves appearing on either side of his mouth and between his eyebrows.

Next to him, Beth shifted uncomfortably in her chair. "What is it, Niel?" she murmured, breaking the tense silence. "What does the Sutherland have to say?"

Niel lowered the parchment. He then inhaled slowly, and deeply, clearly attempting to rein in his temper. "He 'officially' claims the Lochaver as his own" —he rasped out finally, his words echoing down the table— "and declares that if we don't vacate the lands before the eve of Samhuinn, he will raze them, kill any Mackay tenants his men find … and take the territory by force."

Silence fell then, and the mood in the great hall of Castle Varrich shifted. The faces of the warriors seated at the tables beneath the dais turned hard, and both Reay and Iver scowled.

Eventually, the chieftain of Dun Ugadale spoke up, his tone incredulous. "But the Lochnaver is *yers.*"

"Aye, it is," Niel growled. "And Sutherland knows it."

"It's just a ploy, Niel," Beth said. Her voice was subdued, her hazel eyes shadowed. "He's trying to draw ye into battle. It's not just the Lochnaver he wants ... it's revenge."

A muscle feathered in the clan-chief's jaw. "Whatever his motives, Sutherland will take Lochnaver over my dead body."

Beth's face paled at this declaration, yet she said nothing. Reaching out, for she sat just a couple of feet from her sister, Eilidh placed a reassuring hand over her forearm and squeezed gently.

She knew how much Beth feared Niel going to war again. Her sister was tough, indomitable—yet her terror of losing her husband in battle was her Achille's Heel.

"Samhuinn is only a fortnight away, Mackay," Captain Reay pointed out then. "How will ye raise a sizeable force in time?"

"Sending this at the last moment is deliberate," Iver muttered, his own expression stony now. "Sutherland wants ye to be at a disadvantage."

"Meanwhile, he's had months to prepare for battle," Reay agreed.

Niel spat a curse and lunged to his feet, fury bristling off his lean form. "Reay ... send out riders immediately to Farr, Achness, Melness, Loch Stach, and Balnakeil," he ordered. "Send word to Foulis Castle too ... for George Munro will aid us."

"Da's men might not reach us in time, Niel," Beth pointed out huskily.

Her husband nodded, his movements jerky. "Aye, Sutherland will be counting on it."

"Are there any other favors ye can call in?" Eilidh ventured timidly. It was rare she spoke up at the table when her menfolk were discussing important matters. Nonetheless, she wanted to ease the tension that crackled around her. "Jean told me once that Melness enjoys a good relationship with the MacLeods ... and they aren't as far away as our clan."

The clan-chief's midnight-blue gaze seized on her. "Aye, Eilidh ... a good idea." He looked to his captain once more. "Send a rider to the MacLeods as well." Niel's face twisted then. “Sutherland may think he has the advantage … but we shall prove him wrong.”

11

FOLLOWING HER HEART

"WHAT ... NO ARD-RI board?"

Will inclined his head, peering through the gloom at where the Mackay stood in the passageway outside his cell. He carried two wooden cups and a skin of drink, but nothing else.

"No," Niel replied roughly. "I'm not in the mood to play games this eve ... I'd prefer to drink."

Surprised by his tone, Will rolled off his pallet and rose to his feet.

The clan-chief waited until the guard had unlocked the gate before he let himself into the cell. Moving over to the low table where they usually played Ard-ri, he slammed down the cups, unstoppered the bladder, and poured. "Sloe wine," he ground out. "The strongest I have."

"What's the occasion then?" Will asked, eyeing Niel.

Over the months, they'd grown increasingly comfortable in each other's presence. Yet this was something new. Didn't the man have someone else he could drown his sorrows with?

Niel's lip curled, and Will could almost taste his simmering rage.

He could also sense an underlying current of desperation, which surprised him.

"We're drinking to Robert Sutherland," Niel growled, holding his cup aloft. "May the whoreson get the flux ... and shit himself to death."

Will snorted. "Aye ... here's to that then." He took a sip and blinked. The wine was so tart it made his eyes water. "And what's Sutherland done to earn such a toast?"

Niel took a deep draft of wine before answering. "He's claimed the Lochnaver as his own ... and threatened to raze the lands if I don't clear it of my tenants and hand it over by Samhuinn."

The clan-chief's words, sharp with bitterness, fell heavily in the cell.

Considering this news, Will took another sip of wine. "Doesn't John Mackay oversee the Lochnaver?"

"Aye."

"So, Sutherland's still got his dirk out for him then?"

"Aye ... he's never forgiven John for thwarting him while I was locked up in Bass Rock." The clan-chief's expression darkened further. "It doesn't help that John's lands border Sutherland territory."

"Those lands have shifted from clan to clan over the years," Will replied. It was the same with the Gunns and their neighbors. Even when they weren't warring with the Mackays, his clan were constantly negotiating or disputing land rights with the Oliphants and the Sinclairs, the two clans bordering their territory to the north. "Sutherland will feel he's in the right."

Niel's mouth twisted. "I should have known not to look for sympathy from a Gunn."

Will shrugged, not offended by the Mackay's aggression. He wasn't one of the clan-chief's loyal warriors; he didn't need to mind his tongue around him. "Did ye really come down here looking for that?"

Niel glared at him before muttering a curse under his breath. "No." Lifting his cup to his lips, he drained the rest of his wine. He then slammed the cup down on the table and promptly refilled it. Will watched him, silently impressed. That wine was sour enough to shrivel Satan's balls, yet the clan-chief didn't even seem to notice.

After a long pause, Will took another experimental sip of wine. "So ye will be meeting Sutherland in battle, I take it?"

Niel gave a brusque nod, hopelessness lighting in his eyes.

Watching him, Will's gaze narrowed. He now understood the man's desperation. Sutherland was a cunning bastard. He hadn't given the Mackays any time to raise a decent army to face him. Will often lost track of time, for his life was a simple, albeit monotonous, one, but just the day before, one of the guards had told him Samhuinn was a fortnight away.

The Mackay was grossly underprepared, and there was nothing he could do to remedy it.

Unless ...

An idea took root in Will's mind—one so bold that his breathing quickened. He didn't voice it for a moment; instead, he turned it over and over in his head, examining it from all angles. And as he did so, his skin prickled.

He took a gulp of wine, trying not to wince at its tartness, and met Niel's eye once more. "Release me, Mackay ... and I shall return to Castle Gunn and raise a warband." He paused then, watching the clan-chief's gaze snap wide, before continuing. "After decades of feuding ... the Gunns and the Mackays shall now fight side by side."

Niel stared back at him, his lean face shuttering.

Will expected such a reaction. He'd come to understand the Mackay a little over the past months. Like Will, he was naturally suspicious of others—and would immediately assume his prisoner was up to something.

A heavy silence settled in the cell, and when Niel eventually broke it, his voice was cool, guarded. "That's quite an offer."

Ignoring his naked mistrust, Will shrugged. "Aye ... and not one I make lightly."

Niel sneered. "Yer brother will never agree to fight with us."

"He will ... once I convince him that we face a common threat," Will replied evenly. "Ye forget we Gunns also share a border with the Sutherlands. If Robert Sutherland has the balls to try and reclaim old territory from ye ... what's to say he won't do the same with us?"

Will wasn't lying. The relationship between the Sutherlands and the Gunns had been uneasy over the years, although his father and Robert Sutherland had agreed to leave each other alone and focus their aggression upon the Mackays instead. But if the Sutherlands bested the Mackays, there was no telling what they might do next.

George Gunn was dead and buried. Tavish ruled the clan now, and he led differently to his father.

Surely, Will could talk his brother around?

But Niel was still favoring him with a hard stare. Before Will would get the opportunity to see Tavish again, he first needed to convince the Mackay clan-chief to free him.

"Ye have a way with words," Niel murmured after a pause, his gaze glinting. "But I'd wager ye are just trying to buy yer freedom."

"Why don't ye trust me and find out?"

Niel snorted. "I trust few men ... especially those who have wronged me."

Will set down his cup on the table between them. "That's wise ... but also blinkered. There are times when a man must let go of the past, or he doesn't see clearly." He leaned forward, his pulse accelerating. "Don't make the mistake of thinking Tavish is like our father. He isn't."

Niel's mouth flattened, making his opinion of George Gunn clear. His reaction didn't offend Will. He knew exactly what his father was.

"Tav isn't a warmonger," Will continued. "He fights because he has to ... yet he's tired of the feuding."

He broke off then, tensing. He was taking a risk, admitting this to the Mackay. Niel might view it as weakness. Nonetheless, the fact remained that Tavish didn't lust to spill Mackay blood. If there was a way to ensure peace settled in the Highlands, his brother would likely take it. Will just had to find a way to convince him.

The two men stared at each other. Niel watched him with a speculative expression now, although his gaze still glinted. "Are ye in earnest, Gunn?"

"Aye," Will replied, his voice roughening. "Ye can take me at my word."

Indeed, he wasn't lying. His incarceration had altered his view on things. When he'd been dragged back to Varrich after battle, he'd been full of hate for the Mackays. However, loathing no longer cramped his gut when he met with Niel. These days, he felt an odd kinship with the man. Will understood how Niel's mind worked.

"Tavish won't have forgotten Ruaig-Shansaid," Niel said after a long pause. "He'll want reckoning for that … as I would in his place."

Will's mouth quirked. "Aye, ye aren't wrong. But Tavish has always used his wits before his fists … he's clever enough to see beyond his resentment." His belly tightened then. He hoped Tavish would indeed listen to him. His brother might have changed in the interim, might have turned bitter and vengeful. However, Will couldn't show any doubt, or he'd never gain his freedom, would never see Castle Gunn again. "It's time for us to bury the axe, Mackay."

There were few times in Eilidh's life when she grappled for something to say, for she loved to chatter away, even if she thought no one was paying attention.

But now was one such occasion.

Casting a glance at the tall blond man who walked at her side, she tried to think of a way to start a conversation. Iver had gone quiet, clearly not needing to fill a silence as she did.

Clearing her throat, Eilidh finally spoke. "It's a lovely eve, is it not?"

The laird of Dun Ugadale smiled. "Aye ... warm for this time of year."

After supper, they'd taken an evening stroll in the walled garden south of the curtain walls. Eilidh had been hoping he wouldn't call on her, especially after the storm that had broken over the castle with the arrival of the Sutherland missive during the noon meal.

Yet the man wasn't easily put off.

And here they were, making their way around the perimeter of the garden, mounting steps that had been carved out of the rock to the flat area that looked down over the terraces of vegetables and herbs.

"So ye shall be staying on at Castle Varrich?" Eilidh asked after another pause. "Now that the Mackays will be going to war against the Sutherlands." Her chest tightened, anxiety wreathing up. Like Beth, she had no wish to see Niel and his chieftains go into battle again. She looked upon Niel as a slightly intimidating elder brother these days and had grown fond of John and Robin Mackay too. The thought of any of them being maimed or killed in the coming days made queasiness churn in her gut.

"Aye," Iver replied, his handsome face growing stern. "It's just as well I brought a band of warriors north with me ... for there'd be no time to return to Kintyre and gather reinforcements." He paused then, drawing to a halt. His gaze fastened upon Eilidh, roaming over her face. "Has Niel spoken to ye of my intentions?"

Feigning ignorance, Eilidh inclined her head. "No."

It wasn't an outright lie. Niel hadn't said anything to her—Beth had.

Discomfort flickered over Iver's features, although he recovered swiftly. "Aye, well, he's had a lot on his mind today." The young laird cleared his throat then. "I didn't make this visit north to see the clan-chief, Eilidh ... but to see ye." His gaze fused with hers. "I wish to offer for ye ... will ye be my wife?"

Those final words rushed out of him, betraying the man's nervousness. Iver was strikingly attractive, and usually gave off an air of supreme confidence. But she saw a different side to him this evening. It wasn't warm outdoors, the air held an autumnal crispness, yet a light sheen of sweat covered his forehead.

Eilidh's breathing grew shallow.

She'd known he'd propose to her during the walk and had steeled herself for it. Nonetheless, hearing the words made the situation real.

"That is a gallant offer, indeed, Iver," she murmured.

She broke eye contact then, dropping her gaze to the ground between them. The laird would think her shy, but she was readying herself to respond. Anxiety churned within her. She didn't want to hurt him, to see disappointment flare in his eyes, but she'd had time to think about what she wanted.

Her sisters had followed their hearts—and so would she.

William Gunn represented everything she yearned for: adventure, passion, and a little danger. Everyone else thought they knew what was best for her, but they didn't understand what she needed.

Drawing in a deep breath, Eilidh raised her chin and faced Iver once more. "I'm greatly flattered by yer esteem," she continued, her voice low and firm, "… but I cannot accept yer proposal."

Iver's gaze shadowed, his jaw tightening.

Aye, she'd hurt him—there was no getting around it.

When the chieftain finally answered, his voice was husky. "Can I ask why?"

Eilidh swallowed. She wanted to tell him the truth—that she was in love with the Mackay clan-chief's prisoner, and that while hope burned in her heart that she might one day be with William Gunn, she could encourage no suitors.

She'd thought much on her last conversation with Will over the past two months. Aye, his rejection had hurt, but with the passing of time, she became increasingly convinced of the wisdom of his actions. He didn't want to damage her reputation or ruin his own chances at gaining his freedom.

The connection between them had been real. She'd seen the warmth on his face, the desire in his eyes, whenever they met. There was something undeniable between them. He felt it too; she knew he did. Niel would release him one day, and then they could be together.

She wouldn't give up on him; instead, she'd wait for as long as it took.

Will was her future.

But she couldn't say any of that to Iver. It would both wound and anger him to hear that she'd chosen the Gunn hostage over him. He might scorn her sentiments; he might go straight to Niel and tell him, and she didn't want that.

What she felt for Will was special. She wouldn't have it ridiculed or put at risk.

No, she would have to give Iver a different explanation.

"We don't know each other," she murmured. "I always told myself I'd wed for love ... as my sisters all have."

Iver's features tensed. "Beth didn't," he pointed out. "Her and Niel's union was an arranged one ... and look how happy they are together."

"Aye ... although things were very difficult for them in the beginning," she answered, silently cursing herself for using such a weak excuse. She'd need to be firmer. "When I choose a husband, I must be sure."

Iver held her gaze. "Then I will make it my mission to win yer heart ... for ye have had mine in yer keeping for a while now."

Eilidh's heart started to pound. *Lord, no.*

"We have two weeks until we leave for the Lochnaver," he went on. "With yer permission, I shall call on ye daily. We shall talk and spend time together." His expression was earnest now, his longing for her clear. "Fear not, lass, I will not pursue ye forever ... if ye truly don't want me ... but will ye at least give me until we depart for battle? If yer answer is still 'nay', I promise to let this lie."

Eilidh stared back at him, thrown by his request.

Her first instinct was to refuse outright. There was no point in letting this drag on. She wanted another man, and that wasn't going to change. However, the sudden vulnerability in his eyes stilled her tongue.

Curse her soft, cowardly heart. She couldn't do it.

After a lengthy pause, she nodded.

12

SO MUCH UNSAID

EILIDH WALKED INTO the clan-chief's solar and came to an abrupt halt.

She'd been seated by the fire in the women's solar, mulling over the awkward situation she'd gotten herself into, when Clara entered with the news that the clan-chief and his wife wished to see her.

Rising to her feet, Eilidh had wrapped a shawl about her shoulders—for, despite a warm day, the evening had grown chill—and made her way downstairs. In truth, she welcomed a break from the mire of her own thoughts; she wasn't sure what to do about Iver.

In agreeing to his request, she'd only drawn things out.

Sometimes Niel and Beth invited her to share a cup of wine with them before bed. However, when Eilidh entered the solar, she discovered they weren't alone.

Iver was standing before the roaring hearth.

But it wasn't his presence that threw Eilidh—but that of the man seated a few feet back from the chieftain of Dun Ugadale.

William Gunn lounged in a high-backed chair, his tall, lean body clad in a loose brown lèine and slate-grey braies.

Eilidh's heart leaped into a flat gallop.

Frantically scurrying to hide her reaction, she glanced over at where Niel was pouring cups of wine at the sideboard. Meanwhile, Beth sat upon the window seat; like Eilidh, she'd wrapped a woolen shawl around her shoulders.

Eilidh threw a questioning look in her sister's direction, but Beth's expression was impossible to read this evening.

Remembering her manners, she greeted both Iver and Will with a polite nod. "Good evening, Iver," she murmured. "Gunn ... this is a surprise."

Iver flashed her a warm smile, while Will's mouth quirked. "Aye, for us both, Lady Eilidh. Ye are looking well."

"As are ye." It was no exaggeration. Freshly shaved and clad in new clothes, Will was every inch a clan-chief's son once more. All the same, she'd always been able to see past the rags and filth that had covered him. She'd wanted him even then.

"I'm releasing Gunn, as ye can see, Eilidh," Niel said, handing her a cup of wine. "He shall be departing Castle Varrich tomorrow."

Panic flared in Eilidh's breast.

Tomorrow!

Struggling to keep her reaction masked, Eilidh glanced back at Will. "So, ye are returning home then?"

Will nodded.

"The Gunns will be uniting with us against the Sutherlands," Niel continued.

Eilidh's lips parted as his words sank in. The Mackays and the Gunns were to be allies—this was indeed a special evening.

Yet she didn't miss the stern look on Iver's face. His gaze was narrowed. Unlike Niel, he wasn't pleased about this development.

Pretending not to notice Iver's disapproval, Eilidh smiled at Niel. A surge of affection for her brother-by-marriage rushed through her; it took a brave man indeed to let go of the past. "Thank ye for inviting me here to celebrate with ye."

"It's indeed a development worth celebrating, lass," Niel replied before favoring her with a wink. "And Iver insisted ye join us."

Eilidh's pulse fluttered in her throat. Her suitor wasn't giving up easily. They'd only spoken a couple of hours earlier, and already he'd begun a campaign to win her over.

Keeping her smile fixed in place, Eilidh glanced back at the young laird. Her chest tightened when she saw Iver watching her intently.

Clearing her throat, Eilidh took a restorative sip of wine. She then shifted her attention to the window once more. Beth still wore a veiled expression. Usually, her sister's feelings were plain to see upon her face, but not so this evening.

Eilidh tensed then, wondering if Beth and Niel had argued over this decision.

Niel moved across to the hearth and handed cups of wine to Iver and Will. He then took the empty chair next to the fire and met Will's eye. "My men will have a fast horse ready for ye at dawn, Gunn ... how long will it take ye to reach Castle Gunn?"

"Three days ... no more."

"How many warriors does yer brother have at his disposal?" Iver asked, his tone clipped.

Will leaned back, crossing his long legs at the ankle in front of him. He'd been barefoot over the past months, yet he now wore supple boots that reached just below the knee. "It's hard to say ... we suffered quite a loss at Ruaig-Shansaid," he replied, his gaze remaining on the clan-chief. If he noted Iver's distrust, he didn't show it. "Nonetheless, Tavish is likely to have at least one hundred men-at-arms close by. And he should be able to raise another two hundred within a few days."

Niel leaned forward in his chair, his features tightening. "I'll need every warrior he can spare."

Will held his eye. "And ye shall get them."

As the men continued their conversation, Eilidh moved across to the window and slid onto the seat next to her sister.

Leaning close, she then murmured, "What's wrong?"

Beth favored her with a sidelong glance. "Niel isn't a man to give his trust lightly," she whispered back. "I wonder if desperation hasn't made him reckless."

Eilidh's chest constricted. Did her sister not believe the Gunns would ride to their aid? She supposed there was a considerable amount of trust involved. But if Niel took Will at his word, then Beth should too.

Eilidh would.

"Ye think Gunn would betray us?"

Beth didn't reply.

"Well, I believe Gunn an honorable man ... he saved my life, after all."

Her sister's mouth pursed.

Irritation arrowed through Eilidh. "Niel's gotten to know Will over the past months," she pointed out. "Yer husband is a fine judge of character."

"Aye, usually ... but I still remember how easily Roy swayed him."

Eilidh frowned. Beth was referring to the incident around two years earlier when Roy Gunn, posing as Roy Morrison—Tongue's new blacksmith—had approached him at a village fair. After a short exchange, he'd convinced the clan-chief to attack Dounreay, disputed land on their north-western border that the Gunns had held at the time.

Misgiving prickled Eilidh's skin. She shifted uncomfortably on her seat and took another sip of wine, focusing once more on the three men across the room. Will, Iver, and Niel were now deep in conversation.

"Will is nothing like Roy," Eilidh whispered after a pause. Indeed, she'd met that brute once or twice in Tongue and had witnessed him try to gut John Mackay. "It's hard to believe the two of them are brothers."

"Maybe ... but they share the same blood, all the same," Beth murmured. "And the apple never falls far from the tree."

Stifling a yawn, Eilidh rose to her feet. She was tiring of talk of clan politics and warfare. However, she'd deliberately lingered in the solar, listening to the men's conversation.

Beth had retired to the bedchamber next door a short while earlier, and Iver had also bid them all goodnight—

while Niel and Will sat opposite each other before the hearth. Observing them, a smile curved Eilidh's lips. She'd known that Niel had visited Will frequently in the dungeon, and that they'd played Ard-ri, yet it seemed incongruous to see them together.

They bantered, knocking barbs across at each other as the conversation flowed from one subject to another.

Her smile widened.

A Gunn and a Mackay. Friends.

Glancing up, Niel's gaze alighted on Eilidh. He'd been so engrossed in his discussion, she imagined he'd forgotten she was even there.

"The hour grows late," he admitted with a grimace. "I suppose it's time all of us found our beds." The clan-chief then unfolded himself from the chair and rose to his feet. "Beth has readied the largest guest chamber for Gunn ... can ye show him the way to it, lass?"

Eilidh's heart leaped, excitement fluttering up. She'd deliberately lingered in the solar, hoping for a chance such as this to come her way. If Will was to depart with the dawn, she needed to speak to him first—alone.

All the same, she kept her expression shuttered. "Aye," she murmured demurely before nodding to Will. "Follow me, then."

Will stood up and flashed Niel a grin. "I shall see ye at sunrise in the stables, Mackay."

Eilidh led the way out of the clan-chief's solar, and into the narrow hallway, illuminated by flickering cressets. She picked up a lantern from a hook on the landing and motioned to the shadowy stairwell. "This way," she said, brownies dancing in her belly.

Neither of them spoke as they mounted the narrow stairs to the top floor of the castle. However, Eilidh was keenly aware of the man following at her heel. Even though they hadn't spent time together since she'd visited him in the dungeon, the tension between them still crackled like the air before a summer storm.

Could he feel it like she did?

She had to know.

It was chill in the corridors of Castle Varrich, and Eilidh pulled her woolen shawl more tightly about her shoulders. "The servants will have lit the hearth in yer chamber," she said, glancing over her shoulder at Will. "Ye'll need it too … we'll have a frost overnight."

"I shall have a cold start at dawn then," he replied.

Eilidh looked away, her breathing quickening. "I knew Niel would release ye … eventually," she admitted softly. "I only wish ye weren't departing so soon."

"I have to, lass," he replied, his tone veiled. "Samhuinn looms … and the Mackay is eager to have my brother's support when he faces the Sutherlands in the Lochnaver. The sooner I return to Castle Gunn the better … my brother may take some convincing."

Eilidh's belly twisted. "Will ye fight too?"

"Aye … that's likely."

Halfway down the passage, Eilidh halted, turning to a door on the left. "Here's yer chamber," she announced. Her pulse started to race once more, a suffocating sensation settling over her, sucking the air from her lungs. Time was running out, and there was so much unsaid.

Will moved toward the door and reached for the handle. "Thank ye, Eilidh." His gaze, storm-dark in the light of the flickering lantern, rested upon her. "I shall never forget yer kindness, yer generosity." His expression turned serious then. "The man who eventually claims ye as his bride will be fortunate, indeed."

The smothering sensation grew stronger, and Eilidh raised her free hand to her chest, forcing herself to take slow, even breaths.

He was talking to her as if they were mere acquaintances now. She didn't want formality. Instead, she wanted honesty.

"Will," she whispered, her heart kicking like a wild thing against her breastbone. "I want *ye* to be that man."

13

BUILDING CASTLES IN THE AIR

SILENCE FELL IN the corridor.

Long moments passed before Will finally answered. "Eilidh." Once again, he said her name in a way that made need arch within her; it rolled off his tongue like a song. "What are ye saying?"

She held his eye. "How I feel … is that wrong?"

He swallowed and then pushed the door to his chamber open. "We need to talk, lass."

Breathing shallowly, Eilidh followed Will into the room. Her pulse quickened when he closed the door behind them.

Perhaps noting her surprise, his expression grew serious. "I'd prefer we weren't overheard … fear not, I won't compromise ye."

Heat flushed through Eilidh. Was it wrong to wish he would?

Unspeaking, she moved over to where the hearth burned brightly. This was indeed the largest and best of all the guest chambers in the castle. A large, canopied bed dominated the room, although she tried not to look at it. Suddenly, she felt seriously out of her depth.

Will's presence filled the chamber, and it was an effort not to drop her gaze to her slippered feet.

She was no longer as confident as she'd been out in the corridor.

Will hadn't reacted to her admission as she'd hoped, and she couldn't imagine what he wanted to say to her.

"Ye don't feel the same way, do ye?" she murmured after a weighty pause.

Will raked his hands through his hair and muttered an oath. He still wore his dark hair long—although washed and brushed, it was no longer a wild, tangled mane. "How I feel is of no importance," he replied, his voice roughening. "This can't go any further between us. I thought I'd made our relationship clear?"

Eilidh's cheeks started to burn as she relived their last conversation in the dungeon. Aye, he'd sent her away, but she'd thought it was out of consideration for her, and fear of retribution if the clan-chief discovered their burgeoning connection. Ever since, she'd nursed the hope things would be different once he was free.

"But that was when ye were a prisoner," she said, forcing herself to hold his eye as her face glowed like a coal. Lord, she was making a goose of herself. "Ye are a free man now." She clenched her hands by her sides before edging away from the fire, heading toward the door. "I've clearly misread the situation … my apologies. I shall bid ye 'good eve' now."

It was a cowardly thing to do, to flee like a frightened hare—but the back of her eyes had started to burn. Eilidh could feel tears welling. She had to get away from him before he saw her desperation.

Will side-stepped, blocking her path. "Not yet, lass," he said softly. Something laced his voice. Was it regret? "I need to tell ye something first."

Eilidh blinked rapidly and swallowed hard to loosen her tight throat. She wasn't going to like what was coming; she knew it in her gut. "Go on then," she whispered.

"I'm married," he said bluntly. "Even if I wished to, I can't take ye as my wife."

Eilidh stopped breathing. She wasn't sure what she'd expected him to say, but it wasn't this. "A wife," she repeated stupidly. "Why did ye never say?"

Will drew in a deep breath. "Our conversations didn't stray in that direction … but if they had, I'd have told ye." He paused then, a muscle feathering in his jaw. "Ye are lovelier than a summer's dawn, Eilidh Munro, but I cannot give ye what ye seek."

Eilidh stared back at him, nausea rolling over her. If he'd struck her across the face, it would have hurt less.

A wife!

"What's her name?" she asked, her voice barely above a whisper.

Will stiffened. "Allison."

Allison. A beautiful name. Eilidh couldn't help it; she imagined a bonnie lass standing upon lonely battements, gazing longingly east, her hair catching in the wind. "She will be anxious for yer return."

Will's face shuttered, grooves appearing on either side of his mouth. He then nodded.

Eilidh's chest constricted, jealousy knifing through her like a red-hot blade.

She recalled then, how Will had extricated himself from her that day when she'd stretched her hand through the bars into his cell and held his hand. The caution she'd seen in his eyes wasn't for the reasons she'd thought.

He'd pulled away because he was married.

The queasiness that churned in Eilidh's belly increased. Drawing in a deep breath, she prayed to the saints that she'd manage to keep her composure. Will had complimented her, favored her with warm, sensual smiles—and had saved her life—but she'd taken those things and run with them, building castles in the air.

The crackling of the hearth was the only sound in the room. She'd shifted her gaze to the wall yet could feel Will's gaze upon her.

"Eilidh." His voice was husky now. "Please look at me."

Clenching her jaw, she obeyed. His expression hadn't changed, although his storm-grey eyes were shadowed, betraying that this wasn't easy for him either. "I am sorry. I can see ye are hurt."

Eilidh shrugged, even as her heart slammed painfully against her ribs. "Only because I'm daft," she said, trying to force a light tone and failing. Her voice caught, and her eyes started burning once more. "This is what comes of being a spoiled chit." She dragged in another deep breath. "It's I who should apologize, not ye." She shifted then, circuiting him. And this time, he didn't move to stop her. "I wish ye a safe journey home … and all the best for the future."

"I wish ye all the best too," he replied softly.

Eilidh nodded yet didn't slow as she headed for the door. Suddenly, it seemed furlongs distant. She wanted to dive for it, but instead, forced herself to keep a slow, measured step. She had to cling to her last shreds of dignity.

Her surroundings blurred as tears filled her eyes. She felt sick, as if he'd just punched her hard in the stomach.

Instead, he'd set fire to her dreams. Humiliation burned like a brand on her soul, but she couldn't let him see the depths of it.

Will Gunn was forbidden to her.

Eilidh left his bedchamber without a backward glance, closing the door firmly behind her. When she returned to her room, Clara was dozing on her pallet near the fire.

Her maid sat up as she entered, blinking owl-like. "Lady Eilidh," she greeted. "Sorry, I fell asleep."

"Of course, ye did," Eilidh replied. "It's terribly late."

Clara pushed over the covers and went to rise, but Eilidh held out a hand to forestall her. "Go back to sleep … I shall ready myself for bed tonight."

"But—"

"Goodnight, Clara."

Eilidh then turned her back on the maid, making it clear their exchange was at an end. She wasn't normally so brusque with Clara; usually, the pair of them gossiped about the day's events while the maid brushed Eilidh's hair.

"Goodnight, Lady Eilidh."

Swallowing hard, Eilidh unlaced her kirtle and wriggled out of it. She hadn't brushed her hair, but she didn't care. She'd go to bed with it knotted tonight. Climbing naked into bed, she blew out the candle next to her bed and pulled the covers high around her chin.

And then she lay there, staring up at the canopy above her.

Her belly hurt. How she longed to weep. If she'd been alone in this chamber, she'd have howled like a bairn. But allowing the sobs that welled up in her breast to break free would just bring Clara running. And then the maid would be full of questions she didn't want to answer.

Why had she fallen for a married man?

Why had she acted so recklessly?

Despite her best efforts, tears trickled down Eilidh's cheeks, pooling in her hair. Indeed, she did behave as if nothing bad could ever touch her. As if hurt and disappointment only happened to other folk.

But now she, too, tasted regret—and it was as bitter as gall.

Will stared at the closed door for a long while after Eilidh departed.

And then, eventually, he breathed a curse. "Clod-head," he muttered.

He should have told her about Allison from the start—but he hadn't.

Of course, actions had consequences. Hadn't life already taught him that—too many times to count?

Will hadn't spent a lot of time in his thirty winters considering the thoughts and needs of others—he'd grown up in an environment where such behavior would have been considered a weakness—but it occurred to him now that he'd unwittingly hurt Eilidh.

He shouldn't have encouraged the lass's interest in him, yet he had. Right from the beginning, he'd been unable to take his gaze off her. He'd held her eye for far longer than was seemly, and he'd favored her with flirtatious smiles.

But he'd been a prisoner then, and it had seemed safe to act that way, knowing that nothing could ever come of it.

Will crossed to the fireplace and braced his hands upon the mantel, fixing his gaze upon the flickering flames.

I'm a free man ... and can go home.

When the guards had removed his shackles and set him free earlier in the day, victory had thrilled through him. They'd brought him boots and a fresh set of clothes, and he'd walked out of those dungeons, head held high, a grin upon his face.

Life was looking brighter than it had in a long while. He didn't have an easy task ahead: Tavish wouldn't be as easy to convince as he'd made out to Niel. However, he was determined he wouldn't let the Mackay down. In truth, he hadn't spared Eilidh any thought at all today.

Until she'd entered the clan-chief's solar.

His gaze had tracked her, devoured her. Dressed in a dove-grey kirtle, her unbound hair flowing across her shoulders, she was even lovelier than he remembered.

Regret tugged at him then, for he was leaving in the morning. And even while he'd conversed with Niel and Iver, he'd been aware of her, sitting at the window a few yards distant. She'd watched him with those limpid oaken eyes he could easily drown in.

God's teeth, if only she knew how much he wanted her.

Will squeezed his eyes shut.

It was just as well he hadn't told her.

He'd revealed nothing about his relationship with Allison either. He could have told her the truth—that they were unhappily married—but how would that help?

Allison.

He hadn't missed her during his incarceration. And he'd wager she hadn't pined for him either.

It wasn't his wife's fault. The pair of them had wed in haste six years earlier and repented at their leisure ever since.

Will's eyes flickered open, and his mouth thinned. His imprisonment had given Will much time to reflect— and one of the conclusions he'd reached was that he was a selfish bastard.

Aye, he'd taken a wife, yet Allison had never been his priority. She was a fine field to plow, and lust had driven him into the marriage. For the rest, he'd neglected her, preferring to spend time drinking, fighting, hawking, and dicing with the other warriors at Castle Gunn rather than with his wife.

Allison had quickly tired of being taken for granted, revealing that her passionate nature had another side to it: a shrew's tongue.

Will sucked in a deep breath and pushed himself off the mantelpiece. He wasn't looking forward to seeing Allison again—but it was time he faced up to his responsibilities.

She was his wife, and when he returned home, they'd start again, afresh. Life wouldn't have been easy for Allison during his absence either, and he hoped his brothers' wives had supported her.

Turning away from the fire, Will started to undress for bed.

An image returned to him, of Eilidh staring at him, pain suffusing her warm brown eyes, her heart-shaped face going rigid with shock. He'd unintentionally wounded her deeply and was sorry for it.

In a different life, he'd have offered for her—would have wooed her.

But Will had already made his bed, and now he had to lie in it.

14

DELUDED

WIND WHIPPED OFF the kyle, barreling through the outskirts of Tongue village.

Eilidh dipped her head and pulled her flapping woolen cloak close. This hadn't been the best choice of morning to visit Ava, yet she'd doggedly donned a cloak and fur-lined boots before venturing out into the stinging wind.

She needed to see her friend.

Ava knew how she felt about Will; she was the only one Eilidh could confide in.

Another gust of wind pummeled her, and she shivered. There was a harsh bite to the air this morning, and the sky was a chaotic jumble of clouds—some of them ominously purple-grey.

Like William Gunn's eyes.

Jaw tightening, Eilidh marched on, closing the last few yards to the mill.

Curse him, everything would remind her of that man now.

She'd risen from her bed early but had broken her fast in the women's solar to avoid him. By the time she'd ventured out into the bailey, basket tucked under one arm, Gunn had long departed.

An empty sensation had settled deep in her chest then.

It's over.

No—it had never begun.

She'd woven girlish fantasies in her head about a man she didn't really know. She felt like a fool. It should have occurred to her that he might have a wife back at Castle Gunn. Why wouldn't he? The man was around a decade older than her. Of course, he'd be wed.

But such thoughts hadn't entered her mind.

He could have told her—but why would he? Clearly, he didn't feel the way about her that she did about him.

She'd been deluded.

Ahead, Eilidh spied Ava hanging out flapping washing. The lass hadn't yet seen her.

"Ava!"

Her friend turned, squinting at her, before a smile blossomed across her thin features. "Eilidh! It's been days! I heard the Mackays are marching to war against the Sutherlands ... is it true?"

"Aye." Eilidh halted a few feet distant before patting the basket under her arm. "I'm sorry I've neglected ye ... I brought ye fresh bread to make amends."

Ava's smile remained, although there was a brittle edge to it now. "I've told ye that ye don't always need to bring me food when ye visit ... yer company is enough."

"I know," Eilidh replied, feeling chastised. "But I know how much ye love Beth's oaten bread ... and yer Da needs to keep up his strength."

Ava's smile faded, although her gaze softened. "Ye are kind," she murmured. Stepping away from the washing line, she moved close so she could see Eilidh's face. A crease appeared between her eyebrows then, not a squint but a frown. "Ye have been weeping ... are ye worried about the coming battle?"

Eilidh drew in a deep, shaky breath. All the way here, she'd told herself she wouldn't break down in front of Ava. But under her friend's concern, her resolve was crumbling.

"I wish the Mackays weren't going to war ... but it's other news that has upset me even more," she admitted. "The clan-chief has given William Gunn his freedom."

Ava gasped. "But that's good ... isn't it?"

"It would be ... if he wasn't married."

Ava's face froze. "He has a wife?"

Eilidh nodded.

"And he never said anything?"

Eilidh shook her head.

Ava's features tightened.

Eilidh swallowed hard as tears threatened. Her vision misted then, and she blinked furiously. "Ye know he warned me off two months ago … I should have heeded him, Ava. Instead, I pushed things. I confronted him yester eve … confessed my feelings … and that's when he told me."

Lord, it was hard to relive every encounter, and yet she forced herself to. And this time, she saw the past as it really was—instead of with infatuation-misted vision. Grief twisted hard under her ribcage, the pressure steadily building.

"And now … Iver Mackay has made his interest in me clear." Her pulse quickened. Heavens she'd made a mess of that too. "I tried to tell him I wasn't interested … but now he thinks I'm flighty … that I need more time."

Ava inclined her head. "Ye didn't turn him down outright?"

"I should have … but I didn't want to wound him."

Ava pursed her lips.

"I know I should have been blunter," Eilidh went on, her voice catching. She could feel her friend's censure. "All I've done is give him hope. Iver isn't a man to give up easily."

"Ava!" The miller appeared in the doorway behind his daughter. "Where's the—" Cormac Bain broke off as his gaze alighted upon his daughter and her friend. His ruddy face split into a warm smile. "Greetings, Lady Eilidh."

"Good morning, Cormac." Eilidh held up her basket. "I brought ye and Ava some fresh bread."

His smile widened. "That's kind of ye, lass."

"What did ye want, Da?" Ava asked.

"I can't find the broom."

"It's leaning up next to the hearth."

He nodded before a paroxysm of coughing seized him. Hacking loudly, Cormac turned and lumbered back indoors.

Eilidh watched him go, her brow furrowing. She didn't like the sound of that cough. "How fares yer father these days?" she asked, turning back to her friend.

Ava sighed. "He's exhausted every evening." Her face tensed then. "The healer believes his heart is ailing him. He works too hard."

An awkward silence fell between the two young women. Then Ava pulled a face.

Eilidh's frown deepened. "What?"

"Most women would kill to have yer problems," Ava replied. Her voice was soft, yet there was no mistaking the chagrin in it. "Aye, Gunn has spurned ye, but ye told me yerself that Iver Mackay is handsome, brave, and kind. Ye could do much worse."

Eilidh's breathing caught. "Ye sound like Beth," she said stiffly. "She, too, thinks I'm difficult ... contrary."

Ava's blue eyes shadowed then, her thin body tensing.

They stared at each other for an instant before a prickling sensation crept over Eilidh's chest. Shame. Right from their first meeting, it was her, not Ava, who'd pushed this friendship. When she was younger, Eilidh hadn't kept secrets from any of her sisters—but these days, she felt judged by Beth. Eager for a confidant, she'd poured out her heart to Ava instead.

But her friend's response just now highlighted the gulf between them; indeed, Eilidh must appear spoiled and self-indulgent. She wasn't the one local men spurned. The one with an ailing father. The one who worked her fingers to the bone.

"I'm sorry," Eilidh said huskily. She reached out then and clasped Ava's hand, squeezing firmly. "I know ye mean well."

"I do," Ava whispered, her own voice catching. "And like Beth ... I just want ye to be happy."

Slowing his courser to a walk, Will gave a rueful smile as he surveyed the cluster of sod-roofed stone cottages on the shore of the glittering loch. The Lochnaver was bonnie country—was it any wonder Robert Sutherland coveted it?

Indeed, this village appeared prosperous, with well-tended dwellings, rosy-cheeked bairns playing outdoors, and mobs of black-faced sheep grazing on the lush hills behind the houses.

The delicious aroma of roasting mutton beckoned then, and Will's stomach rumbled, reminding him that he'd hardly eaten all day.

Above him, the last of a violet and gold sunset was fading, and he lifted his chin to watch it.

Will didn't take things for granted these days—not after so long in irons, shuffling back and forth from his squalid cell to back-breaking days of work in the fields. It was a thrill to ride free on a fast horse, with the wind in his face.

He'd slept rough the night before and had lain staring up at the stars for a long while. He hadn't realized how much he'd missed the night sky. However, he didn't wish to camp outdoors tonight. He had coin in a pouch at his waist, and he'd use it for a hot meal and a comfortable bed.

Will shifted in the saddle then before wincing. He was halfway into his journey to Castle Gunn, and the muscles in his backside and thighs were protesting.

Dismounting, he led his horse across to a long, low-slung building made of stacked stone at the roadside. A faded sign hung above the entrance: *Grummore Inn*.

The aroma of cooking grew stronger, and Will's mouth filled with saliva. Aye, this was exactly what he'd been looking for.

He stabled Dusk, the leggy grey mare Niel had gifted him, in the stables out back, before making his way indoors.

Seating himself by the flickering hearth, Will welcomed the tankard of ale and plate of hearty food the inn-keeper's wife brought him. "It's quiet in here, this eve," he observed as she placed the trencher of mutton and gravy before him.

The woman pulled a face. "Aye … ever since the Sutherlands started worrying these lands, folk travel north by other roads." She paused then, eyeing him curiously. "Where have ye journeyed from?"

"Castle Varrich."

Her gaze gleamed with interest. "Oh, aye? Any news?"

Will hesitated, wondering if he should warn the woman of the coming storm. Word obviously hadn't reached this part of the Lochnaver yet. He decided that he should; these folk needed to be prepared.

"Aye, but it's ill-tidings," he said after a pause. "The Sutherlands and the Mackays are to meet in battle upon the Lochnaver … at Samhuinn."

The inn-keeper's wife gasped, her spine snapping straight. "God's blood … why?"

"Robert Sutherland has declared these lands as his own … and Niel Mackay disputes his claim."

She muttered another oath under her breath. "Why won't those Sutherland dogs let us be?"

Will didn't answer. It seemed there was a complex web of reasons why the Sutherland had claimed the Lochnaver, but he didn't feel like going into them now.

The woman's jaw tightened then, her blue eyes glinting. "I thank ye for the warning … I must let everyone know."

"Aye … that's wise."

She inclined her head then. "Can I ask yer name?"

"William." Will paused then. He was tempted to tell her he was a Gunn; after so long in captivity, he longed to be able to declare himself. He was a free man, after all. Even so, his clansmen wouldn't be welcomed here, and so Will's mouth tugged into a half-smile. "Mackay."

Watching the inn-keeper's wife bustle off, Will sighed. The brief exchange was a reminder—not that he needed one—of the difficult task that lay ahead. Tavish would be incensed when he learned of the promise his younger brother had made on his behalf. He didn't want to disappoint Tav; his brother's good opinion mattered to him. It would take all his powers of persuasion to convince him to aid the Mackays.

Pushing aside the lingering worry, Will picked up his tankard and took a large gulp. The ale was cold and bitter, just the way he liked it. However, now that his mood had shifted, he struggled to regain his earlier sense of well-being

Remembering his vow to Niel made him think about Castle Varrich—and Eilidh. The lass haunted him. The memory of her hurt gaze, the mortification on her face as she'd left his bedchamber, made the ale turn to vinegar in his mouth. He hadn't wanted to take his leave of her that way.

Shaking his head to clear it of crrant thoughts that would do him no good, Will started on his meal. He had to put Eilidh out of his mind entirely.

Allison is just over a day away now.

Thinking about his wife was a mistake too, for his belly suddenly tightened.

Things hadn't been good between them when he'd left Castle Gunn to march into battle at Tavish's side. On the morning of his departure, they'd argued—he couldn't even remember the reason for it—and Allison had thrown a rolling pin at him. He'd ducked the missile easily and laughed. His wife's insults had followed him down the stairs, ringing off stone, as he'd left her.

Will's mouth twisted as he tore off a hunk of coarse bread and dipped it in gravy. He wasn't proud of himself.

I'll be a better husband this time, he vowed silently. *I'll make it up to her.*

15

YE DESERVED BETTER

WILL SMELLED THE sea before he set eyes on Castle Gunn again. The scent of brine caught at the back of his throat, and the scream of gulls echoed across the green hills of Caithness.

A smile tugged at the corners of his mouth.

Home. Finally.

The Lochnaver now lay behind him—for the moment—and he rode upon Gunn lands once more. When the familiar bulk of Castle Gunn appeared on the northern horizon, Will's heart started to pound, goosebumps prickling his skin.

Not all his memories of this place were pleasant ones, yet this castle still had a visceral effect on him.

It was the seat of the Gunn clan, and he was a clan-chief's son.

Urging Dusk into a canter, Will rode in across rolling hills where sheep grazed placidly, his attention never wavering from the high curtain walls. Like Varrich, it perched above the lands it commanded, although Castle Gunn had a grimmer air than the Mackay stronghold.

It had a precarious position, teetering upon a finger of land that was connected to the mainland by a rickety wooden bridge. Eventually slowing his mare to a trot, Will approached the bridge. He spied the outlines of men standing upon the guard tower, watching him. The portcullis was raised at this time of day, although he could see some of the men held crossbows aloft.

The Gunns were a suspicious lot; they were one of the smallest clans in the Highlands, yet easily the most aggressive toward outsiders.

"Ho!" One of them shouted out, his voice echoing across the chasm between them. "State yer name, stranger!"

Will drew his horse to a halt at the foot of the bridge. Below, waves boiled against sheer cliffs, the roar filling his ears. The breathless sensation that had caught him in its thrall as he approached increased, his pulse now pounding in his ears. "I'm no stranger," he called back. "It's Will Gunn ... back from the dead!"

Will rode into the wide bailey and drew his courser up.

Around him, he could already hear the excited chatter of voices. News of his arrival was spreading through the fortress like fire on dry tinder.

Soon it would reach the clan-chief's ears.

Grinning, Will swung down from the saddle, turning to face the guards who'd come down from the walls to greet him. The delighted smiles etched upon their faces warmed Will; there had been times during his incarceration when he'd wondered if anyone here actually missed him.

Sometimes he believed they'd given up on him.

"It's good to have ye back, lad!" One of the older, grizzled warriors slapped him heartily on the back. "Did ye escape?"

Will shook his head. "The Mackay decided it was time to let me go."

"He did?"

A rumble of disbelief rippled through the gathering crowd, and Will's smile turned rueful.

Wait until ye all hear why. He was aware many of them wouldn't like it—and for that reason, he'd let Tavish be the one to inform them they'd soon be marching to war, not *against* the Mackays, but at their side.

Amongst the guards, he spied his brother-by-marriage, Archie Keene.

And unlike the others, the warrior wasn't smiling.

"Archie!" Will stepped forward, reaching out to clasp arms with the man. However, Archie kept his arms by his sides.

Now that he drew close, Will noted that his brother-by-marriage looked enraged: his mouth was a tight, thin line, his blue eyes narrow slits.

Will's skin prickled once more, his expression sobering. "Is something amiss?" he asked. "How is Allison?"

Even as he asked the question, Will's gut clenched. The muscle flickering in Archie's jaw warned him he wasn't going to like the answer. Even so, he was unprepared for the man's rough response. "She's dead."

For a few instants, Will merely stared at the warrior. Around them, conversation died. However, Will's gaze never left Archie's face. A strange light-headed sensation swept over him. "When?"

Archie's mouth twisted. "Last year."

Will's heart started to pound in his ears. God's teeth, had his wife died in childbirth? Allison might have been with bairn when he was captured, and he'd have had no idea. Long moments passed before he managed to ask, "How?"

"Her lover beat her to death."

Archie's words fell like hammer blows in the now silent bailey.

Will's breathing caught before he rasped, "What?"

It shouldn't have surprised him that Allison had taken a lover after his imprisonment. She'd been a passionate woman who adored male attention. Even so, the news of her demise at a lover's hands shocked him.

Archie took another step toward him, his expression menacing now. The warrior's meaty hands fisted at his sides. He looked like he wanted to take a swing at him. Will scowled. He didn't understand Archie's aggression.

"Ye were a poor husband to my sister," his brother-by-marriage growled. "Ye neglected her ... went away on hunts for weeks at a time without even informing Allison first and ignored her when ye were at home. Is it any surprise she ran into another man's arms in the end?"

A chill feathered across Will's skin. All these accusations were true, although he didn't want his relationship aired like this in front of a gawking crowd. Servants emerged into the bailey now to see the youngest Gunn brother's return. He could almost hear the ears flapping around him.

Folding his arms across his chest, Will's gaze narrowed. "My relationship with my wife is none of yer business."

Two high spots of color appeared on Archie's cheeks. "Aye, it is. She was *my* kin." He spat on the ground between them then. "Ye always were a selfish bastard."

"Watch yer tongue, Keene," Will growled back, his anger quickening. He was still in shock, yet this warrior clearly forgot himself.

Archie swung for him, his large fist slicing through the air.

Will ducked, but the warrior's knuckles collided with his cheek, nonetheless, snapping his head back.

A roar went up amongst the watching crowd when Will snarled a curse and went for Archie, head-butting him.

A heartbeat later, the two men were slugging at each other, the thud of knuckles colliding with flesh, and grunts of pain, echoing through the bailey.

Among his six brothers, Will was the shortest in stature and the leanest in build. However, most of the Gunn males were beasts of men, so that didn't make him small. Archie Keene had a hulking build, and he liked to fight dirty—which made him difficult to best.

It had been a while since Will had been in a scrap, yet his toil in the fields below Varrich had kept his body strong. His blood sang as he landed a hard punch in his opponent's belly.

Archie responded by barreling into him, head-down.

Both men went down in a tangle of limbs and flying fists.

"What's this then?" A rough, yet faintly amused, voice cut through the din of male voices—as the watching guards urged them on and took bets on who would win. "I should have known that I'd find ye in the midst of trouble, little brother."

Climbing to his feet, Will shook his head to clear it. Archie had just landed a punch to his jaw that made his ears ring. Reaching up, he wiped his bleeding nose with the back of his hand.

On the ground, Archie Keene groaned, still curled up from where Will had kneed him in the cods.

He, too, could fight dirty.

However, Will's attention wasn't on the warrior, but on the tall, dark-haired man who'd just elbowed his way through the throng and now stood facing him.

Tavish Gunn eyed his younger brother before glancing down at where Archie was wheezing curses. "Keene has told ye about yer wife then?"

The clan-chief's words were matter of fact, yet Will spied the shadow that flitted across his grey eyes.

"Aye," Will replied roughly. "It seems I'm to blame."

"Ye are," Archie ground out as he tried to push himself up into a sitting position. "Ye drove her into that brute's arms."

"Enough, Keene," Tavish rumbled. His gaze roamed Will's face. He then stepped forward, and the two brothers clasped arms. Behind him, Will spied two more familiar faces. His two hulking other brothers who resided at Castle Gunn—Blair and Evan—approached, incredulous grins upon their faces.

"Never thought we'd see yer face again, lad," Blair greeted him.

"Aye," Will replied, glancing back at where Tavish was still studying him, his gaze veiled. "There were times when I wondered the same."

"So, Niel Mackay gave ye yer freedom?" Evan asked. Both he and Blair stepped up next to Tavish, taking their turns to clasp Will's arm in greeting.

"Aye." The urge to reveal the circumstances of his release reared up within Will. Nevertheless, good sense checked him. He'd just arrived and was still reeling from the news that his wife was dead. He was also still trying to stem the bleeding in his nose after his fight with Archie.

It would be wise to speak to Tavish about the conditions of his release when they were alone. Reactions to what he'd agreed to would cause an explosive reaction within the keep. He needed to manage this with care.

"The Mackay decided two years was long enough," he replied, wiping his nose once more. "The man knows what it's like to rot in a dungeon, I suppose."

Tavish grunted. "I'd have expected ye to look like a scarecrow after being locked up in a cell for so long." His gaze roamed over Will's shoulders before he frowned. "And yet ye are strong?"

Will nodded. "I nearly died of lung sickness in my first winter at Varrich ... the dungeon is carved into the rock under the castle ... a dank, airless place. Once spring arrived, the Mackay surprised me by ensuring I had better food and warmer clothing. He also sent me to work in the fields each day."

Tavish's mouth pursed. "Why would he do that?"

Will flashed him a wry smile. "A dead Gunn hostage isn't any good to him, is it?"

Tavish snorted. "No, I suppose not." He paused then, a slow smile stretching his mouth. "It's good to have ye home, Will."

Will climbed the stairs to the tower where he and Allison had once lived together. Situated on the sea-facing corner of the walls, and formally guards' lodgings, the tower was drafty and bitterly cold in winter. But it was Will's. Tavish had turfed his men out and housed them elsewhere after Will's marriage so that his brother and wife could make it their home.

After his time away, it felt strange to climb these stairs once more. He almost expected to hear the lilt of Allison's voice as she sang to herself while she cooked his supper—but this afternoon, the tower was eerily silent.

Reaching the chamber that had served as their kitchen and eating space, Tavish halted.

The space was spotlessly clean, as it had always been. The air smelled faintly of lye soap, even after months of no one living here.

Will's chest constricted then.

Archie had been twisted up with bitterness and grief and looking for someone to blame, but there had been truth to his words.

Will had never raised a hand to his wife or gone with other women, but he'd been a distant husband. She was merely there to cook him meals and warm his bed. He hadn't wanted anything else from her; he hadn't given her the emotional closeness that women craved.

Will's attention shifted to the ladder on the far side of the kitchen then, his chin rising as he followed it up to the loft where he and his wife had once slept.

He wouldn't go up to that space—not at present.

Did Allison bring her lover here?

With him gone, there would have been little to prevent her.

Will's jaw clenched then. He'd been a little nervous about facing Allison again, and had prepared himself to be humbled, to make amends for the past.

But he'd never expected this.

Tavish had informed him that Allison's lover had been hanged for his crime—his corpse strung up on the walls for the crows to peck clean.

Will shifted his attention to the empty hearth. Satan's cods, it was cold in here, for a north wind whistled in through the open window. However, it wasn't the weather that chilled him to the marrow, but the knowledge that this tower was full of ghosts.

Was Allison's shade watching him, cursing him for being a poor husband?

Mouth twisting, he raked his hands through his hair and moved to the window, staring out at the whitecaps and the clouds that chased each other across the sky.

"Archie was right," he murmured. "Ye deserved better, lass."

A heaviness settled in the pit of Will's gut. This wasn't the homecoming he'd envisaged. As his incarceration drew out, he'd often imagined his return to Castle Gunn, and the sense of belonging he'd feel when he saw his brothers again. Tavish, Blair, and Evan understood him. Their brutal upbringing had bonded them.

But Will didn't feel the connection he'd expected. It wasn't just the tragedy of Allison's death either. His time away had changed him—and as a result, the place he thought was a part of him had altered as well.

16

WILL'S PROMISE

"IT'S SUCH A relief to have ye home, Will!" The slender dark-haired woman flew across the clan-chief's solar and clasped her brother-by-marriage in a surprisingly fierce hug. "We've all been so worried about ye!"

Drawing back, Will smiled. "It's good to see ye again, Robina." His throat tightened then; his sister-by-marriage's warm welcome touched him. He'd always been fond of Robina. Her marriage to Tavish had been an arranged one, and the woman, who was the Oliphant clan-chief's daughter, had been reluctant to bind herself to his clan. But, over a decade on, she and Tavish had a brood of four sons, and the clan-chief's wife still glowed with happiness.

Scanning Robina's elfin face, Will noted that her eyes gleamed with emotion. He'd known that Robina cared for him, yet—like many things—he'd taken it for granted. Her welcome eased the odd sense of dislocation that had settled upon him since leaving the tower.

He cleared his throat then. "How are the lads?"

"Growing like weeds," Tavish answered. His brother was pouring them cups of wine at the nearby sideboard. The solar's shutters were closed at this hour, for it was dark outdoors. Supper had been and gone, and Tavish had invited Will to join him and Robina for a cup of wine before bed.

Will was pleased—finally, he'd get an opportunity to tell him of the promise he'd made to Niel.

"Finn takes after ye," his brother continued, his mouth quirking. "The lad has an impudent tongue that's always getting him thrashed by his older brothers."

Will grinned. "That's what comes from being the youngest," he replied. "Ye grow up fighting."

He'd seen his four nephews at supper. Indeed, Knox, Mungo, Laurie, and Finn had all sprouted up since he'd seen them last.

Taking the cup of wine from Tavish, Will met his eye. "Knox reminds me of Alex."

Tavish nodded, although his expression hardened at the mention of their eldest, estranged brother. They never usually discussed Alexander.

Will took a sip of wine. "I saw him, ye know … at Farr Castle, after Ruaig-Shansaid."

Tavish stilled. "Ye did?"

"Aye, I was locked up in one of the cages on the cliff-face beneath the castle when he paid me a visit."

"Came to gloat, did he?" Tavish growled, his fingers tightening around the cup of wine he'd yet to take a sip from.

"I accused him of that," Will admitted, "but I think it was curiosity that brought him to me. He wanted to know how we were all faring."

Tavish snorted at that. He then crossed to the glowing hearth and folded his long, lean body into one of the high-backed chairs before it. "Bit late for that now."

Will drew in a deep breath, readying himself for what needed to be said. He'd dreaded this moment, but Niel was relying on him—and the promise Will had made him suddenly mattered even more than it had when he'd left Castle Varrich. Tavish wasn't going to like what he had to say, yet he'd gain nothing by putting this off.

"There is something I must tell ye, Tav," he said after a pause.

Tavish glanced up from where he'd been watching the dancing flames. "Aye?"

"I didn't want to say anything earlier, not in front of yer men and our brothers … but the reason I gave for my release wasn't the truth."

The Gunn clan-chief stilled, his gaze narrowing. "Go on."

Will took a large swallow of wine. "Niel Mackay and I have developed an 'understanding' of sorts over the past months." Tavish's dark brows crashed together, warning him that, indeed, his brother wasn't going to welcome his next words. Yet Will pressed on. "He even brought an Ard-ri board down to my cell sometimes … and we'd play a few games."

Robina's eyes went as wide as moons at this revelation, while Tavish gave an incredulous snort. "All those years at Bass Rock clearly didn't do him any good … the man's cracked."

Will's mouth curved. "No, he's still as sharp as a blade." He halted there, considering his next words carefully. "The Mackays and the Sutherlands are in dispute over the Lochnaver … they will be facing each other in battle at Samhuinn."

Tavish inclined his head, gaze hooding. "Aye?"

Will nodded. "Robert Sutherland deliberately waited until a few days ago before announcing his intention to raze those lands and claim them as his own … giving the Mackays little time to prepare for battle."

"A canny move," Tavish replied, his mouth curving into a smug smile. "Serves the whoresons right."

Will took another drink of wine, uneasiness tightening his gut. "Niel Mackay is scrambling to call his nearest allies to him, but when they face the Sutherlands, the Mackays will be at a considerable disadvantage." He paused there, before finally admitting, "I told him that if he gave me my freedom, the Gunns would ride into battle against the Sutherlands with him."

Silence fell in the solar.

A veil dropped over Tavish's gaze, and his face turned stony.

Will's breathing grew shallow. He didn't want Tav to be disappointed in him, but he stared at him now as if a changeling had just appeared in his brother's place.

Robina's face had also frozen, the warmth leeching from her features. Will knew what she was thinking—that he'd lost his mind.

But he hadn't.

"Judas," Tavish eventually growled, setting his wine down with a thud and pushing himself out of his chair in one smooth movement. "How dare ye make such a promise?"

He stalked over to Will then, going eye-to-eye with him. Will tensed. He didn't want to brawl with his brother. He had to make him see past the hate he bore his neighbors.

"The Sutherlands are a threat to us all," Will replied, his tone low and even. "We must unite with the Mackays against them."

"After Ruaig-Shansaid?" Tavish growled. "I shall rip out Niel Mackay's guts with my bare hands before I'll ever fight at his side."

Will cocked an eyebrow. "Ye know who ye sound like?"

Tavish's lean body tensed.

George Gunn.

They'd all hated their father. He'd been a bully, who'd lived for war. In truth, Tavish wasn't anything like him, but Will's comment had been deliberate. A warning.

He stepped closer to his brother then. "Put aside yer hate for the moment, Tav, and see what ye will gain from this alliance. Don't forget that we share a long border with the Sutherlands. The Lochnaver is but a stone's throw from here." He paused then, letting his words sink in. "Who's to say that once he's taken those lands, Robert Sutherland won't turn his attention upon us?"

"I think we should turn back now," Eilidh called out. "From the look of the sky, rain is on its way."

Twisting in the saddle, Iver Mackay's gaze lifted north to where ominous-looking grey clouds were rolling in. He pulled a face. "Aye, ye are right," he replied. "Come on then."

The pair of them turned their mounts—her on Gypsie, him on a temperamental stallion with a glossy peat-brown coat—and headed back along the shore of the kyle. The dark outline of Castle Varrich was still some distance off, and as the riders made their way toward it, Eilidh felt spits of moisture upon her face.

They weren't likely to beat the rain.

"Sorry, it probably wasn't the best afternoon to take a ride," Iver said, slowing his stallion so she drew up alongside him.

Eilidh shrugged and smiled. "No need to apologize, Iver ... ye know how capricious the weather is in the Highlands. The sky looked clear enough when we set out."

Iver smiled back, and Eilidh shifted uncomfortably in the saddle, nervousness bubbling up.

Nearly a fortnight had passed since Robert Sutherland's missive, and since William Gunn's departure. To her surprise, and relief, she hadn't seen much of Iver in that time. The laird of Dun Ugadale had been caught up, helping Niel prepare for war.

But with the Mackays marching out the following dawn, he'd finally cornered her after the noon meal the day before and requested they took a ride together. Indeed, it would be his last chance to spend any time with her before his departure.

Not for the first time, guilt constricted Eilidh's chest.

Ava's counsel rang in her ears. Iver was a good man. Most women—lasses who weren't daft like she was— would leap at the opportunity to become his wife. Will was lost to her, after all; the man had never been hers, to begin with.

She'd be wise not to dismiss Iver so lightly.

Glancing back at her companion, Eilidh met his eye and smiled, resolving to try and look to the future rather than the past. "Tell me a little of Dun Ugadale, Iver."

He grinned back. "Have ye ever been to the Kintyre peninsula?"

She shook her head.

"Aye, well, it's a bonnie corner of Scotland indeed … with windswept hills, long golden-sand beaches, and views of the sea." He paused then, his gaze shining. Iver clearly loved his home. "My broch sits on the site of an ancient fort, perched upon a low promontory, looking out to sea."

Eilidh's smile widened. "And what of yer kin … do ye have any siblings?"

Iver's mouth quirked. "Aye … three younger brothers … Lennox, Kerr, and Brodie."

There was warmth in his dark-blue eyes, and Eilidh sensed he had a good rapport with his brothers—something else that went in his favor.

Aye, she'd be a fool to refuse this man.

Shifting her gaze ahead, Eilidh surveyed the tents camped around the base of the rocky promontory upon which the castle perched. Nervousness fluttered within her.

"How many men has the Mackay been able to raise?" she asked.

"Too few, unfortunately," the young laird muttered. "The MacLeods aren't willing to assist us … and even with all the men Achness, Loch Stach, Farr, and Balnakeil could spare, we are below four hundred."

Eilidh's breathing quickened. Four hundred sounded like a large number to her; yet, what if Sutherland had gathered twice that number?

It would be a massacre.

Cold sweat beaded across her skin, and she shivered, pulling her cloak close. They were on the cusp of the bitter season now. Soon the warmth of summer would be but a distant memory.

"Ye will be relying on support from the Gunns then?" she said after a pause.

Iver didn't answer immediately, and when she glanced his way, she saw the tense cast to his features. "Aye … and that bothers me," he muttered.

Eilidh frowned. "Ye don't trust William Gunn's word?"

Iver's mouth thinned. "Not in the slightest. Never trust a Gunn."

Eilidh's pulse accelerated. She wanted to speak up, to defend Will, yet she bit back the words. Iver would wonder why she spoke so passionately on Gunn's behalf. All the same, she couldn't let the statement go unanswered. "Yer clan-chief is no fool," she pointed out cautiously, "he wouldn't have released Gunn if he thought he'd betray him."

"Niel was desperate," Iver replied, his tone cooling. He paused then before exhaling sharply. "Let us not talk of such things, Lady Eilidh. Tomorrow, I shall depart with the rest of the Mackays to battle ... but I'd prefer to focus on other matters this afternoon."

There was no mistaking the sudden intimacy of his tone.

Iver wasn't giving up on her. She knew then that he intended to propose to her—again.

They rode into the encampment, past where warriors sparred with dirks and claidheamh-mòrs, the aroma of roasting meat drifting through the clusters of tents.

Along the way, they passed Connor Mackay, laird of Farr, taking his men through drills.

Spying Iver, Connor turned and waved.

The chieftain of Dun Ugadale grinned back. "Readying yer rabble, eh, Connor?"

"Aye," the chieftain of Farr replied, his mouth curving in a wry smile. "This lot can't wait to spill some Sutherland blood."

Iver nodded, his gaze sweeping over the cluster of warriors who'd been sparring with bound sword blades behind Connor. An instant later, Iver stilled, his jaw tightening. Following his stare, Eilidh's attention alighted upon a big, heavily-muscled man with shaggy black hair, a scar on his cheek, and grey eyes.

Eilidh's breathing hitched.

Those eyes were the exact same hue as Will's.

This man was a Gunn.

Her mind scrabbled, as she tried to make sense of it, before she realized this must be the infamous Alexander Gunn.

Alexander met Iver's stare and held it boldly, his handsome face impassive.

Jaw clenching, Iver eventually jerked his attention away and focused on Connor once more. "They'll get their chance soon enough."

He then urged his stallion on, continuing his path through the camp. Wordlessly, Eilidh followed. Her brow furrowed; indeed, Iver didn't trust the Gunns one bit. Any of them.

17

RESOLVED

LEAVING THE CAMP behind, Eilidh and Iver ascended the path toward the castle.

The rain hit when she was halfway up, driving across the land in heavy curtains.

Cursing under her breath, Eilidh yanked up her hood and bowed her head, crouching low over her garron's neck. Gypsie doggedly plodded up the path, ears back.

The squall battered them viciously, splinters of ice amongst the pelting rain—and by the time they clattered into the bailey, Eilidh's hands were numb, her cheeks stinging.

Swinging down from her pony's back, she pulled Gypsie toward the stables. Iver was close behind, soothing his stallion as the beast tossed its head and pawed at the ground. Despite herself, Eilidh was impressed how he handled the courser; the horse always seemed on the brink of throwing its rider, yet Iver managed to keep its energy leashed.

Out of the slashing rain, Eilidh pushed back her hood and led Gypsie into a stall. She then started removing her tack, cursing her numb fingers that kept fumbling.

"Here ... let me help with that." Iver appeared at her shoulder. He'd tied up his stallion in the stall opposite and noted her struggles. In a deft movement, he unbuckled the saddle and removed it from the garron's broad back.

"Thank ye," Eilidh murmured, embarrassed by her ineptitude. "My fingers have gone numb from cold."

"I really shouldn't have insisted we went so far," Iver replied, his gaze shadowing as he turned to her.

And then he reached out and took her hands, thawing them between his.

Iver's touch was warm and strong—and yet it didn't make her pulse race, didn't make her breathing catch or belly dive.

Curse Gunn, would she always compare her reactions to men with the effect Will had wielded on her? Couldn't he leave her be?

Eilidh clenched her jaw. Will was married. Right now, he was back in his wife's arms, not giving her a second thought. Why was she pining over him? Why was she comparing Iver to him?

It wasn't right. Iver had no idea she was measuring him against another man and finding him lacking.

Goose-wit, she chided herself. *Are ye going to let a fantasy ruin yer life?*

"Eilidh." Iver's voice was husky, full of longing. "I know I said I'd give ye time … but I ride out tomorrow. Before I do, can ye tell me if there is any hope? Do I woo ye in vain?"

Eilidh drew in a slow, steadying breath. This was her chance. If she was going to dash his hopes forever, now was the moment.

However, she hesitated.

She'd had plenty of time to think over the last two weeks, time to consider her behavior over the last year and marvel at her naiveté. Disappointment soured her belly, and longing caused a permanent ache to settle under her breastbone, but it was foolish to give such thoughts free rein.

Will was gone. She'd never likely see him again.

But Iver was here, and most importantly, he wanted her. Wasn't that what really mattered?

She'd tried to follow her own path, to reach for her dreams, but life had crushed her spirit as only it could.

And so, she held the laird's gaze and whispered, "Aye … there's still hope."

Iver stared back at her a moment, his gaze turning limpid. "Then I shall ask ye one last time, Eilidh ... will ye be my wife?"

Lifting her chin, she favored him with a soft smile. "I will."

Jean cast her sewing aside and leaped to her feet. "I'm glad to hear ye have come to yer senses ... at last!" She then rushed to Eilidh and threw her arms around her, squeezing hard. When she drew back, Jean was smiling. "Iver is an excellent choice."

"He's a bit arrogant though, don't ye think?" Neave quipped from the window seat.

Eilidh glanced to where her sister sat nursing her bairn. Lyla Mackay of Aberach had been born barely a month previous. She was a small babe, with soft, fluffy brown hair and lay cradled against her mother's exposed breast.

Neave wore a wicked grin upon her lips, making it clear she was teasing her younger sister.

"All our husbands are arrogant, Neave," Beth pointed out from where she sat by the fire, a pile of mending on her lap. "As are most warriors."

Jean snorted at this. "Robin's not as cocky as Niel."

Beth pulled a face before fixing her attention on Eilidh. She smiled, yet the expression was a trifle strained. "Ye chose well."

Eilidh smiled back, warmth flooding through her. Her sisters' approval had always meant a lot to her—too much perhaps, she'd come to realize. Still, their happy faces made her lingering anxiety about her decision to wed Iver fade.

Resolve hardened within her. It was time to grow up, to appreciate what she had instead of wasting time on foolish daydreams.

"Have ye set a date yet?" Jean asked then.

Eilidh shook her head. "The Mackays must face the Sutherlands before we can turn our thoughts to such things."

The moment she uttered those words, she regretted them.

All three of her sisters stiffened, a shadow falling over their faces.

Neave dropped her gaze, her mouth compressing, while Jean swallowed hard. By the fire, Beth went still, color leeching from her face.

Eilidh's breathing quickened, worry flickering through her. "Beth?" She went to her eldest sister and lowered herself before her, grasping her hands. Beth's fingers were ice-cold. "I'm sorry … that was insensitive of me."

Her sister attempted a smile, although it was more of a grimace. "For a short while, I'd almost forgotten," she murmured, "that they're riding out tomorrow."

"Ye are worried about Niel," Eilidh replied, gently squeezing her hand. "That's understandable."

"We *all* worry about her husbands," Neave reminded them, her voice tight. "I've just given birth … do ye think I want John to go off to war?" There was an uncharacteristic edge to Neave's voice, and when Eilidh glanced her way, she marked the tears glistening in Neave's eyes. Likewise, Jean looked as if she might start weeping at any moment.

"Och, don't fret so," Eilidh said, attempting to lighten the atmosphere of gloom that had settled over the women's solar. "Our men are all warriors of renown. They will return to us."

"Aye, but only if the Gunns uphold their end of the bargain," Beth replied, her voice roughening.

Eilidh's belly contracted. Like Iver, her sister doubted William Gunn's word.

It was ironic really. Despite that they hadn't parted under the best of circumstances, Eilidh still trusted Will.

But, apart from Niel, few others did.

"Have faith that they will, dear sister," Eilidh murmured. "The Gunns will ride into battle with the Mackays. Ye shall see."

Their gazes fused and held before Beth slowly nodded. She then reached down with her free hand and cupped her belly, her expression softening. "I hope so, lass," she whispered, "because Niel will soon be a father again."

Chaos reigned in the bailey of Castle Varrich. The clatter of shod hooves and the boom of rough male voices echoed against stone. Niel was readying his men to ride out. Their blood was up—male aggression hung heavily in the damp air.

Standing on the steps above the bailey, Eilidh watched them.

Iver wasn't there, for he'd gone down to the base of the promontory, where his men had camped, to ready them for departure. However, before leaving that morning, he'd come to the clan-chief's solar to bid her farewell. Eilidh had wished the chieftain well, and then he'd taken her hand, lightly kissed the back of it, and promised her he'd return to her.

"Ready, Niel?" John Mackay of Aberach twisted in the saddle and fixed his clan-chief with a penetrating look. As always, John's eye patch lent him a roguish air. Usually, Eilidh's brother-by-marriage wore a smile upon his face, but his expression was set hard this morning.

Niel flashed his cousin a feral smile. "Aye." He then swung up onto the back of his courser—a fiery bay stallion named Stoirm—and drew his dirk, holding it aloft. The morning light—dim as it was today, for heavy clouds hung over Varrich—glinted off the wickedly sharp blade. "We ride for the Lochnaver," he shouted, his voice thundering through the bailey and quietening the chaos around him, "to show Robert Sutherland what happens when he tries to take what belongs to us!"

Shouts and whistles rang out, lifting high above the curtain wall.

Eilidh shivered at the bloodlust she heard there. Misgiving rippled over her.

Growing up, her father had often warned her that war was an ugly thing, that it turned even gentle-hearted men into savages. She'd listened to him, nodding at his wisdom, but she'd never truly understood him. Until now.

The Saints preserve her, she hoped Will would be successful in convincing his brother to join them in battle. If he wasn't, there was a good chance she'd never see these brave warriors again.

Eilidh sucked in a deep breath. *I know ye can do it, Will. I believe in ye.*

And she did. Despite that she'd let Will go, she couldn't bring herself to think ill of him. He was trustworthy and would prove himself.

Eilidh stepped close to Beth then and slid her arm through hers. Her sister held Angus upon her hip; of course, she was still early into her pregnancy and wasn't yet showing.

"Did ye tell Niel," Eilidh murmured to her sister, "about the bairn?"

"Of course," Beth whispered back. "Last night."

"And?"

Beth's eyelashes fluttered. She then reached up and knuckled away a tear. "He was overjoyed ... said it was a good portent for the coming battle."

Niel turned in the saddle then, his gaze cutting across the throng to his wife. An intense look passed between them—and Eilidh's breathing caught.

It was as if the rest of the world disappeared.

An ache rose under her breastbone.

How she'd longed for a connection like the one Niel and Beth shared. The passing of time only seemed to grow their love, to make deep roots spread beneath them.

Ye shall have that with Iver, one day ... ye'll see.

Eilidh slowly released the breath she'd been holding, watching as Niel favored his wife with a lingering smile. And then he turned, shouted to his men, and urged Stoirm toward the archway that led out of the bailey.

Beth's gaze never wavered from him. She tracked her husband's path until he disappeared.

18

AUSPICIOUS OMENS

"LOOK ... TWO BLACKBIRDS sitting together. That's an auspicious omen if ever I saw one."

Niel shifted his attention left to where his cousin flanked him. John was pointing at a birch on the roadside. The tree had almost finished dropping its leaves, revealing the silvery, mottled trunk.

And indeed, two blackbirds sat side-by-side upon a branch, watching them ride by.

Niel observed the birds, the lingering tension he'd felt upon leaving Varrich easing just a little. Seeing his wife standing on the steps before the castle—their son perched on her hip, her eyes glittering with tears—had caused his chest to ache.

God's teeth, he hated goodbyes.

But Beth had just revealed she was with bairn, news that had filled his heart with joy—and now John had pointed out another good sign. Blackbirds were territorial birds; it was rare to see them sitting together so companionably. But these two were—and it boded well.

The two men rode at the head of the snaking column of men-at-arms. Most of the Mackay warriors traveled on foot, their pikes bristling through the mist that swirled across the surrounding glen. The pike-wielding warriors were an essential part of his army, for they would form the schiltron—a shield wall—against the enemy during battle.

Twisting in the saddle, Niel surveyed the army he'd amassed. His mouth thinned, frustration simmering within him. He hadn't been given much time, but he'd called in every favor he had to gather the four hundred warriors who marched with him.

Four hundred isn't enough.

Robert Sutherland would have already amassed a much bigger force before he'd sent that missive to Castle Varrich. It was just as well they'd have the Gunns at their side. Without them, Niel would be leading his warriors into a battle they couldn't win.

The clan-chief fought a scowl then. A few people—his wife and Captain Reay included—had questioned the trust he'd put in his former hostage, but he knew what he was doing. These days, he felt an odd sort of kinship with Gunn. He'd initially visited the prisoner in the dungeon out of curiosity, yet the man's proud defiance—so much like his own—had drawn him back repeatedly. And when he'd clasped arms with him that evening in the dungeon, and held the man's eye, he'd known he could depend on him.

"Have ye had word from Castle Gunn?"

The clan-chief turned from surveying his army to see that Iver had ridden up next to him. Schooling his features into an inscrutable expression, even as irritation spiked through him, Niel shook his head. "No ... I didn't expect to."

It was true. When Will set off for Castle Gunn, there had been little time. Niel had preferred that the Gunns focus on raising a warband in time for Samhuinn, rather than sending him missives. Yet he knew what the young chieftain was getting at.

He wanted assurances their former enemies would join them.

Niel couldn't give him any. They would just have to trust that he wouldn't lead them into battle against the Sutherlands without support.

Tension rippled across the laird of Dun Ugadale's face. Nonetheless, he knew better than to question Niel. All his chieftains did. Breac Mackay of Balnakeil rode directly behind them, alongside Robin Mackay of

Melness, while Hugh Mackay of Loch Stach and Connor Mackay of Farr both traveled in the midst of the column.

Niel didn't want to discuss his decision, for Iver would get the sharp edge of his tongue if he continued to question him. The Mackay's word was final. It was best they changed the subject.

The men rode in silence for a few moments before Niel's mouth quirked. "I've heard whispers that congratulations are in order?"

Warmth ignited in Iver's eyes, and his mouth stretched into a grin. "Aye ... Eilidh has agreed to wed me."

"She will make ye a fine wife."

"The lass was reticent at first," Iver admitted. "In truth, I thought she was going to refuse me."

Niel's smile widened. "Och, she can be a flighty, at times ... but she's big-hearted, as are all her sisters. I don't think she'd toy with ye."

"It seems strange to think we won't be lighting the Samhuinn bonfire tonight," Eilidh murmured. "Although none of us are in the mood for donning a guise and dancing."

Foreboding settled in her belly as she spoke. The autumn fire festival was her favorite celebration of the year—but this evening, she didn't have the heart for it.

Standing at the solar window next to her, Jean sighed. "Varrich seems so quiet ... it doesn't feel like Samhuinn at all."

The two sisters stood in silence for a few moments, focusing on the view outdoors. A grey dusk had settled over the kyle and rolling hills north of Varrich. At this hour, crowds of villagers would normally be making their way up from the village toward the castle, their torches glowing like fireflies. Usually, the clan-chief hosted the people of Varrich and Tongue here, just outside the walls of the keep, with a great bonfire that lit up the promontory like a beacon.

But not this Samhuinn.

This year, all the men—save a skeleton garrison left behind to watch over the castle—had emptied out of the castle and village and gone to fight the Sutherlands. Only the women, the elderly, and the young were left behind.

A tense, somber air had settled over Varrich this evening.

It was difficult for any of them to relax.

Beth had retired early, citing a headache. However, Eilidh wasn't fooled. Her sister had been pale and on edge ever since she'd watched Niel lead his men out of the bailey.

"Is this what our mother went through," Eilidh said after a long pause, "every time Da went into battle? The worry … the waiting."

"Aye," Jean replied. "I never really understood either … until now. Ma was so strong."

Eilidh's throat tightened as memories of her childhood intruded. Whenever George Munro had ridden away with his men, there had been no doubt in her mind that he'd return—thanks to their mother's unfailing optimism. When Colleen Munro was around, all her daughters had believed nothing bad could touch any of them. But, of course, that wasn't the way of life. Their mother's sickness and death had felt like a betrayal—a crack in the world.

Glancing Jean's way, Eilidh observed her solemn profile as she stared out of the window. Her sister had changed in the past year—in many subtle ways. Jean was both softer and yet more confident. But Eilidh knew she'd be worrying about Robin and wouldn't be able to relax until he returned from battle.

Eilidh's throat tightened then, her thoughts going to Will and Iver: the man she'd once pined for, and the one who'd soon be her husband.

The thought that either might fall made her stomach clench and her pulse race. She wasn't pious like Jean, but tomorrow morning—and every dawn until the men returned—she'd accompany her to the chapel for prayer.

God had to watch over the Mackays—and the Gunns—in the coming days.

19

THE DAY OF RECKONING

SATAN'S CODS, THERE'S a lot of them.

Standing with his men, Niel's gaze swept over the bristling dark bulk of the Sutherland force. Even partially concealed by the fog, the size of their army was impossible to hide.

The two armies had drawn to a halt, around a furlong apart, as dawn rolled over the loch and surrounding hills. Mist swirled about them, curling and drifting like vapor from a witch's cauldron amongst the ranks of warriors.

Niel drew in a slow, deep breath, and cut one last look east.

His gut cramped then. The Gunns weren't coming.

Will hadn't made good on his promise.

If he'd had time to dwell on it, fury would have barreled into Niel like a charging boar—but he needed to focus his aggression on the threat before him.

A vast, well-equipped force that had marched into the Lochnaver with the single purpose of claiming the lands for the Sutherlands.

Inhaling once more, and pushing aside Will's betrayal, Niel emerged from the ranks of his army and strode out to meet the tall figure, clad in a heavy hauberk, who emerged from the Sutherland front line.

Niel hadn't seen Robert Sutherland in a long while—not since that fatal council in Inverness, during which Niel had been sentenced to incarceration at Bass Rock, many years earlier. He remembered the clan-chief as a reserved, observant man, who despite his quiet ways nursed fierce ambitions.

"Sutherland," Niel greeted him, his voice expressionless. "Ready to have yer hide whipped?"

The older man halted and placed his hands on his hips, his gaze raking over Niel in a cool, silent assessment. "Ye were always an arrogant pup," he drawled finally. "I see time hasn't altered that."

Niel grinned. "Let's not bandy words, Robert," he replied, deliberately using the clan-chief's first name—a reminder that although the man was nearly fifteen years his elder, they were equals in every way. Niel was in his mid-thirties now. He wasn't some callow youth. "I ask ye now, and only once, to leave my lands ... never to return."

Sutherland's lip curled. "*Yer* lands? The Lochnaver belongs to my clan ... and I will take it back."

Over my dead body.

A chill skated down Niel's spine then, and a vision of Beth's face intruded, her hazel gaze imploring. Beth was everything to him. These past two and a half years had been the happiest of his life. He hadn't known such joy existed.

Niel dragged in a deep, slow inhale. He had to survive this—for her, Angus, and their unborn bairn.

He had so much to live for. He couldn't die today.

Resolve clenched under Niel's ribcage as his stare with Sutherland drew out. "Yer position is clear then," he growled. "We shall fight."

Sutherland spat on the ground between them. "Aye, and ye shall soon be feeding crows."

Niel's mouth curved into another fierce smile, one that showed his teeth. "We shall see about that."

Howls of rage—and agony—echoed across the still waters of Loch Naver, the clash of steel ringing high into the damp morning air.

Niel fought in the midst of it, his claidheamh-mòr swinging a vicious arc as he cut down any Sutherland who dared cross his path. Sweat poured off him, slicking his body under his gambeson and mail, and running down his face.

Clenching his jaw, he finished off a pikeman who'd just tried to stab him under the armpit, leaped over the fallen warrior, and attempted to gain ground through the press.

But, just like the last battle he'd fought in—in which he'd failed to reach Tavish Gunn—he couldn't seem to get to Robert Sutherland.

The bastard had been swallowed up by the sea of struggling bodies.

Boots sliding on gore, Niel nearly went down. However, he righted himself just in time to see John jam a dirk blade through the eye of a Sutherland warrior.

The significance of that act wasn't lost on him.

John didn't speak about the Battle of Drumnacoub much, yet he hadn't forgotten what the Sutherlands had taken from him—one didn't forget something like that.

All Niel's chieftains fought for their lives this morning.

Robin swung his axe with lethal precision, hooking it over an opponent's blade and ripping it from his hands before finishing him off with a cut to the neck. Iver and Breac fought back-to-back, their faces splattered with blood, while Hugh bore down on the Sutherlands with his heavy broadsword.

A raw cry splintered the air then, just to Niel's right. Whirling, he saw his captain, Ewan Reay, fall.

Two Sutherlands had taken him on; one had stabbed him in the thigh with a pike, while the other drove a dirk under his armpit.

Time slowed as Niel watched the big warrior—a man who had served him, John, and Niel's father loyally for many years—crumple.

A howl ripped from Niel's throat, and he threw himself at the Sutherland warriors. Moments later both were dead, their bodies twitching on the muddy ground beside Reay's. But it was too late for the captain.

Niel had no time to dwell on the loss, for suddenly the enemy surrounded him on all sides. The Sutherlands had surged forward, using their superior numbers to draw a net around the Mackays.

Niel's breathing now came in ragged pants.

They're winning.

Ice settled in his bowels. He'd brought his men into this, with the promise they'd not stand alone against the Sutherlands.

But he'd let them all down.

Niel fought harder than he ever had then. Each blow he struck had the force of rage and grief behind it. Yet it wouldn't be enough. The hoarse shouts from the Sutherlands goaded him, as did the bellow of Robert Sutherland's voice as he urged his warriors on.

Despair clutched at Niel's throat—despite his best efforts to keep it leashed—yet he continued to fight, sweat pouring off him.

"Niel!" John's voice cut through the din of battle. "To the east … look!"

Yanking his blade free of the warrior he'd just killed, Niel swung around, his gaze jerking left.

The battle hadn't been going on long, but the mist had lifted enough to reveal the glistening surface of the loch and the surrounding hills.

And there, along the eastern shore of the loch, he spied horses thundering toward them, banners rippling in the breeze: dull green plaid threaded with crimson.

Niel's breathing caught. An instant later, a savage grin split his face.

The Gunns were coming, after all.

20

DEATH WOULD TAKE HIM FIRST

WILL KNEW, THE moment he spied the fighting that boiled around the southern shore of the loch, that the Mackays were in trouble.

The Sutherlands closed in on their adversaries, surrounding them as they cut off any escape route. A massacre was beginning, the Sutherland war cry reverberating through the air on all sides.

"Sans peur!"

Will cut Tavish a glance before shouting, "We're just in time!"

The Gunn clan-chief nodded, his lean face hardening. Tavish's dark hair streamed behind him as he rode. Their mounted warriors led the way along the loch's northern shore, although their men-at-arms—who'd fight on foot—weren't far behind. The Gunns had always favored their horses, and nearly fifty of them now bore down on the battling warriors.

Tavish drew his longsword—an unwieldy claidheamh-mòr was no good on horseback—and prepared to launch himself into the fray.

"Aut Pax Aut Bellum!" Tavish roared.

Either peace or war—it was the Gunn way.

Heat swept over Will, igniting in his veins. It hadn't been easy to convince Tavish to ride to the Mackay's side. Indeed, it had been the hardest argument he'd ever had. His brother had raged at him, and they'd almost come to blows several times.

But after days of upheaval, he'd managed to convince Tavish that this was his opportunity to secure a better future for his kin, his clan—for the Sutherlands were a threat to their own borders.

They'd departed Castle Gunn at the last moment and ridden hard to reach the Lochnaver. Will had hoped the battle wouldn't start on the very dawn after Samhuinn—but it had.

Robert Sutherland was a man of his word, it seemed.

The Gunns crashed into the Sutherland ranks, scattering men as they went. The Gunn war cry splintered the air, and soon the Mackay's bellowed their own as they took advantage of the commotion the arrival of their allies had created.

"Manu forti!"

With a strong hand.

Will spied Niel amongst the fray. His friend flashed him a toothy grin before he whirled away to deal with a Sutherland axeman.

An instant later, Will was too busy, slashing his way through enraged Sutherlands, to pay the Mackay clan-chief any more attention. The battle had turned against the Mackays, yet their arrival had caused things to shift.

The Mackays had been struggling against despair, but upon seeing the Gunns fight their way into the midst of the melee, their spirits soared once more.

The Sutherlands turned savage, their roars splitting the air. Meanwhile, a group of Robert Sutherland's warriors formed a protective circle around their clan-chief, pulling him out of the heart of the battle and to safety.

But many of the enemy still faced them down—and one of them, a maddened warrior with wild black hair and beard—fought in a frenzy, his broadsword's blade crimson with blood.

Shock jolted through Will as the man slashed his way closer.

Roy!

It had been years, yet he'd recognize kin anywhere. Even from a distance, his brother's pewter eyes were unmistakable, as was the grimace of hatred that twisted his face.

What was Roy doing fighting with the Sutherlands?

Niel had told Will about the man's deeds over the past couple of years. The man had hung around in the Highlands like a foul stench, despite suffering terrible wounds at John Mackay's hand.

Will's mouth twisted. Of course, Roy was a Gunn—and out of the brothers, he was the one who took after their father the most. He was malevolent, bitter, and driven by a hunger for revenge.

Roy believed he'd been wronged by his kin—and by the Mackays. He hadn't been able to let the past go, and he never would.

Death would take him first.

And then, Roy's gaze fixed on Tavish fighting only a few yards distant. Still upon his horse, the Gunn clan-chief had just driven his longsword through a Sutherland's throat.

Roy's face twisted. The hatred he held for the Mackays paled in comparison to his loathing for his own kin. He'd once tried, and failed, to kill his elder brother—and been cast out of clan Gunn as a result. He likely blamed Tavish for every ill that had befallen him ever since.

Roy shoved his way through the chaos of battle, his gaze never leaving Tavish.

Alarm rippled through Will, for Tavish hadn't seen Roy approach. He was too busy fending off two Sutherlands who were attempting to pull him off his horse.

Will reined his own horse sharply right, barreling toward them. He cut one of the Sutherlands down before shouting to Tavish, "To yer right!"

His brother whirled just in time. He dug his heels into his horse's flanks, causing the beast to lunge forward, narrowly missing the sweep of Roy's broadsword. They were in the midst of the battle now. The initial advantage of fighting from horseback had ended, and so both

Tavish and Will swung down from their mounts to continue the fight on foot.

Without even glancing to the east, Will knew that their men-at-arms would have caught up with them now.

He no longer heard Sutherland war cries. Only Gunn and Mackay.

Tavish and Roy were locked in battle, their grunts and curses rending the air.

However, Roy's actions were choppy and stiff; it wasn't just blinding fury that twisted his face, but discomfort.

Will narrowly sidestepped the stab of a Sutherland dirk and was forced to turn on his assailant to avoid being gutted.

When he shifted his focus once more to his brothers, they were still battling it out.

Then Roy lunged under Tavish's guard, stabbing at his guts.

Only the clan-chief's quick reflexes saved him. Nonetheless, the blade caught his forearm, cutting through the leather bracer he wore upon his right wrist— his sword arm.

Cursing, Tavish stumbled back, his sword slipping from his fingers.

Snarling, Roy closed in on him.

An instant later, a tall, dark-haired man barreled into Roy, knocking him sideways.

Niel rolled to his feet as Roy fell, face first, into the mud. And then the Mackay clan-chief flashed Will a grin. "He's all yers."

Roy scrambled to his feet, growling a vicious oath. He whirled around, clutching his side, his gaze alighting on Will. "Whelp," he rasped. "Come for another beating? This time, I'll crush yer skull." Not waiting for Will's answer, Roy lunged for him, claidheamh-mòr swinging.

Will blocked the blow, although the impact of their blades meeting jolted him to the marrow of his bones.

Christ's teeth, he'd forgotten how strong Roy was. The man was a mountain; years of work as a blacksmith had bulked him up so he was even bigger than Will remembered.

But strength wasn't everything in a fight.

Ducking the next swipe of the broadsword, Will dropped his sword, drew his dirk, and went in low, driving the long, thin blade into Roy's groin.

His brother's howl rent the air, and he tumbled backward, taking Will with him.

Yanking his dagger free, Will climbed up Roy's body and stabbed him again, this time through the throat.

And while the roar of battle continued around them, Will watched his brother die.

21

BREAKING THE CHAINS

IN THE AFTERMATH of battle, the Mackays and the Gunns amassed at the northern end of the loch, close to the Mackay encampment, leaving the dead strewn across the churned-up ground next to the shore. Soon, they'd begin the unpleasant task of gathering up the corpses.

The world seemed unnaturally still and quiet. Now that the cheers of victory had died and everyone gathered to hear the Mackay clan-chief speak, Will was aware of the whine of the wind, the far-off cry of a kite wheeling above them.

The Sutherlands had retreated, hauling their clan-chief to safety. However, many of their warriors lay dead upon the battlefield. Robert Sutherland's mighty army had still outnumbered its foe—even with the Gunn's arrival—but they hadn't been prepared to see two old enemies unite.

"Today will be remembered among my clan until the end of days." Niel's voice, gruff with exhaustion and emotion, echoed across the battlefield. "The day the Mackays and the Gunns fought shoulder-to-shoulder and emerged victorious."

A wave of noise rippled across the shore of the loch—the thunder of elated, exhausted male voices.

And Will joined them, shouting until his throat was raw.

Elation constricted his chest, making it ache. It was odd. Why did fighting alongside his clan's former enemies make him feel as if he'd come home? His skin hadn't even prickled like this when he'd ridden through the gates of Castle Gunn.

"Tavish Gunn." The Mackay clan-chief swiveled to the Gunn clan-chief standing a few yards away. Tavish's right arm had been bandaged and now hung in a sling, but that was the only injury he carried from the battle. "I thank ye for coming to our aid. I swear here, before all our men, that should the Gunns ever need us, we will ride to yer side without hesitation."

There was no mistaking the sincerity in Niel's voice, and the clamor of voices around them quietened, all gazes flicking between the two clan leaders.

Will surveyed his brother's face, a little of his elation dimming. Tavish wasn't smiling, and there was a glint in his eye that Will knew well.

Aye, he'd come to Niel Mackay's aid, but that didn't mean he'd forgiven him for Ruaig-Shansaid, or for anything else.

Long moments passed, and then Tavish gave a curt nod. "Yer pledge is heard, and accepted, Mackay," he replied. He then glanced over at Will, his expression rueful. "Although it's my younger brother ye must thank. Will had to work hard to convince me to rally a warband."

"And I'm relieved he did," Niel replied, his own expression sobering. "The time has come for a new day between our clans. I don't want my children to grow up hating the Gunns, as I did. Someone must break the chains ... and it will be us."

Will's skin prickled once more at these words. He hadn't realized Niel could be so eloquent.

Yet Tavish's expression didn't change. He merely held the Mackay's eye, his lean jaw hardening.

A heavy silence followed.

"My brothers!"

Will was enjoying a much-needed tankard of ale with Tavish, Blair, and Evan when a deep, rumbling voice hailed them. Turning, his gaze alighted on a big, brawny man with shaggy black hair and eyes the color of a stormy sky.

Will stilled. He hadn't realized his eldest brother had been fighting with the Mackays. "Alex?"

Alexander was blood-splattered, yet unharmed, and he strode toward them, a cup of ale in one hand, with the same unbridled arrogance that Will remembered. The last time they'd seen each other, Will had been injured and locked in a cage under Farr Castle. But now, here they were, face-to-face, without iron bars dividing them.

Tavish, Blair, and Evan all tensed at Alex's approach.

Stopping a couple of yards away, the Gunn firstborn's gaze swept over his brothers' faces. The scar on his cheek had silvered even further, visible under the dark shadow of stubble.

"I hear celebrations are in order," Alex rumbled, "… and not just for our victory against the Sutherlands. Roy's now eating dirt."

Will's mouth curved. Anyone listening in on their exchange would think them heartless bastards. He'd killed his own brother, and they were all crowing about it—but then, unless someone had grown up in Castle Gunn, and lived under their father's tyranny, they wouldn't understand.

The world was a better place for being rid of Roy.

Tavish shifted then, approaching his eldest brother. His fingers were now clenched tightly around his wooden cup, the only sign that Alexander's appearance had shaken him. Alex and Tavish's relationship had always been an odd one in the past—they'd been rivals, and yet they'd understood each other. Will wondered whether time had changed anything between them.

However, when Tavish spoke, his tone was cool, "I never thought to see yer face again in this lifetime."

Alex cocked his head, his gaze settling upon the clan-chief's face. "It's been a while."

"A lot of water under the bridge," Tavish replied.

A heartbeat passed, and then Alex's mouth curved. "Aye."

"I can't believe it," Jean murmured, squeezing Eilidh's arm tightly. "Look … Gunns and Mackays drinking together."

"Aye," Eilidh agreed. "It's quite a sight."

The two sisters were walking arm in arm, through the crowd before the bonfire upon Beltaine Hill. Around them, men and women celebrated raucously, laughter and singing rising high into the night. The wail of a Highland pipe joined in then, followed by whoops of joy and mirth.

The Mackays had beaten the Sutherlands—although they'd never have done so without the Gunns' assistance. This was a great day for them all, one that forged a new beginning in this corner of the Highlands.

"I wouldn't be surprised if a few brawls break out this eve," Jean continued. "Things are still new, raw. It'll take time for old resentments to die."

Eilidh's mood sobered a little. Of course, Jean—ever practical in her assessment of situations—was right.

Just one victory couldn't end decades of bad blood between the two clans. Indeed, she spied two warriors shoving each other now, as what had clearly started out as banter escalated into aggression.

Iver stepped in then, planting his muscular frame between the men, and talking them down.

Pale hair rippling down his back, his dark-blue eyes narrowed, Iver cut a striking figure as he spoke to the warriors. Moments later, the men stood down. The chieftain then glanced up and saw the two sisters approaching.

Iver grinned, raising a hand in greeting.

Eilidh waved back, smiling.

She'd been relieved to see her intended return to Castle Varrich—unharmed and victorious. Iver left the warriors with a stern word then and cut his way through the crowd toward them.

Smoke from the bonfire behind him drifted across the hilltop. Above, the sky was clear, revealing a glittering swathe of stars. The shell of a waxing moon cast a hoary light over the celebrations.

Nervousness fluttered under Eilidh's ribs as Iver approached. Now he was back at Varrich, they'd soon set a wedding date. Mother Mary, this was starting to feel very real.

"Good eve, bonnie Eilidh," Iver greeted her. He had a cup of ale in hand, and there was a faint color to his cheeks. Like most of the men here, he was already well into his cups. He then nodded to her sister. "And greetings too, Jean."

"Evening, Iver," Jean replied, unlinking her arm from around Eilidh's. "Robin tells me ye fought bravely at Lochnaver."

"As did yer husband," Iver replied with a grin. "I swear, Robin is a terrifying sight with that axe."

"He tells me all the men of his family have fought with an axe through the generations ... a legacy from his Norse forbears."

"I, too, have Norse blood in my veins," Iver answered, pride lacing his voice.

That admission didn't surprise Eilidh. Iver's build and coloring gave him away. She could easily imagine his great-great-grandfather standing at the prow of a Viking drakkar, his long white-blond hair flying behind him.

"Speaking of my husband, I must go and find him," Jean continued, flashing them both a smile as she moved away. "I trust ye shall take good care of my sister, Iver."

He grinned back. "Aye."

Jean's gaze caught Eilidh's then, a gleam in her eye. An instant later, Jean was bustling off through the crowd, in search of Robin, leaving Iver and Eilidh alone.

Nearby, a man started singing, his resonant voice carrying across the crowd. Twisting, Eilidh spied her brother-by-marriage John standing, arm around his wife's shoulders, as he sang a ballad about brothers-in-arms and the women who waited for them at home. After the first verse, Neave chimed in, her sweet, lilting voice lifting high into the crisp night air.

Eilidh's breathing caught, as it always did when she heard Neave sing. Her sister had a lovely voice.

"They make a fine couple, do they not?" Iver said after a spell as the song concluded.

Shifting her attention back to the chieftain, Eilidh smiled once more. "Aye, they are a good match. John and Neave were close friends, even before they fell in love."

Iver's gaze fused with hers. "I want us to grow close too."

Eilidh stared back at him, suddenly tongue-tied. Their conversation had gone from light to intense in an instant, and she wasn't sure what to say.

"I thought of ye the entire time I was away," Iver continued, his voice lowering. "I long for ye."

Eilidh's breathing caught. "Iver," she began softly. "I—"

"I want ye to feel the same way about me."

"I will," she murmured. "Just give me a little time." She meant it too; she'd made a commitment to him, and she'd honor it.

Iver continued to study her. However, his expression now shadowed. "There's still a reserve in ye, lass," he observed softly. "Is there someone else?"

Heat flushed through Eilidh, and her heart started to race. "No," she whispered.

Iver inclined his head. "Are ye certain?"

Eilidh stared back at him. Iver was no fool—not that she'd ever thought him a dullard—but he was wrong.

There *wasn't* anyone else. Not anymore.

Silence stretched between them before she finally answered, firmly this time. "I'm certain." She then cleared her throat and coughed. "This smoke stings the throat … I don't suppose ye could fetch me some wine?"

Iver smiled back. "Of course." He then nodded to the left, where a woman was dispensing drink from oaken barrels a few yards distant. "Wait here ... I shall be back shortly."

"Thank ye."

Eilidh watched the chieftain move off, her pulse still galloping. God's blood, she'd put her daft infatuation for William Gunn behind her, yet suddenly Iver doubted her.

I should have been warmer ... more flirtatious.

Jaw clenching, she resolved to reassure him as soon as he returned to her side.

But then her gaze alighted upon a man across the crowd—and her belly did a steep dive.

22

HOW FARES YER WIFE?

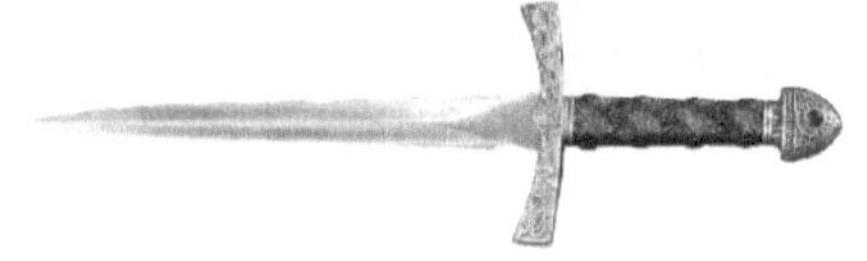

OF COURSE, HE'D been looking out for her.

Will was drinking and bantering with the other warriors, yet he'd been restless all evening. His gaze constantly roamed the crowd, searching for Eilidh.

And there she was, standing alone.

Their gazes met, and Will's breathing slowed. She was even lovelier than he recalled. Eilidh possessed an elegant beauty that the ruddy glow of the firelight only enhanced. Her oaken hair was unbound, falling over her slender shoulders in soft waves. Her cheeks were slightly flushed, her large brown eyes huge upon her heart-shaped face—and those soft pink lips parted slightly as their stare drew out.

Without thinking, Will moved through the crowd toward her, halting when they stood a few feet apart. The scent of lavender drifted over him, and he dragged it deep into his lungs.

"Lady Eilidh," he greeted her, surprised to find his voice had roughened. "It's good to see ye again."

"Will," she murmured. "I didn't think ye'd be here."

His mouth curved. "After our victory at Lochnaver, the Mackay invited all of us back to Varrich for a grand celebration."

Eilidh cleared her throat. "Congratulations ... I knew Niel could rely on ye."

Will grew still. "Thank ye." Her words and faith in him were touching. "I'd say ye were one of the few who did believe I'd make good on my promise."

She inclined her head. "Was yer brother hard to convince?"

Will huffed a laugh. "Ye could say that." He paused then, searching her face. Eilidh's expression was composed, her gaze veiled. She was more reserved than the lass he'd bid farewell to in his bedchamber a few weeks earlier. "Have ye been well?" he asked finally. The question was stilted, yet he suddenly felt awkward, and a little embarrassed.

"Aye, thank ye." Her response was polite, yet distant.

"Eilidh." He took a step closer. "I didn't like the way we parted ... and it has played on my mind ever since."

Eilidh's mouth compressed, even if he noted the way her pulse fluttered at the hollow of her throat. "I imagine ye have been too busy of late to spare me much thought."

Will tensed. There was no mistaking the edge to her voice. As he'd suspected, she resented him now.

"That isn't the case, lass," he replied after a pause. It was the truth. Thoughts of Eilidh, and the hurt and disappointment that gleamed in her soulful brown eyes the last time he'd seen her, stole upon him often these days, especially in the aftermath of the battle. He couldn't deny he'd looked forward to seeing her again.

The faint blush upon her cheeks deepened then. "Tell me, Will," she began, her tone clipped. "How fares yer wife?"

Will sucked in a sharp breath. "Eilidh," he began. "There is something I must—"

"What's this?" Iver stepped up next to Eilidh then, passing her a cup of wine. "I turn my back for an instant and find a Gunn sniffing around my intended?"

The laird of Dun Ugadale's greeting punched the air out of Will's lungs.

Intended?

Iver's tone wasn't friendly—but that came as no surprise. The chieftain hadn't hidden his disdain for Will over the past weeks.

Eilidh turned to Iver, flashing him a smile. Only the lingering tension around her eyes, and her flushed cheeks, gave her away. "William was just telling me about the battle."

"I'm sure he was," Iver drawled. "Boasting were ye, Gunn?"

Will folded his arms across his chest.

Two could play at this game. "No need, Mackay ... my brave deeds speak for themselves."

"Aye ... although ye left yer arrival late."

"And brought ye victory," Will reminded him.

Iver snorted, slinging a possessive arm around Eilidh's slender shoulders. Will tensed. There was no doubt about it—they made a beautiful couple.

He should be happy for Eilidh. Iver was certainly a fine choice of husband.

But even as Will told himself such, the red-hot blade of jealousy stabbed him through the chest.

"Niel will never forget what ye did for the Mackays," Eilidh interjected then, casting Iver a look of censure. "Ye are his friend for life now, I believe."

Will flashed her a tight smile. "And it's an honor to be named such." He glanced then at Iver, to see the chieftain was scowling. Taking a step back, Will nodded to the couple. "Congratulations to ye both ... now, if ye will excuse me ... I shall return to my brother's side."

Without awaiting their response, Will turned on his heel and walked away.

"More mead?" Niel held up the drinking horn, swaying unsteadily in his chair as he did so. "Let's see ... if I can drink ye under the table as easily I did yer brother!"

That last sentence was so slurred it was barely intelligible.

However, Will had understood. And the crowing Mackay clan-chief was right. Tavish now lay slumped over the table, in a drunken slumber. His snores reverberated across the great hall, blending with those of the warriors stretched out on the rush-strewn floor.

Will eyed his brother, relieved that a surfeit of mead hadn't loosened his tongue around Niel. Instead, the more he'd drunk, the quieter he'd become. Yet as the drinking games had drawn out, Will hadn't missed the dark looks Tavish cast the Mackay.

Resentment still simmered, yet Niel seemed intent on ignoring it.

Once the celebrations on the hillside under the castle had died away, and revelers retired to their beds, Niel had invited his chieftains and the Gunn brothers to drink with him and his men in the great hall.

Evan and Blair had taken part in the drinking games for a while before both admitted defeat. The pair now slept on the floor, upon the dais, just a few feet from the table.

Only Niel and Will remained.

Grasping the horn of mead, Will tried to focus. In truth, he wasn't sure he could stomach one more gulp of the stuff. The hall was starting to spin unsteadily around him, and nausea rose, making bile sting the back of his throat.

"That's it," he slurred. "I'm done … ye've bested me, ye bastard."

With that, he poured the contents of the drinking horn into the jug in front of him.

A grin of victory split Niel's swarthy face. Reclining in his carven chair, he swung his booted feet up onto the table, crossing them at the ankle. "It seems the Gunn lads can't hold their drink." The clan-chief's eyes closed, and he fell silent. Will thought he'd fallen asleep, yet Niel continued speaking moments later. "Victory in battle is always bitter-sweet, isn't it?"

Will grunted, wondering at Niel's shift in mood. He shouldn't have been surprised; drink often turned men maudlin. He knew what Niel meant though.

"I lost the Captain of the Varrich guard … Ewan Reay … at Lochnaver," Niel continued. "A good man … he will be missed."

Will pulled a face. "Ye lost a few good men in that battle … as did we."

It was the truth. Aye, they'd emerged the victors, but the Mackay losses had been heavy, nonetheless. Several women were now widows.

"Reay served my father before me," Niel continued, his eyes flickering open. "He could be cantankerous, yet there are few men as loyal as he was."

Will nodded. Tavish had often told him how much he also valued such allegiance. In a world where a clan-chief's rivals were always sharpening their dirks, ready to stab him between the shoulder blades, a devoted warrior was something to be cherished. "Aye, trustworthy men are a rarity," he agreed.

Leaning forward, Will rested his elbows on the tabletop, sticky with spilled ale and mead, and leaned his forehead against his clenched hands. Christ, that mead was strong. He now felt dangerously bilious.

"Ye may not realize ... but I'm not one to trust easily," Niel admitted then.

Will huffed a laugh, and instantly regretted it; his stomach churned. "I'd noted that."

A companionable silence fell between the two men. It was getting late now—the witching hour had come and gone a while ago. It was time for them both to find their beds.

"What say ye to becoming my captain, Will?"

The question, softly uttered, made Will straighten up, his attention sliding to Niel. "What?"

Niel's mouth quirked. He still reclined in his chair, yet his dark-blue eyes were focused. He seemed to have sobered up. In contrast, Will's head felt as if it were stuffed full of wool.

"Remain here at Varrich," Niel went on, still favoring him with a half-smile. "Reay's chambers are in the west tower ... they're comfortable enough ... ye wouldn't have to share quarters with the other warriors."

Will snorted. He didn't care about that—he was more concerned about the first part.

Staying on at Varrich.

He'd planned on remaining here for a couple of days before returning to Caithness with his kin. Yet whenever he thought of home, a hollow sensation settled under his ribs. Over the past days, he'd come to realize that he didn't belong there anymore.

But did he belong here either?

"Of course, if yer heart lies at Castle Gunn, I understand," Niel said eventually. "I never asked if ye have a wife … but if ye do, bring her here."

"I was wedded," Will replied gruffly. "Although she died while I was in gaol."

Niel stiffened, his smile fading. He then dragged a hand down his face, as if trying to sober himself up. "I'm sorry."

"Don't be … her death wasn't yer doing." Suddenly, Will wished he'd downed that final horn of mead. He wasn't drunk enough to prevent the clutch of guilt in his gut. Memories still had sharp edges, and they dug at him.

Niel cocked a dark eyebrow. "So, what's keeping ye at Castle Gunn … other than loyalty to yer brother?"

Their stare drew out while Will considered the question. He'd been born and raised within the walls of that mighty keep, and before Ruaig-Shansaid would have laughed in the face of anyone who suggested he live elsewhere. But something had shifted in him of late. Castle Gunn held too many ghosts. He'd find it hard to make a new start there.

He and his brothers were bound by blood—but was that enough?

Will heaved a deep sigh. "I don't imagine yer men will welcome a Gunn leading them."

"They won't," Niel replied without hesitation. "Relations between our clans are still raw … fragile." He glanced over at where Tavish slumbered, oblivious to their conversation, his brow furrowing. "But I don't want things to go back to how they were. If I choose a Gunn to lead my guard, I'm making a gesture of good faith, am I not?"

Their gazes met once more, and Will's mouth curved into a half-smile. "Ye are."

23

A BRAVE CHOICE

EILIDH SLOWLY PUT down the piece of buttered bannock she'd been about to take a bite of—her lips parting in surprise. "William Gunn is staying on?"

"Aye." Niel took a sip of warmed milk and winced. The man's face bore the strain of too much drink and too little sleep this morning. However, next to him, Beth's expression was serene as she fed Angus porridge from a wooden spoon. "I need someone I can trust to replace Reay."

"But *Gunn*?"

Niel frowned. "I thought ye liked the man?"

"He proved himself honorable, aye," Eilidh replied, deliberately skirting around the question. Beth's gaze had flicked her way as well, and her sister was observing her with a sharp look. "But will yer warriors welcome a Gunn as their captain?"

Niel's mouth pursed. "They'll be reluctant at first, but Gunn proved himself at Lochnaver." He paused then, pushing away his untouched bowl of porridge. "Tavish Gunn still views me like I'm a rabid dog ... this will be an opportunity for us to build strong links between our clans."

"It's a brave choice." Beth's brow furrowed. "Did Gunn require much convincing?"

Niel shook his head before giving another wince. He then reached up and gingerly rubbed his temples. "The light's bright in here," he mumbled.

"No, it's not," Beth replied with an arch look.

Indeed. Outdoors, the morning was grey and chill. The daylight filtering in through the glassed window was watery, yet Niel looked as if he wished to crawl back to bed.

"I'm never touching mead again," the clan-chief muttered. His attention then fixed on where Angus was watching him. "Hear that lad? Stay away from strong drink ... it rots the gut."

Beth snorted. "Aye, but ye have a short memory for such things, my love."

"Da ... Da ... Da," the bairn sang, wriggling on his mother's lap.

Niel's mouth curved. Reaching out, he took Angus from his wife. "Next time I suggest drinking games, ye are to slap me soundly, mo chridhe."

Beth laughed, the merry sound echoing through the solar. "With pleasure."

Watching the three of them interact, Eilidh suddenly felt as if she were intruding. They were such a happy family—and in a few months, there would be another addition to it.

Picking up her piece of bannock, she took a bite and chewed doggedly. Seeing Will again—and hearing he was to become Captain of the Varrich Guard—had unsettled her, but she had to remind herself of her own plans.

Soon Iver and I will be wed ... soon we will start a family of our own.

They hadn't decided on a wedding date, but she would approach him today about the matter. It was best they didn't delay things. She was eager to leave Varrich and go to live at Dun Ugadale on the Kintyre peninsula.

She'd be happy with Iver, would bear his bairns and make a new life for herself.

Far from this corner of the Highlands.

Far from Will Gunn.

"Have ye lost yer mind?"

"I don't think so."

"So why the hell would ye accept such a position?"

Will regarded Tavish a moment, considering his reply. They stood in the bailey, where the clan-chief was saddling his courser, readying himself for the journey back to Castle Gunn.

His youngest brother wasn't going with him.

Tavish's face was pale this morning, and he looked a bit peaky. Will was sure *he* didn't look any better. He'd woken up with a dry mouth, sour belly, and a pounding head. A tankard of boiled water and some bannock had improved things, although any abrupt movement made it feel as if vindictive imps had just taken hammers to his temples.

"The Mackay wishes to build an alliance between us," Will answered eventually. "He believes hiring me to captain his guard will help ... and I agree with him."

Tavish folded his arms across his chest and looked down his nose at his younger brother. "Ye're both taking things too far."

"Trust has to start somewhere."

Tavish scowled before his gaze roamed over Will's face. "Ye have changed," he muttered. "Before Ruaig-Shansaid, ye'd have taken a blade to yer own throat rather than work for Niel Mackay."

Will held his eye. "Ye're right ... I'm not the same man I was. When I was back at Castle Gunn, it dawned on me that I don't belong there anymore."

Tavish snorted. "Of course, ye do ... ye are a *Gunn*."

His brother's emphasis on their clan name wasn't lost on Will. Tavish was trying to guilt him, as if he'd forgotten who he was.

But Will hadn't.

"Aye, and I'll always be proud to carry our name," Will replied after a pause. "But the time has come for me to strike out on my own."

"Are ye really going through with this?"

"Aye."

His brother cast him a sly look then. "I suppose having a spy in the enemy camp could have its benefits."

Will stiffened. "I'm not spying on the Mackays."

Tavish's dark brows crashed together. "Why not?"

"Because I now consider Niel a friend … I'll not betray his trust."

"A *friend*?" A muscle flexed in Tavish's jaw. "And what about loyalty to yer own blood?"

"I'll always be loyal to ye, Tav," Will ground out. He'd always been proud to follow Tavish—yet a gulf yawned between them today. Things would never be the same between them, and he was sorry for it. "But not like this."

Silence fell between the brothers then before Tavish shook his head, disdain glinting in his eyes. "I was right," he muttered. "Ye *have* gone mad."

Will's gaze swept over the long row of warriors standing before him in the bailey. His mouth thinned then. He'd only just stepped into his new role as Captain of the Varrich Guard, and already things had gone into a downward spiral.

He'd been about to ask his men their names when two of them walked.

"Come on, lads," he muttered after a lengthy pause. "I know the clan-chief gave ye the freedom to choose whether ye follow me or not … but this is ridiculous."

A cold silence greeted him.

Will silently cursed Niel. He'd had the easy part. The clan-chief had stridden into the bailey a short while earlier and informed the men that William Gunn would be leading them from now. Niel's gaze had narrowed as he let them know that any who didn't like his decision were released from service.

He'd then departed, leaving his men—and Will— stunned.

The silence drew out before one of the older warriors stepped out of line and spat on the cobbles. "I'm leaving," he snarled. "I'd rather die than follow a Gunn."

Will eyed the man. "That's a little ungrateful, don't ye think? After we came to yer aid."

The warrior's face twisted, the veins on his temples bulging. Without another word, he turned and stormed from the bailey, shoulders hunched. Will watched him pass under the archway before he turned to survey the remaining warriors.

He was tempted to demand if anyone else lacked the balls to follow him. However, he choked the words down. He was unpopular as it was—best he didn't insult them, or he'd end up with no Guard at all.

Instead, Will stepped up to the first man in the row. "Right," he said roughly. "Now that's over with … it's time we made some introductions." He met the guard's eye, a man around ten years Will's senior. "Yer name?"

"Kirk," the warrior growled.

Ignoring the man's surly tone, Will moved down the line, getting each guard to introduce himself.

Rory, Blaine, Colin, Logan, Fife, Brodie, Fergus—Will took note of each one.

They were sullen bastards though, some of them barely grunting their name.

"We'll go up onto the wall shortly, lads," Will announced when he reached the end of the line. He stepped back and ran a critical eye over the men he now commanded. "First though, I want to see what yer skills are like." He flashed them a tight smile. Aye, the morning hadn't started well, but it could only get better from here on. "Break off into pairs and bind yer knuckles … let's see if any of ye can swing a punch."

"When's the wedding then, Iver?"

"Soon."

Will glanced up from where he was spooning honey onto his morning porridge, his gaze alighting upon the tall blond man seated at the opposite end of the table. The chieftain was breaking his fast with the guards in the great hall.

Iver ignored him. Instead, he smiled at Kirk, the guard who'd spoken. "We have set the date for a fortnight hence."

Will stiffened. The smug look on Iver's face irked him.

He supposed he too would wear such an expression if Eilidh had agreed to be his wife.

She wanted ye, remember, but ye spurned her.

Aye, he had—but he'd been married then. He'd had no choice.

Two days had passed since Will had taken on the role of Captain of the Varrich Guard. He'd wanted to seek Eilidh out, to continue the explanation Iver had interrupted before the bonfire, but his new duties had utterly absorbed him. His men were proving hard work.

"The lady is eager then, eh?" Kirk gave a chuckle and winked at Iver.

In response, Iver cast him another smile, this one veiled, and took a bite of bannock. "Aye, but we must both send word to our kin at Foulis and Dun Ugadale." The chieftain paused then. "I'd like my brothers to attend the wedding ... and Lady Eilidh wants her father to be present."

Will looked down at his rapidly congealing porridge. He'd been hungry when he'd sat down at the table—but now his belly had closed.

"Watch yer defense, Rory!" Will bellowed. "Flailing around like a landed pike will get ye gutted like one."

Snorts of derisive laughter rumbled through the bailey, the sound mixing with the whine of the wind. It was a raw morning; icy fingers dug through the thick padded gambeson Will wore over his lèine, prickling the flesh underneath. He was overseeing his men at swordplay. Two of them, Rory and Fife, were going at each other with wooden practice swords.

However, the former's style left a lot to be desired.

Will's gaze swept over the men watching the sword practice. The past couple of days had been tough, and he'd deliberately trained them hard. After losing three warriors on his first morning, he had quite a task before him. Even so, it wasn't one he shirked from. Will was bluntly spoken and swift to deal with insubordination, but he was fair. Experience had taught him the men he commanded would thaw eventually.

He sensed now that barking orders from the sidelines wasn't the way to earn respect. He was going to have to get his hands dirty.

Picking up a practice sword of his own, Will strode into the ring and positioned himself next to the lanky young warrior, who'd now gone red in the face. "If ye go into a fight on the attack, ye will end up dead within moments," he explained, meeting Rory's eye. "Any fight, be it with yer fists, a sword, or a dirk is about making sure yer defense is strong ... ye want to ensure it's safe to strike without yer opponent gaining the advantage."

Gripping the wooden broadsword with both hands, Will raised it across his body, moving into a defensive posture. He then nodded to Rory to do the same. "That's right," he said, "but widen yer stance ... ground yerself, man."

They went through a sequence of defensive moves, and as he instructed, Will was aware of his men's gazes tracking him.

And now, as he taught Rory how to prevent getting himself skewered on an enemy broadsword, he sensed he was slowly gaining ground.

Finishing his lesson, he moved to the sidelines once more, calling out for the warriors to resume their sparring.

They did, and this time Rory blocked his opponent's blade effectively before landing good strikes of his own.

They'd nearly finished when a flash of color to Will's right caught his attention. He looked away from the two sparring men to see Eilidh walking toward the archway, basket under one arm. Dressed in a moss-green kirtle, with a heavy fur cloak around her shoulders, the lass's cheeks were flushed with cold.

She didn't glance his way.

Will's heart bucked against his breastbone.

He didn't like being ignored.

Let her go, the voice of commonsense cautioned. *She's Iver's woman … not yers.*

His hand clenched around the hilt of the practice sword he still held.

Aye, he should let things be, but his gaze still tracked Eilidh's path as she crossed the bailey. She'd be off to market, on foot today rather than upon her fat pony.

Eilidh disappeared through the archway, and Will's gaze snapped back to the fight, to see Rory slam the flat of his blade into Fife's belly, bringing the older man to his knees.

Whoops went up at Rory's victory, while Will allowed himself a small smile. "Good job," he said when the cheering subsided. "That's it for this morning … get back to yer posts."

Handing one of the warriors the practice sword, Will then headed toward the bailey gates. He'd join his men on the walls soon enough—but Eilidh couldn't wait.

24

A MAN OF HONOR

"LADY EILIDH!" A man's voice echoed down the hillside. "Wait up."

Slowing her pace, Eilidh cast a glance over her shoulder. Upon spying Will approaching, she tensed. The path was steep in places, yet he jogged down, his booted feet navigating the rough surface with ease.

"Good morning, Captain." Eilidh straightened her spine, clutching her basket tightly to her as if it could protect her from him.

"Off to market?" he asked, drawing to a halt before her. He was uphill, and Eilidh had to angle her head back to hold his gaze.

"Aye," she replied coolly.

"Unescorted?"

She nodded, irritated. It was none of his business where she went or whether she had an escort. She'd already had a similar discussion with Iver; indeed, she'd sneaked out of the keep this morning to go to market on her own. If her intended spotted her leaving, he'd insist on accompanying her. Eilidh wished to go down to Tongue alone, especially because after shopping at the market, she planned to visit Ava.

And there was plenty to update her friend about.

The wedding date was now set. Tomorrow morning, riders would leave for both Dun Ugadale and Foulis, to let Iver's brother and her father know they were expected at Varrich in a fortnight.

The last person she wished to see this morning was Will Gunn.

Holding his eye and trying not to be drawn in by their smoky depths, she firmed her jaw. "Did ye want something?"

"Aye, lass." He flashed her a smile—the one that made his cheek dimple. "A few moments of yer time."

"Aye, well … I'm busy this morning, so make it quick." Her response was rude, yet she didn't care. Gunn was a married man, and he had no business following a woman who was promised to another.

Will's smile faded.

Eilidh resisted the urge to shuffle back, to distance herself from him farther. Lord, how awkward it was between them now. The infatuated lass she'd been earlier in the year seemed a distant memory. In truth, her behavior now embarrassed her; she'd shown no propriety or restraint and had ended up looking like a goose.

And every time she set eyes on Will, she was reminded of her humiliation.

"Ye are vexed with me," he murmured, his gaze searching her face. "Why?"

Eilidh pulled a face. "I'm not vexed."

And she wasn't. She just wanted to move on with her life and forget the past. Clearing her throat, she took a step back, teetering slightly as her boots slid on gravel.

Will moved forward, his hand closing over her upper arm, to steady her.

His firm grip, the heat of his palm, which she felt even through the wool of her kirtle, made her breathing hitch.

"Eilidh." His face was serious now. "It took a lot of courage for ye to say what ye did that evening before I left Varrich, and I'm sorry if my response hurt ye. I can be callous sometimes."

Eilidh stared up at him, her pulse quickening. They were standing too close now. Anyone looking down from the walls might see them. Strange how propriety hadn't mattered at all to her during the summer. All she'd cared about was being in his company. She'd lived to hear the rumble of his voice, to feel his sensual gaze upon her.

"Fear not," she replied, cursing the way her voice caught. "I've forgotten all about that."

His gaze trapped hers. "Ye have?"

"When's yer wife arriving?" The question burst from her. She had to remind him of the reality of their relationship; maybe then, he'd back away and leave her be.

Their gazes held, and Will's hold on her arm relaxed. However, he didn't let go of her.

"She's dead," he murmured.

Eilidh stared up at him. *Dead?* Long moments passed before she found her tongue. "Oh, Will … I'm so sorry. When?"

"Late last year … I didn't learn of it until I returned to Castle Gunn."

"How awful for ye."

He cleared his throat. "Allison and I weren't happily wed … I wasn't the best of husbands."

Eilidh frowned. She could hear the guilt in his voice. "I'm sure ye did yer best," he murmured.

Will's mouth twisted, his fingers tightening around her arm once more. "Those are kind words … but the truth is I was selfish and inconsiderate."

Eilidh's breathing grew shallow. His hand was a brand upon her arm; his nearness drew her in. "Ye are neither of those things, Will," she whispered. "Lochnaver proved ye are a man of honor."

"I wish that were true," he replied, stepping into her. His free hand came up to cup her cheek then. "But an honorable man wouldn't do this."

He lowered his head, his lips grazing over hers.

Eilidh gasped at the touch, her body going rigid.

She shouldn't allow him such liberties—she was promised to another man.

She should reel back, should push him away.

Yet she didn't—instead, she swayed into him.

Murmuring a curse under his breath, Will brushed his lips against hers once more. And then he kissed her with slow sensuality, his lips and teeth teasing her.

A moment later, his tongue slid into her mouth and Eilidh gave a soft, needy whimper.

Will gathered her close. One hand cupped the back of her head, while the other slid down her back, holding her fast against him.

Mother Mary, his mouth was so hot, his tongue so wickedly sensual. He devoured her in a deep, languid embrace that made Eilidh's toes curl in her boots. It was a raw day and exposed out here on the promontory. A gelid wind swirled around them, tugging at their cloaks, yet they were both oblivious to it.

Eilidh clung onto him, her fingers sliding up and grasping his gambeson.

Heat roared through her veins and bathed her skin.

God's blood, what are ye doing?

Reality hit her in an icy blast—as if she'd just been dunked headfirst into a freezing loch.

She hadn't even kissed Iver yet, and here she was tangling tongues with a man who wasn't her intended. Worse still, they were standing out here, in the open, where anyone might see them.

Balling her hands into fists, she pushed back against Will's chest.

He let her go easily, and they drew apart, both out of breath.

Will's grey eyes had deepened to purple, and his lean face was all taut angles. He looked like a starving man, and she the feast.

"I apologize," he rasped, his chest rising and falling sharply now. "I shouldn't have done that."

"No," she whispered, aghast at her own lusty behavior. "Ye shouldn't."

However, she couldn't lay the blame entirely at his feet—for she'd responded to his kiss as hungrily as he'd given it.

"Eilidh," he breathed her name like a prayer. "I didn't plan any of this ... but I had to see ye, before—"

Eilidh raised her hand, her fingers resting upon his lips to still them. She couldn't let him go on.

Before it's too late.

It already was—didn't he realize that?

The back of Eilidh's neck prickled then, and her chin kicked up, her gaze alighting upon the curtain wall that reared above them. An instant later, she sucked in a sharp breath and dropped her hand from Will's mouth.

She felt his fingers close around her forearm, squeezing gently. "What is it?"

Eilidh didn't answer. She couldn't. Her tongue suddenly felt cloven to the roof of her mouth—for there, high upon the battlements, his white-blond hair snapping in the wind, was Iver Mackay.

And he was staring down at them.

Will entered the bailey ahead of Eilidh.

He'd hoped she wouldn't follow him inside, that she'd continue down to Tongue and let him and Iver confront each other on their own.

But such a wish was like praying the sun set to the east instead of the west.

Eilidh walked smartly at his heel, her boots pattering on stone. She'd already pleaded with him not to re-enter the bailey, but to accompany her to Tongue instead. His confrontation with Iver could wait.

But some things couldn't be put off. The chieftain would be waiting for him.

Passing under the archway, Will slowed his pace, his gaze sweeping the wide, cobbled space. And there, a few feet before the steps that led down from the walls, stood Iver, arms folded across his chest.

The man's face was taut, his gaze narrowed, and he stood dangerously still—a stance that made Will's hackles rise.

"Explain yerself, Gunn," Iver ground out.

Will halted a few feet back from the younger man. "I can't," he replied. "Other than to say that I forgot myself."

"Ye did more than forget yerself, man. Ye just stuck yer tongue down the throat of my future wife."

Will's mouth thinned. There was no getting away from what he'd done. Aye, he hadn't planned that embrace, yet he'd known anyone could see him from atop the walls when he'd pulled Eilidh into his arms and kissed her for all the world to see.

Did he hope Iver might witness it?

Part of him itched to give Iver a drubbing, for the man had rubbed him up the wrong way for a while now. Right from the day Niel had granted Will his freedom, Iver had made little effort to hide his distrust, his disdain, for him. Even so, Will didn't want to cause a scene in front of Eilidh, and nor did he want to set a poor example for his men.

"Iver." Eilidh halted to Will's right, her hands fluttering nervously as she made a placating gesture. "I can explain. We—"

"We shall discuss this later," Iver cut her off smoothly, his gaze never leaving Will's face. "After I deal with this whoreson."

And with that, the chieftain started rolling up the sleeves of his gambeson.

25

THE FIGHT IS ON

"ARE YE SURE ye want to do this now?" Will flashed Iver a thin smile. "In front of the lady?"

Eilidh's pulse quickened. God's blood, the pair of them were about to brawl.

Iver was incensed, and she didn't like the gleam in Will's eye; it reminded her that the Gunn males had a reputation.

Iver nodded brusquely. "Go inside, Eilidh," he commanded, his voice emotionless.

"No," she choked out, heat washing over her. Curse them, she wouldn't be sent away like a bairn.

Iver tore his attention from Will then and glanced her way. Eilidh's breathing caught at the hurt in his dark-blue eyes. "Ye shouldn't bear witness to this."

"Bear witness to what exactly?" she shot back, shoving down her guilt. "To ye beating each other senseless?"

"Eilidh." Will moved toward her. "Please go indoors."

However, she shook her head and backed away, holding up her basket to ward him off. "No! This is pointless and stupid. I forbid it!"

"Ye can't," Iver replied, his voice roughening. "Gunn has dishonored ye, lass ... and he must pay the price."

"The devil take my honor," Eilidh growled back. Iver's blue eyes snapped wide at her show of temper, yet she plowed on. "If either of ye cared about such things ... ye'd listen to me!"

Will rolled his shoulders, readying himself to trade blows. "It seems the lady is staying … do ye still want a fight, Mackay?"

"Aye," Iver growled. "More than ever."

Fury grabbed Eilidh in a chokehold then. She was almost tempted to storm off, to fetch Niel so he could stop this from going any further. However, stubbornness kept her rooted to the spot. Glancing right, she spied one of the scullery maids standing in front of the kitchen door, watching the scene unfold with wide-eyed fascination.

Eilidh mouthed a command to her: *go fetch the Mackay.*

Disappointment clouded the maid's face, for she clearly wished to stay and watch the fight. Yet she nodded, picked up her skirts, and hurried past Eilidh, taking the steps up into the keep two at a time.

Satisfied that help was on its way, Eilidh turned back to see that Will and Iver were eyeing each other like two stags about to lock horns.

She marked the way Iver's gaze glittered, watching as Will rolled up his own sleeves. A few men-at-arms had noticed the argument and were drawing close, curiosity on their faces.

"A silver penny on Mackay."

Eilidh's mouth thinned. Heavens, they were taking bets. She could try to order them to return to their posts, yet they weren't likely to obey—most men loved to watch a good fight.

Especially one between a Gunn and a Mackay.

Will cast Eilidh another sidelong look. "Ye might want to give us some space, lass … this shall get bloody."

Eilidh glared back at him. Did he think this was a game? Blistering words bubbled up inside her, on the verge of spilling out. However, she choked them down and shifted back toward the steps to the castle.

Both men were deaf to her protests. Railing against them now wasn't going to help.

But she would later.

Will and Iver circled each other then, fists raised.

Eilidh noted that they were of the same height, although Iver was of a slightly more muscular build. They appeared equally matched.

Her belly clenched.

Hurry up, Niel.

Iver attacked first, striking hard with his right fist. Will jumped back, yet the blow glanced off his shoulder. He counter-attacked with vicious swiftness, catching Iver on the jaw.

His opponent's head snapped back.

The surrounding crowd of gathered men-at-arms, stable lads, and kitchen servants let out a collective roar.

The fight was on.

Still circling each other, fists held high, the two men traded blows. Sometimes they missed the mark, sometimes they didn't—and grunts and the meaty thud of blows landing drifted across the bailey.

And with each one, queasiness rose within Eilidh.

She hated violence, and she hated being the cause of it.

Both men's bare knuckles were bloodied now; their hands would be throbbing from the hits they'd already landed, yet neither showed any discomfort. Instead, each man's gaze was fixed upon his adversary.

Eilidh didn't like the steely expression on either of their faces.

God's blood, they look like they want to kill each other.

She knew fights like these could be dangerous. She recalled an incident during her childhood at Foulis, where two stable lads had brawled over a lass—it was always over a woman—and one had landed a haymaker punch that had sent his opponent sprawling backward over the cobbles. The fall cracked his skull and killed him.

Iver's left eye was starting to swell, while blood trickled from Will's nose.

Iver struck hard once more, his fist colliding with Will's cheek. Sidestepping as the chieftain followed up with a second punch with his left fist, Will flashed him a feral grin. "Come on, Mackay ... ye are too young to be that slow."

Eilidh clenched her fists at her sides, swallowing as queasiness slammed into her once again. Iver hadn't been slow at all. What in Hades was Will doing? It was as if he was deliberately goading Iver, encouraging him to lose control.

With a growled oath, Iver went for him, throwing a vicious right hook, and then a left.

One caught Will in the side of the face once more, throwing him off-balance. But an instant later, he launched himself at his opponent, striking fast, and head-butting him.

Shouts echoed off the surrounding stone, as Iver staggered backward, one hand rising to his nose.

Blood now streamed from his nostrils.

"Stop this!" The cry tore from Eilidh's throat, tears stinging her eyes. She didn't want to see the pair beat each other to a pulp. But her plea was lost in the roar of the crowd.

The men-at-arms were cheering loudly now, and the kitchen servants were whooping as if they were watching dancers performing a lively jig.

Was she the only one horrified by the fight?

Snarling curses, Iver launched himself at Will, colliding with him. The two men sprawled to the ground, their grunts and insults ringing through the bailey as they punched, gouged, and kicked.

A tall, lean figure elbowed his way through the crowd then, making for the struggling figures.

Niel's expression was hooded. In one hand he carried a wooden pail. Water, that he'd just drawn from the trough behind him, sloshed over the brim as he walked.

However, Iver and Will paid his approach no mind.

Iver had managed to get Will under him, and was landing heavy punches, but his opponent twisted like an eel, bringing his knee up into Iver's groin. The chieftain grunted, slackening his grip just enough for Will to shove him aside and reverse their positions.

An instant later, a wave of water hit them.

Will, who'd just drawn back his fist to punch Iver in the face, froze—as did the man under him.

Dripping, the pair lowered their fists, their gazes cutting to where Niel stood a yard back, the empty bucket at his feet.

The clan-chief folded his arms across his chest and looked down his nose at them. "Ye two had better have a good reason for brawling like pit dogs in my bailey," he greeted them. Niel's voice was quiet, controlled. Eilidh had seen him like this before and knew it was a sign he was angry.

And clearly, Will and Iver did too, for neither of them answered.

"Get off him, Gunn," Niel growled.

Will nodded, rolling to his feet with a wince. Blood still trickled from his nose, one of his cheekbones was swollen, and a bruise was coming up on his jaw. Even so, Iver looked worse. His left eye was completely swollen shut, and his mouth was bloodied and swollen, as was his nose. Even from a distance, Eilidh could see his nose was broken.

Iver pushed himself up from the cobbles, biting back a groan of pain as he stood up.

Niel observed them, taking in their shuttered expressions and bloodied faces. Tension crackled through the air, and the watching crowd fell silent.

The clan-chief's mouth compressed, and he jerked his chin back toward the keep. "I'll not air yer grievances here," he said after a long pause. "Upstairs ... now."

Will massaged his aching jaw as he turned to follow Niel and Iver into the keep. God's teeth, the man had a powerful right hook. It felt as if he'd loosened a couple of teeth.

His gaze fell then, for the first time since the fight had begun, upon the slender figure standing to the right of the steps.

Eilidh stood there, pale and tense.

She exchanged a long look with Iver, as the chieftain walked by, and Will's gut clenched. It served him right really—this fight was his fault—but he didn't want her looking at the man he'd just fought. He wanted her to look at him.

And as he approached, she finally did.

Will's breathing grew shallow as their gazes locked. "Eilidh," he murmured, halting before her. "I—"

She brought a hand up in a sharp motion, cutting him off. "Not now," she said, biting out the words. Her oak-brown eyes were narrowed, high spots of color flaring upon her pale cheeks.

Will tensed, misgiving feathering through him. She was truly vexed—with him.

Eilidh turned away then and walked off without another word.

26

THE HEART WANTS WHAT IT WANTS

"I SHOULD HAVE known," Niel muttered. The clan-chief's dark brows then crashed together. "Ye were brawling over a lass."

"Eilidh is my intended," Iver ground out, a muscle feathering upon his bruised jaw. His speech was slightly muffled due to his swollen lips. However, his gaze still glittered with outrage. "Gunn dishonored her."

Niel's gaze cut to Will. "Is this true?"

Will inhaled deeply before nodding. There was no use in denying it. "I kissed her," he admitted.

Niel muttered a curse before raking a hand through his long dark hair. "Didn't ye know that Eilidh has agreed to marry Iver?"

"Aye, he knew, all right," Iver ground out. The chieftain's bloodied face went taut, his bruised and split knuckles clenching at his sides. "That's why he did it."

Niel scowled, his jaw tightening. "Will?"

Drawing in a deep breath, Will met the clan-chief's eye. "It was an impulsive act ... one I regret."

"As do I," Niel muttered. "Ye raised yer fists to one of my chieftains and made a spectacle of yerself in front of yer men. Do ye think that's the way to earn their respect?"

Will didn't answer; Niel didn't expect him to. The rebuke stung, yet he weathered it. He deserved it.

The disappointment shadowing the clan-chief's gaze concerned him. He'd indeed overstepped. He didn't want this to sour his relationship with Niel, nor did he want to lose his position here. Yet his behavior put them both in peril.

Will tensed then, waiting for the axe to fall, for Niel to dismiss him from his role and send him back to his clan in disgrace.

After long moments, Niel pulled a face. "Get out of here and return to yer post, Gunn … I'll decide what to do with ye when my temper has cooled."

"Hold still, Iver … I'm almost finished."

Eilidh dipped her cloth in the bowl of warm water and wrung it out. She then dabbed delicately at the blood crusting Iver's mouth.

He winced. "Ow."

Eilidh frowned. It never failed to amaze her, how men could beat each other senseless without uttering a squeak, but the moment a woman tended to their wounds, they whimpered like bairns. Lips compressed, she completed her ministrations and drew back.

An awkward silence settled in the women's solar. The pair of them sat at the small table in the center of the space. Eilidh's maid, Clara, stood a few feet away, a basket of unguents and bandages clasped before her. The lass's gaze was riveted upon the chieftain's battered face.

Indeed, Iver looked a mess.

Reaching up, Eilidh gently felt Iver's nose. "Aye … that's broken all right," she murmured. "Shall I call for the healer?"

"No," Iver grunted. "I doubt they'll be able to do much about it."

Eilidh nodded. Their gazes met then and held.

"Why did ye let him kiss ye?"

Eilidh sucked in a breath at Iver's bald question.

Of course, she'd known it was coming—but she wasn't ready to answer it.

Stiffening, she cast a glance in her maid's direction. The lass was watching them, wide-eyed. "Clara … can ye fetch me some clean, warm water from the kitchen?" she asked.

The lass's brow furrowed. "But I thought ye'd finished?"

"Not yet."

Casting Eilidh a look of chagrin, for the maid knew she merely wanted her out of the way, Clara departed the solar.

However, she left the door to the chamber open.

That didn't matter to Eilidh. It was enough that she and Iver now had a little privacy. This wasn't going to be a pleasant exchange, and they didn't need witnesses.

Straightening her shoulders, Eilidh met Iver's eye. "When ye returned from the Lochnaver, ye asked me if there was someone else," she said softly. "Do ye remember?"

Iver's bruised jaw tightened, his gaze guttering before he rasped, "William Gunn?"

Eilidh nodded. "Months ago, while Gunn was still a Mackay prisoner ... we got to know each other ... and a bond formed between us."

Eilidh's throat constricted then. Thinking about Will caused a volley of conflicting emotions to pepper her like quarrels: fury, hurt, and a longing that infuriated her beyond words.

"I don't understand," Iver rasped. "How—"

"We only ever had a handful of conversations," she admitted huskily, "but it was enough ... and that's why ye found me so difficult to woo initially." Eilidh broke off there. She didn't want to recount the rest of this tale, yet it was unfinished. Iver had to know everything now. "After Gunn was released from the dungeons, I went to him ... on the eve of his return to his clan ... and confessed my feelings. He revealed then that he was married ... and that he couldn't return my affection."

Iver's battered mouth thinned. "Filthy shit-weasel," he growled. "How dare he—"

"He never touched me," Eilidh cut him off, panic fluttering up. The last thing she wanted was for Iver to defend her honor again. "The only kiss between us was the one ye witnessed today." She broke off then, marshaling her thoughts. "Will's wife died last year, while he was in prison."

Iver's lip curled, an expression that made him wince. "So, he's free to wed again." The bitterness in the laird's voice cut Eilidh deep. She didn't want to wound Iver.

"I shouldn't have let Gunn kiss me," she replied, a knot twisting under her ribcage. "And I'm sorry for it." She paused then, her heart racing now. "I thought I'd put him behind me."

Iver stared back at her, and the pain in those midnight-blue eyes made it hard to breathe. She'd never hurt anyone like this before, and it sickened her. "But ye hadn't," he replied hoarsely. "Why did ye agree to my proposal, Eilidh?"

"Because I *wanted* to wed ye," she replied, taking his hand, and squeezing it. "I swear I did, Iver. I never meant to hurt ye."

Iver gently withdrew his hand from hers. "I've seen the way ye look at him … I watched the pair of ye kiss." He paused then, a nerve flickering on his cheek. "I love ye and would have treated ye like a queen … but I could never compete in a contest that has already been won. The heart wants what it wants, Eilidh … and yer heart never wanted me."

Will was standing on the walls, watching the sun slide behind the mountains to the west, when the scuff of footfalls warned him that he was no longer alone. Turning, his gaze alighted upon a slight figure bundled up in fur.

Despite that the wind had died, it was a chill evening. A frost would settle early tonight; his breathing was already clouding the air like steam. Will's pulse quickened at the sight of Eilidh, cheeks flushed, eyes bright, her brown hair cascading over the fur mantle about her shoulders.

His chest started to ache. How he longed to draw her into his arms, to kiss her once more. But now wasn't the time—not after his brawl with Iver. The fury he'd witnessed upon her face in the bailey earlier warned him that he'd have to work hard to regain her trust, and indeed, her good opinion of him.

In the meantime, he had his future at Varrich to worry about. Niel hadn't yet called for him—but he would. Will might not be Captain of the Varrich Guard for much longer.

Yet he was pleased Eilidh had sought him out. It was a promising sign.

"Ye didn't need to come looking for me on the walls, lass," he greeted her with a smile. "It's freezing up here."

"I don't mind the cold," she replied, her tone clipped. "And I didn't climb up here for a chat." Her jaw firmed. "I want an explanation. I asked ye—no, I *begged* ye—not to fight Iver, but ye ignored me. Why?"

Taken aback by the vehemence in her voice, Will's smile faded. "I had to fight him ... he left me with no choice."

"Aye, he did. There's always a choice, Gunn!"

Two of his men, standing upon the southern guard tower a few feet away, turned from their posts and gawked at them. Will scowled up at them. "Get back to work," he growled.

The guards did as bid—although not without smirks.

Will shifted his attention back to Eilidh. "That's not how it is between men ... Mackay issued a challenge, and I couldn't back down from it without looking weak."

Eilidh's full mouth thinned, and she crossed her arms, raising her chin. "Aye, but ye couldn't wait to pummel him with yer fists, could ye? I saw the gleam in yer eye. Ye *wanted* to fight him."

Will's mouth compressed. She was right. There wasn't any point in lying about it. "Iver has always had a problem with me," he admitted roughly. "The bastard had it coming."

Eilidh growled an unladylike curse, and Will jolted in surprise. He had no idea the lass knew coarse phrases like that.

"Ye aren't sorry at all?" she ground out, the flush on her cheeks deepening.

Will pulled a face, wincing as pain shot through his bruised jaw. "Aye, I'm sorrier than ye'll ever know."

Eilidh snorted.

Silence fell on the wall, stretching out for a few moments before Will exhaled sharply. "The truth is … I was jealous."

Eilidh's eyes narrowed. "Aye, ye don't like being denied things, do ye?"

"No," he murmured. There was little point in lying to her. "But don't think that kiss was premeditated … I acted on reckless impulse."

A shutter came down over Eilidh's face, and she took a smart step backward.

Will followed Eilidh, reaching for her, yet she moved out of range. He'd never seen her like this, and he didn't like it. When she spoke once more, her voice held a brittle edge. "That's all I am to ye, an *impulse*?"

"No … I mean … I acted without thinking." Christ's teeth, he was stuttering like a halfwit. "Of course, ye mean more to me than that. I'm—"

"Did ye know Iver was up on the walls?" she demanded then, cutting him off.

"No."

"I don't believe ye."

Will scowled, his own anger quickening. "Are ye calling me a liar, Eilidh Munro?"

"No, I'm calling ye a conceited knave." She broke off then, breathing hard. "Ye'll be pleased to hear yer ruse worked. Iver and I have broken off our plans to wed."

Relief, sweet and heady, barreled into Will. However, he wisely shielded his response. Folding his arms across his chest, he eyed her. "Ye don't love Iver … ye shouldn't have accepted his proposal anyway."

"How dare ye tell me whom I do or don't love?" she shouted, her voice ringing across the battlements. Will was aware his men had turned once more to gawk at him and Eilidh. He didn't bark at them this time, didn't tear his attention from the furious woman before him. Yet she wasn't done. "Once again, ye prove how self-seeking ye really are."

"No, I—"

"Go to the devil, Gunn!"

Will stared, struck speechless, as Eilidh turned, gathered her furs around her, and stalked from the wall.

27

MAKING AMENDS

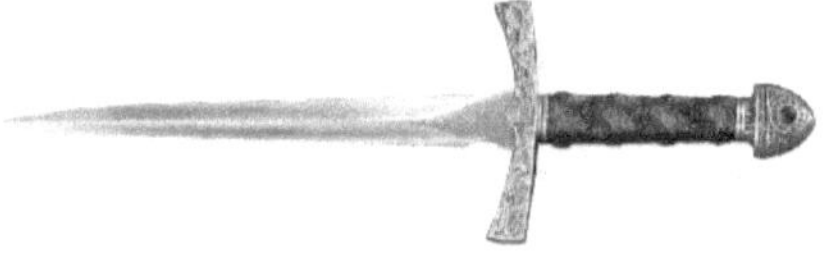

EILIDH WAS WEEPING upon her bed when a soft knock sounded on her door.

She ignored it.

Long moments passed, and then her visitor knocked once more. "Eilidh," Beth's concerned voice filtered into the bedchamber, muffled by the thick oaken door. "Can I come in?"

Eilidh raised her face from the pillow, scrubbing at her eyes to clear her vision. "Aye," she hiccoughed.

Behind her, she heard the door open and the soft pad of Beth's slippered feet. The ropes then creaked when her sister perched on the side of the bed. An instant later, she felt Beth's gentle hand on her shoulder.

"I'm sorry, lass," she whispered.

Eilidh swallowed a sob, burying her face in her pillow once more.

Beth couldn't be as sorry as she was.

They sat in silence for a few moments while Beth stroked her back. She was grateful her sister didn't try to offer her advice or attempt to remonstrate with her. The whole keep would be abuzz with the news that she'd gone up onto the wall and shrieked at the Captain of the Guard like a scold.

She'd hidden in her chamber ever since and had even sent Clara away when her maid tried to comfort her.

Guilt twisted her innards in knots.

Iver didn't deserve the humiliation he'd received at Will's hand—and at her own. There wasn't a soul within the keep who didn't know that Will had kissed her before he and Iver attempted to beat each other senseless.

Upon the dawn, she and Iver had planned to send out riders to their respective kin, to announce the happy news.

Yet there would be no wedding now.

Raising her face once more, Eilidh rolled over onto her side to look at Beth. Her sister's hazel eyes were clouded. "Are ye weeping because Iver has broken things off?"

Eilidh stared back at Beth, her chest constricting. Curse her sister—she always saw the truth, even when Eilidh tried to hide it from herself. "No," she whispered, "but I feel to blame. Ye should have seen his face, Beth … I've broken his heart."

Her sister's features tensed. "A warrior's pride is a fragile thing," she murmured.

"It's not just that." Eilidh swallowed hard. "I told him about Will."

Beth's brows crashed together. "What about him?"

"That I'd carried a torch for him … but then discovered he was married before he returned to Castle Gunn."

"What?" Beth snapped upright. "Ye never said anything at the time."

Eilidh grimaced. "There seemed little point … I already felt like a fool … and didn't need more witnesses to my folly." She sucked in a deep breath then. "Will's a widower now … he told me yesterday."

Beth's gaze narrowed. "Right before he kissed ye?"

"Aye."

Silence fell in the bedchamber then. A lump rose in Eilidh's throat. However, she scrubbed away the fresh tears that welled; weeping wasn't going to change anything.

"I heard what happened up on the walls," Beth said finally, a rueful edge to her voice. "The whole keep is talking about it."

Heat flushed across Eilidh's cheeks. "I'm sure they are," she muttered.

"It sounds like Gunn deserved the tongue-lashing ye gave him."

"He did." Eilidh pushed herself upright, fixing her sister with a level look. "What's yer opinion of him?"

Beth's mouth lifted at the corners. "He's cocky ... headstrong ... not that different to Niel really."

Eilidh snorted. Beth wasn't wrong there. It didn't surprise her that the two men got on so well. "And do ye believe Gunn can be trusted?"

Beth's smile widened. "Niel trusts him ... and after Lochnaver, I do as well." She paused then, her expression sobering. "However, that doesn't mean I condone what he did today."

Eilidh's hands balled into fists, her nails biting into her palms as ire pulsed in her belly once more. "Neither do I."

"I should make an example of ye."

Tensing, Will closed the door to the solar behind him.

The Mackay stood at the window. He had his back to Will, staring out at where the last glow of a fiery sunset faded from the sky.

Wordlessly, Will approached him, drawing to a halt before the window. The glass pane protected them from the chill wind, but even so, the cold seeped in like an icy breath.

Niel didn't appear to notice it. His profile was austere in the fading light.

"Do it then," Will said finally. His face ached this eve, and his mood was dark. When the clan-chief had called for him, he'd gone without hesitation. Nonetheless, he was growing weary of apologizing to folk, only to have them throw it back in his face.

Tonight, he just wished to retire to his tower and lick his wounds in private.

Niel cut him a sharp look. "Why did ye make a spectacle of yerself today?"

Will scratched his chin before wincing. His jaw would be black and blue in the morning. "Jealousy," he murmured. "Pride."

Niel's gaze narrowed. "Ye want Eilidh for yerself?"

Will's pulse quickened. He hadn't visited the clan-chief to lay himself bare before him. His feelings for Eilidh weren't to be bandied about. Yet the glint in Niel's eye warned him from trying to avoid the question. "Aye," he murmured after a long pause. "But it matters not ... she can't stand the sight of me now."

Niel huffed a laugh. "She'll forgive ye ... eventually."

Will frowned. He wasn't so sure about that; the fury in the lass's eyes had a finality about it. He'd lost her good opinion and didn't know how to reclaim it.

A hush fell in the solar then. Standing at Niel's side, listening to the creak of the windowpane in the wind and the crackling of the hearth behind them, Will considered his situation—and what really mattered to him.

"I wish to stay on here," he said eventually. "If ye'll have me."

Niel turned his attention to him once more. "Do ye promise not to pick any more fights with my chieftains ... and to set a proper example to the guard?"

Will held his eye. "I do."

Niel's mouth quirked then. "They'll accept ye eventually, ye know ... I've been watching ye over the past days. Ye know how to lead men."

The clan-chief's praise caused a kernel of warmth to germinate within Will, and he smiled. "They're not a bad lot ... for Mackays."

Will stared up at the rafters, watching as the first rays of dawn filtered into his bedchamber. He'd slept poorly overnight. Aye, his face had pained him, yet that hadn't been the cause.

Instead, the events of the previous day weighed on his mind. His conscience was bothering him.

Muttering a curse, Will threw off the blankets and rolled out of bed. There was little point in lying there, mulling over his many mistakes. Today, he had to set about making amends.

And he'd start right now.

It was bitterly cold in the tower. The lump of peat that had burned in the hearth overnight had gone out. Will's breathing clouded in front of him as he dressed in layers of linen and wool, before donning a quilted gambeson and a heavy fur-lined cloak. Then, pulling on his boots, he descended the tower, stepping out into a grey dawn.

Tilting his head up, he observed the colorless sky above. The air had a dank odor to it—a smell that promised ice and snow. Winter almost had them entirely in its grip; it was now just over six weeks until Yuletide.

Instead of striding across the bailey and entering the keep, where he'd break his fast in the great hall with his men, Will turned left and made his way to the stables.

Iver was saddling his stallion, a toey-looking beast that snorted and pawed the straw-covered ground.

Around him, the rest of the chieftain's men were also readying their mounts for the long journey ahead. Dun Ugadale was over a week's ride to the south.

Some of the warriors turned to look at him when Will entered. Ignoring their stares, he crossed his arms and leaned up against the entrance to the stall, watching as the stallion nearly stomped on Iver's booted foot.

"He looks a handful," Will observed.

Iver's chin jerked up, and he swiveled to face him before growling, "What the devil are ye doing here?"

It wasn't a warm welcome, although Will hadn't expected one.

Iver's face looked a mess this morning: one of the chieftain's eyes was dark purple, his nose was swollen, and his lips crusted with newly formed scabs.

Will was sure *he* didn't look any prettier.

Even so, the aggression in Iver's voice made his blood quicken.

There was a part of him—which had developed during a difficult childhood—that made him want to go for the throat when faced with aggression.

It was a reaction that had likely guaranteed his survival over the years. Even so, he wasn't sure it had earned him many friends.

Going on the attack had always been his default reaction to conflict. But today he shoved the instinct down and met Iver's eye squarely. "I owe ye an apology, Mackay," he admitted gruffly. His gut twisted then; this was harder than he'd thought. "I knew Lady Eilidh was yer intended ... and I should have respected that."

Iver stared back at him, his gaze narrowing further. His hands, with their bruised, split knuckles, clenched into fists at his sides. "Aye, ye should have," he replied, his voice sharp-edged. "Are ye here to ask forgiveness though ... or to crow?"

Will cocked an eyebrow. "Crow? About what exactly?"

Iver's expression didn't change, although Will caught the vindictive glint in his eye. "I heard Lady Eilidh paid ye a visit on the wall."

Will stiffened. Of course, Iver would have heard about the scene. It was likely every villager in Tongue had, too, by now. "Aye, well ... she's upset with me at present."

Iver's bruised face hardened. "Ye don't deserve her, Gunn."

"And ye do?" It was a provocative response, yet Will couldn't help it. Iver always managed to rub him up the wrong way.

Iver stepped forward, fists tightening further at his sides.

Will held his ground.

As apologies went, this was a failure. He had to try a bit harder.

"Ye are right," he admitted then, his voice roughening. "Ye *are* the worthier man."

Iver's jaw clenched, and Will didn't miss the wince he tried to stifle. "Why didn't ye leave her alone then?"

The question fell heavily in the now silent stables. Unsurprisingly, Iver's men had stopped saddling their horses so they could listen in on the exchange.

Will tensed. He couldn't answer the chieftain, not without making himself vulnerable. The reasons for his behavior the day before were complicated. In truth, he didn't fully understand them himself.

A tense pause drew out before Iver's face twisted. "It's ye she wants, anyway ... not me." A nerve jumped in his cheek. "It was never me." The bitterness in the chieftain's voice was so tangible that Will could almost taste it.

"It matters not now," Will replied gruffly. "After yesterday, Eilidh won't have anything to do with me."

Iver snorted before turning back to tighten the girth of his stallion. The beast tossed its head in the air, showing the whites of its eyes. The chieftain ignored it. When he answered, his voice was flat. "Ye'll bring her around."

28

THE GAME CAN WAIT

AVA PICKED UP the turnip, bringing it close to her face so she could see it properly.

"What are ye doing, lass?" The vegetable vendor asked with a snigger. "Sniffing it?"

Ava lowered the turnip, her cheeks flushing. "I wasn't."

The man's eyes glinted. "Next thing I know, ye'll be wanting to take a bite. I'll charge ye for that, mind."

Behind him, a woman selling eggs gave an amused titter.

"She was checking ye aren't selling her rotten vegetables," Eilidh said, cutting the man a stern look. "Which makes her canny ... not worthy of yer ridicule."

The vendor's grin faded. However, Eilidh raised her chin before hooking an arm through Ava's. "Come on," she announced. "We'll buy our vegetables elsewhere."

The two women moved away from the stall, although Ava's face now glowed like a coal. "God's blood, Eilidh," she muttered under her breath. "Ye're not making me any friends here today."

Eilidh caught the annoyance in her friend's voice and tensed. "I'm only sticking up for ye," she murmured. Nonetheless, Ava had a point. Eilidh had also just had words with the baker, who'd placed four currant buns in Ava's basket when she'd paid for six. She was aghast that folk took advantage of the fact that Ava couldn't see well, but they did. "When folk mistreat ye, I can't keep my tongue leashed. They should be ashamed of themselves."

"I don't disagree with ye … but please let me fight my own battles. Ye don't have to live alongside these people … *I* do."

Eilidh swallowed, hurt constricting her chest. It dawned on her then that she wasn't that different to her sisters, after all. The Munro women all had a knack for meddling in the affairs of others. Their hearts were in the right place—for they only wanted to help—but they often rushed in without thinking.

Just as she had.

The realization was a slap to the face. As the youngest sibling, she'd often lamented having overbearing sisters, yet ever since she and Ava had become friends, she'd taken on the role of her protector.

Falling silent, Eilidh shadowed Ava as she continued her shopping. Fortunately, there were a few other vegetable vendors at market this morning, so Ava was able to purchase what she needed. Meanwhile, Eilidh bought some walnuts—an autumnal treat she always looked forward to. Their baskets filled, the friends then headed back toward the mill.

It was a bright morning, although the remnants of a hard frost sparkled around them. The sky above was a swathe of unblemished blue, which was a rarity this time of year.

Eilidh sucked in the fresh air as they walked, hoping it would ease the tightness in her chest. They were halfway back to the mill when Ava glanced her way, her blue eyes clouded. "I hope I haven't offended ye?"

"Och, no," Eilidh replied hurriedly. "In truth, I'm vexed with myself. I'm just as bossy as Beth, it seems."

Ava flashed her a smile. "Ye are, but ye're still my friend."

Eilidh managed a strained smile. "I've missed our chats," she admitted. "How are things at the mill?" She was keen to turn the conversation away from herself.

"Busy … everyone's readying their winter stores."

Eilidh noted how tired Ava's face looked. It wasn't surprising that Ava's mother had died young; the poor woman had likely worn herself out, as her daughter would too. "Ye work too hard," she said softly.

Ava shrugged. "No more than most folk," she replied, and Eilidh caught the warning note in her voice once more. She didn't want to be fussed over. Ava squinted at her then. "Enough about me … when are ye going to tell me about what happened last week?"

Eilidh huffed a sigh. "Do I have to? I'm sure the gossip has reached the mill."

"It has … but I wish to hear the tale from ye."

Eilidh grimaced. She'd tried to keep herself distracted of late, anything to avoid dwelling on what had happened. "In truth, I just want to put the incident behind me."

The two friends fell silent. They passed behind the kirk and took the path along the riverbank. Eventually, Ava cleared her throat. "So, Iver's gone?"

"Aye."

It had been over a week since Iver had departed Varrich. She'd let him go without fanfare. There was nothing left to be said, and if she'd shown her face in the bailey as he'd prepared to ride out, it would have just made things even more awkward. Even so, she was ashamed of her reckless behavior with Will. She hadn't wanted to wound Iver, yet she had. Some women reveled in male attention and loved pitting suitors against each other—but she didn't.

"And have ye spoken to Gunn again?"

Eilidh shook her head.

Of late, she'd retreated to her loom and focused on finishing the detailed tapestry she'd begun a month after her arrival at Varrich nearly three years earlier.

Just that morning, she'd completed it.

Beth had admired the tapestry, had complimented her sister on her talent—but despite a sense of satisfaction at a completed project, Eilidh felt little else.

Everything was flat these days.

Of course, she'd taken to the women's solar to avoid Will, and she'd succeeded, although she couldn't keep indoors on a morning such as this. Gunn wouldn't make her a hostage in her own home. Usually, a sparkling late autumn morning like this one would fill her with joy. Instead, she was tense, out of sorts.

Sooner or later, their paths would cross again, and she'd need to brace herself.

"Ye're still in love with him … aren't ye?"

Ava's question was softly spoken, yet it made Eilidh flinch. Of late, Beth had deliberately avoided bringing up the new Captain of the Varrich Guard in conversation, sensing that her sister wished to avoid the subject. However, Ava had no such qualms.

Eilidh's throat thickened, and she blinked rapidly as her vision blurred. Mother Mary, she was about to cry. Sorrow welled up inside her, and there was nothing she could do to prevent it.

Halting on the path, she brought up a hand, clapping it over her mouth, choking off a sob.

"Eilidh!" Ava stepped close, her blue eyes flying wide with alarm. "What is it?"

"It's a mess," she gasped, "all of it … and I don't know what to do."

"God's bones, it's cold enough out there to freeze off yer bollocks!"

Will stepped inside the clan-chief's solar, chafing his hands together. He'd just come from the walls, where he and his men huddled under layers of furs, fingers numb with cold. The weather had indeed taken a wintry turn. Icy gusts, full of stinging sleet, currently slashed across the bailey.

In here was another matter. Warmth barreled into him, and he inhaled the scent of clove and the fruity aroma of warm wine. But an instant later, as he looked up, Will realized the clan-chief wasn't alone as he'd anticipated.

Niel sat at a table in the center of the space, readying the board where they'd play Ard-ri, while Beth and Eilidh flanked the roaring hearth, fingers wrapped around cups of what was likely mulled wine.

They all looked his way.

Aware that he'd made quite an entrance, Will favored them with a sheepish smile. "Good evening." He cleared his throat then. "Lady Beth … Lady Eilidh."

The clan-chief's wife flashed him a smile in greeting, while Eilidh lowered her gaze, her lovely face unusually inscrutable.

Will's heart lurched. He hadn't seen Eilidh in over a week, and certainly hadn't expected to see her in here this evening; she'd been avoiding him, that much was clear. He imagined she spent time in the women's solar after supper. However, it was a freezing evening, and this chamber was easily the warmest one in the keep. It made sense that she'd join her kin in here.

Niel eyed him, taking in the layers of wool, fur, and leather that encased his captain. "Bitter night to be leading the watch?"

Will pulled a face. "Aye."

Turning away, he divested himself of his heavy fur cloak and used the distraction to compose himself. Being in Eilidh's presence again reminded him of how she'd railed at him. Embarrassment prickled his skin at the memory.

His reaction irritated him. Will wasn't a man easily flustered—especially by women. The truth was though, he *was* embarrassed by his behavior.

It was why he'd let Eilidh be ever since, despite that he longed to talk to her, to make things right between them.

He needed to ask the lass for her forgiveness.

However, he wouldn't do it right now, not with Niel and Beth present.

"Cup of mulled wine, Will?" Beth asked.

"Aye, thank ye."

The clan-chief's wife rose to her feet and retrieved a fresh cup from the sideboard. She then ladled some wine into it from an iron pot that sat on the edge of the hearth, keeping warm. "Here."

Will flashed Beth a smile, a sigh escaping him when he wrapped his fingers around its welcome warmth. His hands ached with cold.

"How is yer new role going, Will?" Beth asked then, catching his eye as she settled back into her seat.

"Well enough, thank ye," he replied.

Niel glanced up once more from placing the king figurine at the center of the board. "I saw ye leading the men through drills this morning," he said casually. "They're improving fast."

Will smiled. "They've finally decided that a Gunn might be worth listening to, after all," he quipped. In truth, some of the younger men's skills had been sorely lacking—a few of the Varrich Guard fell at Lochnaver, and some of the warriors they'd taken on afterward were as green as saplings.

The clan-chief grinned. "Good. Take a seat then … and ready yerself for a beating."

"Over-confident, as always," Will muttered, pulling out a chair opposite the clan-chief. As he spoke, Will's gaze flicked across the solar to where Eilidh sat, still and silent. She sipped at her wine, her attention riveted upon the dancing flames in the hearth, as if he hadn't even spoken.

Will's spine stiffened.

He didn't like being ignored—especially by her.

Taking a gulp of mulled wine and savoring the flavor of cinnamon and clove, Will shifted his attention back to the board.

Niel was watching him, a glint in his eye. "Attack or defense?"

Will flashed Niel a thin smile. "I'll attack."

The rustle of skirts a few feet away caught his attention then. Eilidh had put her cup of wine aside and was rising to her feet.

Will rose with her, without thinking.

"I think I shall retire now," she said, looking past him and meeting Niel's eye.

Beth's brow furrowed. "So early?"

"Aye ... I'm weary."

Eilidh's face did appear a trifle pale and strained, although Will knew it wasn't due to fatigue.

His presence was the reason.

"Sleep well, Lady Eilidh," he murmured.

Eilidh did look his way then, meeting his gaze briefly for the first time since he'd entered the solar. In the past, her oak-brown eyes had been soft when she looked upon him, welcoming. However, tonight, they were as veiled as her expression. Full mouth compressing, she nodded. "Goodnight."

Eilidh left the solar then, the door whispering closed behind her.

Will sat down once more.

Curse it, he hated feeling so inadequate.

Eilidh had withdrawn from him, and he was completely at sea on how to breach the gulf between them.

"Go after her then."

Surprised, Will glanced the clan-chief's way. Niel was watching him, his expression shuttered now. "Excuse me?" He wasn't sure he'd heard the man right.

Niel's mouth quirked. "The game can wait ... this can't."

29

PERFECT

"EILIDH!" WILL'S VOICE hailed her as she reached the top step of the landing. Swiveling around, Eilidh put a hand on the damp wall to steady herself, her gaze alighting upon the man she'd just fled from.

"What are ye doing?" she greeted him, cursing the panicked edge to her voice. "I thought ye were playing Ard-ri with Niel?"

"The game hasn't started yet ... and he gave me leave to talk to ye first."

Eilidh's heart started hammering in her ears. *Damn ye, Niel.* He thought he was helping, yet he wasn't.

The last thing she wanted this evening was to talk to Will Gunn. Two days had passed since she'd broken down in front of Ava, and she still felt raw. She hadn't realized Niel had invited him to play Ard-ri this evening. And after Will had entered the solar, the wine she'd been drinking tasted like vinegar on her tongue.

But now he'd followed Eilidh and was climbing the steps toward her. Swallowing, she moved up onto the landing, where there was more space. She didn't want him looming over her in the narrow stairwell.

A draft breathed through the passageway in which they now stood, the nearby cressets guttering. The air was chill, and Eilidh was glad of the wool cloak she wore about her shoulders. Will hadn't retrieved his own cloak before following her, although he didn't seem to notice the cold.

Instead, his pewter gaze burned into hers with an intensity that made heat shiver across her skin.

"What?" she gasped, forcing herself not to step backward. There was nowhere to go, though—save the alcove behind her. And entering that shadowy space with this man wasn't a wise idea.

"I've been hoping our paths would cross," Will's voice held a rasp, betraying his discomfort. "Please don't run away from me."

"I'm not," she replied stiffly. "I'm tired."

Will grimaced. "Aye ... of my company."

Eilidh pursed her lips. "Well, ye have 'crossed paths' with me now, and I shall bid ye 'good eve' ... again." She attempted to edge past him then, but Will sidestepped, preventing her from walking away.

Eilidh's chin kicked up, anger punching her in the throat. "Let me pass, Will."

"I shall, lass," he replied, his gaze ensnaring hers once more, "but first we must speak. I do not want a war between us."

"There is no war," she replied, biting out the words. "Not if we avoid each other."

"Eilidh." He said her name with such tenderness that her chest started to ache. "Do ye hate me now?"

Her heart started to pound wildly at these words. Mother Mary, she wasn't ready to have this conversation. It was strange really. The last time they'd spoken in this passageway seemed an age ago. She'd been fearless then, so sure of her love and that he felt the same way. His response had knocked her confidence from her, and she'd never recovered from it.

She didn't trust him.

She didn't trust herself.

"No, I don't hate ye," she managed, her voice coming out in a strangled bleat.

"But ye look at me as if I'm a leper," he replied, his gaze never leaving hers. "I know I'm not perfect ... but am I abhorrent to ye?"

Heat flushed over Eilidh. "Of course, ye aren't."

"I behaved badly," he admitted softly, a muscle feathering upon his jaw. "I'm not proud of what I did."

Dragging in a deep breath, Eilidh eyed him.

His throat bobbed. "As I said … I'm not perfect … but I wish to be a better man … for ye."

The ache inside Eilidh's chest intensified. Was that what she wanted? Right from the beginning, she'd enjoyed the breathless risk that being around Will Gunn brought. He had a wild edge that drew her in, and he'd represented escape from a life that stifled her.

Will brought out something in Eilidh that both excited and thrilled her.

Silence swelled between them before she heaved a sigh. "I don't want to change ye, Will."

His gaze widened. "Ye don't?"

"No." The events on the fateful day he'd kissed her had stripped them both back to the bone, exposed them for who they really were. She'd recoiled at what she'd seen—but she didn't retreat now. Will wasn't perfect, yet neither was she. "If there's anything I've learned of late, it's that we shouldn't fool ourselves about who we really are." She sucked in a deep breath then. "When Iver first proposed, I hesitated. I should have followed my gut, yet I lied to myself … and it got me into trouble."

"None of this is yer fault, lass." The huskiness in his voice made the ache in her chest spread to her throat. "I take full responsibility for what happened with Iver." Will stepped closer then, the heat of his body wrapping around her. "I've been a fool about a great many things over the years … but of one thing I'm certain. I know, to the marrow of my bones, that ye were meant for me, Eilidh." He reached up then, his fingers brushing the line of her jaw.

She stared up at him, her feet rooted to the spot. His admission rendered her speechless.

However, Will wasn't finished. The pad of his thumb skimmed across her lower lip as he whispered, "I'd protect ye with my life, and I shall love ye until I drag in my last breath."

Eilidh stopped breathing.

Will's mouth quirked, even as his eyes gleamed. His hand fell away from her face, coming to rest upon her shoulder—a steady, grounding weight. "Aye … I love ye …

and I ache to make ye mine. Would ye take me as yer husband, mo chridhe?"

Eilidh stared up at him, her chest aching now. His words had torn her open, had ripped down the shield she'd raised between them. The breath she'd been holding gusted out of her. "Aye," she gasped.

Whispering her name once more, Will hauled her against him.

Their mouths crushed together, hungry, wild. His arms went about her, molding the length of her body against his. The lean, muscled length of him pressed—chest to thigh—against her softness, and fire flared deep in her belly.

She kissed him back fiercely, her hands sliding up his gambeson, clutching at the quilted material across his chest, yanking him hard against her.

Will responded in kind, his hands sliding down to cup her backside. He pulled their hips together, crushing her against him.

Eilidh felt something—long and hard—pressing against her belly. Excitement quivered through her, heat pooling between her thighs. She was a maid, but she knew what a man did with the rod between his legs. A lass couldn't grow up in a busy keep without hearing the servants whisper or catching glimpses of couples writhing in the shadows at fire festivals.

In the past, she'd been a trifle nervous of coupling—it seemed animalistic and painful—but any reservation swept away at the feel of Will's mouth, his tongue entwining with hers, his teeth gently biting her lower lip.

One of his hands left her backside and ran down her thigh, lifting it so that she pressed even more fully against his arousal.

Eilidh whimpered against his mouth. The Saints forgive her, the sound was so needy, yet she couldn't help it.

She didn't want to fight this.

They were meant to be together—as she'd known for a long while.

Her whimper elicited a low growl from him. Walking her backward, Will took them out of the passageway and into the shadowy alcove beyond. It was less public than the corridor, although anyone walking by might see them. Fortunately though, it was a chill evening, and the inhabitants of Castle Varrich stayed close to their hearths.

Neither Eilidh nor Will cared anyway. They were both too caught in the thrall of desire that had been steadily building between them over the past months.

It was too powerful to deny.

His kisses were hot, consuming, his hands possessive. Eilidh forgot the cold, forgot where they were. Writhing against him, her fingers scrabbled, searching for his skin beneath the layers of clothing.

Ripping his mouth from hers, Will trailed his lips down her jaw to her neck, where he nipped at the sensitive skin with his teeth. "I'm on the edge, lass," he rasped. "If we continue like this, I'll take ye here … and this isn't the place for a coupling."

Somewhere in the back of her mind, Eilidh heard him. Yet her body was aflame; she was having trouble concentrating on anything but the feel of his lips on her neck.

She groaned, dropping her head back to give him better access. Right now, she didn't care. He could yank up her skirts, pin her to the wall, and take what he wanted, and she'd give it willingly. Her limbs were molten, and the blood roared in her ears.

Yet Will had a tighter rein on his self-control, for, taking hold of her shoulders firmly, he pushed himself off her—although not without a whispered curse.

A soft cry of disappointment broke from Eilidh, and she reached for him.

However, he held her firm. Very little light entered the alcove, but she could make out the strained expression on his face. "We can't," he ground out, "not like this … not here, my love."

30

FULL CIRCLE

MY LOVE.

EILIDH'S throat constricted. Reaching up, her fingers curled around the iron strength of his arms. His hands still rested upon her shoulders, his grip firm. "I agree," she whispered huskily. "We need to find somewhere else ... somewhere *private*."

His fingers clenched, their tips digging into her flesh. "Eilidh," he growled softly. "We—"

"Come with me," she murmured back, cutting him off.

It had only taken a few instants for her mind to scrabble through the various possibilities. She couldn't take him back to her bedchamber, for Clara would be there, and someone would see them if they went to his lodgings as they'd have to cross the bailey to reach his tower. The women's solar might have been suitable if there was any way to lock the door, but there wasn't.

But Eilidh knew that Beth—capable chatelaine that she was—always kept the guest chambers prepared, just in case one of Niel's chieftains arrived at Varrich unannounced.

Her hands slid along Will's arms, her fingers closing around his wrists. "Come," she repeated, firmly this time. "I know just the place, where we won't be disturbed."

Wordlessly, he let his hands drop.

Smiling, as excitement thrilled through her, Eilidh led the way out into the passageway. She was aware of him just behind her, the heat of his body burning into her back.

Eilidh quickened her pace, her breathing coming in short gasps now. She needed to be alone with him—to shut the whole world out.

This move was bold indeed, but Eilidh was born to live boldly.

She'd been angry with him, yet she realized now it hadn't been selfish impulse that drove him to kiss her that day.

Her feelings hadn't been one-sided, as she'd believed.

He loved her.

As she did him.

She led them to the largest of the guest chambers, the one Will had stayed in that night after his release from the dungeon. The conversation they'd had that evening had ripped the scales from her eyes. In just a few instants, she went from a naïve lass to a heart-sore woman.

Eilidh could have taken him to a different room, but she wanted it to be this one.

She'd bring things full circle.

"God's teeth, it's cold in here," she muttered as she glanced around the dark space.

"Aye," Will agreed from behind her. His voice held a sensual rasp, yet he didn't touch her. Instead, he retrieved an unlit candle from the bedside table and went outside into the hall to light it from one of the cressets. Bringing the candle back into the chamber, Will closed the door and barred it. Then, as Eilidh looked on, her breathing shallow with need, he crossed to the hearth. One of the servants had already set it, ready for the next guest—and so Will had it blazing within moments.

It was still freezing inside the chamber, although when Will added a lump of peat to the hearth, Eilidh felt the rawness ebb.

Rising from where he'd been crouched, ensuring the fire didn't go out, Will swiveled to Eilidh.

"Apologies for the wait," he said, his voice a sensual drawl as his gaze roamed over her. "But I wish to make this comfortable for ye ... I want this first time between us to be a cherished memory."

Eilidh's pulse quickened, and warmth bathed her skin. She now felt as if she was standing close to the blazing fire.

Wordlessly, she took off her woolen shawl and cast it over a chair a few feet back from the bed. She hadn't examined the bed too closely, for dizziness swept over her—a blend of longing and nerves—whenever she'd glanced over it while Will had been busy lighting the fire.

The bed was a beautiful one, large and canopied, and covered with a soft blanket.

She turned from divesting herself of her cloak to find Will standing over her. With a growl low in his throat, he pulled her into his arms, his hands tangling in her hair as his mouth devoured hers.

Now that they were behind a locked door, there was no restraint between them.

Reaching down, Eilidh tugged at the gambeson and lèine he wore underneath. She wanted them off; she wanted to see him.

Will drew back from her, his mouth curving at her eagerness. He then reached down, his fingers fastening around the hem of his gambeson before he yanked it over his head.

Breathing hard, as if she'd just sprinted up the promontory on which Castle Varrich stood, Eilidh fumbled with the laces of her kirtle. If he was undressing, then so would she.

Moments later, they stood naked facing each other, their clothing pooled around their feet.

Will's gaze raked over her, hot and hungry, from the crown of her head to her feet, his lips parting as he took her in.

Likewise, Eilidh studied every lean line of his body.

He was beautiful.

Months of labor in the fields had built hard muscle on his frame. Will's long dark hair was unbound this evening, falling in a curtain over his broad shoulders.

Swallowing hard, for her mouth had just gone dry, Eilidh reached out, her fingertips trailing over the hard planes of his chest and the light covering of crisp black hair. Her fingers then traveled south, over his flat belly—to where his shaft thrust up to meet her.

Eilidh studied it with the same intensity she had the rest of him. Large and curved, with a swollen tip, his rod fascinated her.

Nervousness fluttered up then, even as heat pulsed between her thighs.

Could something that size fit inside a woman?

Boldness—and curiosity—surged within her then, as she trailed her fingers down over its length, marveling at the heat, and the strength, of him.

Will went still, the rasp of his breathing the only sound in the bedchamber save for the crackling of the fire behind him.

Eilidh licked her suddenly parched lips. She almost tasted the tension emanating from him. Glancing up at his face, she saw the skin was pulled tight across his high cheekbones and his grey eyes looked almost black in the dimly lit room.

With a sigh, Eilidh dropped her gaze once more to his rod. Then, following instinct, she fell to her knees before him so she could study it better. She wasn't sure what to do with the appendage, yet since he was allowing her, she wished to explore it further. Her hand cupped his bollocks, large yet high and tight, and she squeezed gently.

Will groaned, the sound low and feral. His hands, which hung at his sides, clenched into fists.

A wicked smile curved Eilidh's lips. Aye, he was barely holding onto his self-control. She was playing with fire, and it thrilled her. The musky, uniquely-male scent of him made her belly flutter.

She continued to explore the length of his shaft with her fingers before she curled them around his hardness.

"Eilidh," he whispered hoarsely. Smiling, she leaned in, her lips brushing across the swollen head of his rod. And then when her tongue darted out and she tasted him, he made a strangled sound deep in his throat. "Are ye trying to kill me, lass?"

"No," she replied, her voice deliberately teasing. "I'm just exploring."

"Grip me firmer then," he rasped, still not touching her, "and stroke yer hand up and down."

She complied, and to her awe, his rod grew larger still and impossibly hard in her hand. A deep, restless ache set in between her thighs as she leaned in and tasted him once more.

Will's muttered curse filtered over the chamber then, and an instant later, he'd drawn Eilidh to her feet, and into his arms.

Naked bodies flush, they kissed feverishly, tongues tangling, hands roaming at will.

Eilidh marveled at the heat of his skin, the hardness of his body compared to the softness of hers. They contrasted each other beautifully; they were meant to go together.

Mirroring her earlier move, Will tore his mouth from Eilidh's and sank to his knees before her. His gaze was now level with her breasts. Small and pointed, they felt unnaturally heavy, the nipples as hard as two berries. Aye, it was a cold night, but it wasn't the chill that made them stand to attention—and when Will's hot mouth closed around one tip, Eilidh gave a raw cry.

He suckled her before his teeth gently nipped at her nipples. Pleasure arrowed straight down to Eilidh's lower belly, and she trembled against him. Her breathing came in strange, mewing gasps now, her fingers tangling in his long hair.

Eventually, when he'd given both breasts a thorough sucking, Will rose to his feet in a smooth, swift movement and scooped Eilidh up into his arms. His mouth fused with hers, almost bruising in its hunger, as he carried her to the bed.

They sprawled across it, their limbs entwining.

Eilidh's skin shivered with delicious pleasure at the feel of him pressed hard against her. The scent of his skin, the taste of his mouth, the rasp of his stubbled jaw against her cheek as he kissed her, took hold of something deep inside her—something primal.

"I've wanted this," he growled, as his mouth left hers, and he began a long, slow exploration down her trembling body, "... to know how ye'd feel ... how ye'd taste ... for so long." His tongue traveled over the hollow of her navel. "Ye are delicious ... like cream and honey."

His sensual words made Eilidh's breathing hitch. His languorous touches were both delighting and frustrating her. She wanted more—so much more—even though she'd never traveled this path before.

And then he parted her legs, his lips trailing down her inner calf and thigh to the nest of brown curls between them.

Eilidh stopped breathing, her body tensing as he lowered himself—and when he tasted her there, in her most intimate spot, she let out a high, keening cry that rang through the chamber.

It was just as well the walls of Castle Varrich were thick, although at that moment Eilidh couldn't have cared less if everyone inside the keep heard them. All she could focus on was what Will was doing to her, and the flick of his tongue upon the most exquisitely sensitive nub of flesh, that caused her lower belly to tighten. Warm, tingling pleasure spiraled out from where he was touching her, building fast to something wild and intense that had her arching against his face with reckless abandon.

She'd had no idea couples did things like this. Breathless excitement caught her in its thrall, and she cried out again, grinding herself against him. Will's hands slid under her, grasping her backside to hold her steady while he continued his onslaught.

Hot, throbbing pleasure spiked through Eilidh's loins, pulsing in her lower belly, and she cried out again before collapsing against the mattress, her body trembling.

Will drew back from between her thighs, his gaze dark and hungry, before he crawled over her, capturing her mouth in a fierce, demanding kiss.

Eilidh responded in kind, her hands roaming across the planes of his chest before one traveled down to his straining shaft. The head of it was slick was moisture now, and she ran her palm over it, marveling at the sensation.

Will ripped his mouth from hers, his lips traveling down to her neck, where he bit down gently. He then soothed the sting with his tongue, while Eilidh shivered and moaned under him.

"I'm going to take ye now, lass," he ground out. "I'm going to make ye mine."

Eilidh sighed his name and parted her legs wide for him. God's blood, she wished he would. She wanted him so much that it felt as if a fever raged through her. Her gaze moved down, between their bodies, to where she watched him take his rod in hand and position it at her entrance.

And then, with exquisite, aching slowness, he slid inside her.

31

MY HEART IS IN YER HANDS

WILL'S CHEST ACHED, his breathing coming in short, painful gasps. Sweat bathed his skin, and his groin throbbed.

It was taking everything he had to go slowly.

He was exercising a restraint he hadn't even known he possessed. In the past, his tumbles with women had been just that: lusty and fast. He took what he wanted, although he always ensured his lover enjoyed herself too.

But he'd never focused so intently on a woman's needs as he did tonight. As he'd told Eilidh earlier, he wanted their first coupling to be a memory they'd both cherish forever. They'd only get to experience the magic of their first time together once.

Eilidh was his jewel, and he wanted to make this perfect for her.

But the Lord preserve him, it was hard not to plunge his rod deep into her—not to ride her with abandon.

He'd never been with a virgin before, yet even so, he understood how important it was to treat her gently.

And so, he inched his way in, let her stretch and adjust to him.

Like him, sweat coated Eilidh's body. Her slender limbs gleamed in the flickering firelight, a flush had risen upon her cheekbones, and her chest rose and fell sharply—those delectable, pointy tits of hers tempting him with each exhale. They were as delicious as the rest of her.

He'd penetrated her halfway when Eilidh's body tensed. He halted then, holding her tightly against him until she relaxed—and then he fell into her, sliding down to the root in one long, slow movement.

Eilidh let out a guttural cry, and Will stilled. "Have I hurt ye, lass?"

"No," she gasped. "Don't ye dare stop, Will!"

"I won't," he assured her, withdrawing almost to the tip of his rod before sliding home once more. Eilidh cried out his name while he continued taking her in slow, measured thrusts that made heat build at the base of his spine.

It wasn't enough—he needed to be deeper inside her. Rearing back then, Will spread Eilidh wider still and pulled her up to meet him. The different angle made her moan and writhe against him, and when Will reached between her trembling thighs, his thumb finding the spot that had made her shatter against his mouth earlier, Eilidh's lithe body started to tremble.

Her eyes were wide, desperate, as she watched him, her lips parted. She didn't understand what was happening to her, and he loved seeing her unravel. "Do ye know how beautiful ye are?" he rasped, sliding deep inside her once more. "Yer hot, tight quim is driving me insane."

She cried out again then, shuddering as he rolled his hips, changing the angle of penetration once more. "Aye, ye like this, don't ye?"

"Aye ... don't stop, Will!" Her voice was high, frantic. "Harder!"

Her plea untethered him. If hard was what she craved, he'd give it to her.

Lowering her hips to the bed, he leaned forward over Eilidh once more, holding himself above her as he plowed her with single-minded determination.

She splintered under him, writhing and gasping, her fingernails raking down his back—and when Will finally joined her, his vision went dark for a moment.

They lay entwined afterward, their bodies slick with sweat, their breathing coming in rasping pants. Will had collapsed on top of Eilidh after his climax, yet he shifted to her side moments later, for fear of crushing her.

For the longest while, he couldn't speak. Their coupling had been so wild, so emotional, that he felt as if his chest had been ripped open.

The world was spinning around him.

"Will?" Eilidh rolled toward him, propping herself up on an elbow as she regarded him, her brown eyes limpid. "Are ye well?"

"I believe so," he murmured, his voice a rasp. "I just need to catch my breath."

That was a lie; he needed to do much more than that. This coupling had just flung him skyward, breaking him free of his past. He felt lighter, while at the same time fragile.

This woman could break him into tiny pieces if she wished.

He wasn't used to feeling so vulnerable.

Reaching out, he stroked her cheek with the back of his hand, his throat constricting. "In truth, I feel like a newborn bairn right now," he admitted. "My heart is in yer hands, lass."

Eilidh's eyes gleamed, and then a tear escaped, trickling down her cheek. Even so, she was smiling as she reached up and covered his hand with hers. "And mine is in yers, my love."

The tears flowed freely now. Tears of joy. Even so, Will's eyes guttered, his throat working. "I didn't mean to make ye weep, mo chridhe." He reached for her then, gathering her against the wall of his chest.

"Ye haven't," she whispered back, wrapping herself around him. "But the emotions within me can't be contained. I'm so happy, Will."

His arms tightened around her. She laid her cheek upon his chest, feeling the tattoo of his heart against her ear.

The moment was perfect; she wished it could go on forever.

They fell silent for a spell. The fire had warmed the chamber. But as the sweat cooled on their bodies, a chill feathered across Eilidh's skin.

Murmuring an endearment to her, Will pulled a blanket over them both before he drew her close once more.

Eilidh snuggled into her lover's warmth, sighing as he wrapped her in his embrace. There was no safer place than this. "Didn't ye say Niel was waiting for ye?" she asked sleepily.

"Aye."

"Won't he be getting impatient?"

A laugh rumbled through Will's chest. "Most likely ... but he'll give up on me eventually." He paused then, a smile in his voice when he continued, "I don't think he'll be surprised that I didn't return."

"That's a relief ... I don't want ye getting into trouble on my account." Eilidh tipped up her head then, seeking out his gaze. It was dimly lit inside the chamber, yet there was no mistaking the tenderness she spied there. "Although, what we've just done might."

His expression sobered. "Ye don't regret it, do ye?"

"Never." Eilidh's response was instant, fierce, before her lips then curved. "However, this does mean ye *will* have to do the honorable thing ... and wed me."

Will's mouth kicked up into a wide smile. "Fear not, lass ... I intend to do exactly that. I will ask Niel for permission at dawn."

Niel lowered the wedge of bannock, dripping with heather honey, he'd been about to take a bite of.

Watching the clan-chief's face, Eilidh's belly fluttered. She'd expected Niel to smile at Will's declaration that he was in love with the clan-chief's sister-by-marriage—and that he wished them to wed as soon as possible.

Instead, Niel's expression was impossible to read.

Across from him, Beth's hazel eyes had sprung wide. Wee Angus, however, was oblivious to the tension that rippled through the solar. He was too busy trying to feed himself porridge—with his hands.

The lad was making a right mess, although his mother was too distracted at present to notice.

Next to Eilidh, Will's expression sobered. An instant later, his hand tightened around Eilidh's. "Niel?" His voice had lowered.

The clan-chief leaned back in his chair, his gaze sweeping over them both. "I put away my Ard-ri board after ye left me, last eve," he replied, his expression still veiled. He then glanced over at Beth, and they shared a look. "It was obvious ye wouldn't be returning."

Silence fell once more in the solar.

Niel's mouth curved then, his dark-blue eyes glinting. "It seemed ye two had much to discuss."

Relief washed over Eilidh, weakening her limbs. She'd thought the clan-chief was angry that Will had stolen her virtue—Niel was her guardian, after all—yet she saw understanding in his gaze.

Rising from his seat, the clan-chief approached Will. The two men clasped hands, and then Niel pulled him into a hug. He then embraced Eilidh.

An instant later, Beth was there too, Angus perched upon her hip as she wrapped her free arm around her sister and squeezed tight.

Drawing back from the hug, Eilidh saw her sister's eyes sparkle with tears. Likewise, Eilidh was on the verge of weeping. She'd been nervous this morning. Beth knew how she felt about Will, but the scene with Iver had left a sour taste in everyone's mouth.

There had been a part of Eilidh that was worried Niel would deny them.

"Bastard," Will muttered, landing a playful punch upon the clan-chief's shoulder.

However, Niel just laughed. "Aye ... I had ye worried for a few moments there, didn't I?"

Beth cast him a censorious look, and Niel's mirth faded. Stepping close to Will and Eilidh once more, he reached out, placing a firm hand on both of their shoulders. "Apologies ... my sense of humor isn't to everyone's taste." He paused then, his lips curving. "Of course, ye have my blessing. Ye shall be wed tomorrow, if ye wish it?"

"Give us a few days." Will then glanced across at Eilidh, his eyes crinkling at the corners as he smiled. "I imagine ye wish yer kin to attend the wedding?"

Eilidh nodded. "And ye shall want to invite yers too?"

To her surprise, Will's gaze shadowed then, his smile fading. "Tavish and I didn't part well," he admitted after a pause. "There's little point in sending him an invitation ... he's not likely to come."

Eilidh held his gaze, a little of the warmth that glowed within her ebbing. The tension on his face betrayed him. She wasn't sure what had passed between the brothers, but surely it wasn't insurmountable?

Will clearly wanted Tavish at their wedding yet was too proud to ask him.

She reached out then and took his hand, squeezing gently. He wouldn't be sending word to Castle Gunn— but *she* could.

32

ALLIANCE

ROBINA GUNN ENTERED her husband's solar, moving quietly in slippers.

Even so, Tavish heard her. He glanced up from where he was reading a book by the fire. A candle perched on the mantelpiece illuminated the pages in the otherwise dimly lit chamber.

He flashed her a smile. "The lads are all in bed, I take it?"

"Aye ... Finn took some convincing tonight though." Her mouth curved. "He seems to think he doesn't need to sleep."

Tavish snorted a laugh. "I remember Will going through a stage like that." His expression sobered then. "He soon got over it when our father took a stick to him."

"Well, Finn knows ye'd never do that," Robina replied gently. Crossing the solar, she lowered herself into a high-backed chair opposite Tavish, her gaze settling upon her husband. "Speaking of Will ... word came today from Castle Gunn." She withdrew a scroll of parchment from her sleeve and handed it to him.

Tavish's brow furrowed as he took it from her. "The seal's broken."

Robina cast him a withering look. "Aye ... that's because it was addressed to me. It's from Eilidh Munro."

The clan-chief's frown deepened. "Beth Munro's younger sister? Why would she do that?"

"Read the missive for yerself and see."

Mouth compressing, Tavish unfurled the parchment, his gaze scanning the message within. His gaze widened. "God's teeth, my brother works fast."

Robina smiled. "Aye ... the wedding is just a few days away, and we're invited."

"I see that," he replied, lowering the missive.

Robina scanned her husband's face. She and Tavish had been wed over a decade—and over the years, she'd learned to read his moods well. His expression was carefully neutral now, although his grey eyes had darkened, a sure sign emotion churned within.

"Has Will disappointed ye that much?" she asked after a beat.

Tavish pulled a face.

"I didn't realize ye two fell out."

"We didn't."

"But ye can't forgive him for taking up with the Mackays?"

"It's not a question of forgiveness, love," Tavish muttered, rolling up the parchment and handing it back to her. "Will is a Gunn ... his place is *here*, at my side. Instead, he's chosen to follow Niel Mackay."

Tavish growled the clan-chief's name like a curse. Aye, he'd ridden off to fight at the Mackay's side. However, it had been to quash Robert Sutherland's ambitions and prevent him from encroaching on the border the two clans shared.

He hadn't done it out of any sense of loyalty to the Mackay.

He still resented the man for the battle two and a half years earlier, when he'd drawn the Gunns into conflict and then bested them. Tavish had lost a lot of good men at Ruaig-Shansaid—and her husband wasn't about to forget it.

"Ye have Blair and Evan," she reminded him after a pause, turning the rolled parchment over in her hands.

"Aye ... but Will's the best fighter of the three. He let me down."

Robina inhaled deeply. She loved Tavish with everything she was—a love that was stronger than the foundations of this great fortress—but his Gunn pride frustrated her at times.

"Will has always looked up to ye," she said quietly. "He will be disappointed if ye don't attend his wedding."

Tavish frowned once more. "Will he? That missive was from his intended, not from him. I wonder if he even knows Eilidh Munro sent it."

Robina met his eye, her own brow furrowing. "Does it matter?" She paused then, her jaw firming. "This is about more than yer relationship with Will … this is yer chance to put the conflict between ye and the Mackays behind ye. Do ye want yer sons to grow up nursing the same old hates as ye have?"

"These blades wouldn't cut through warm butter," Will said, holding a broadsword up to examine its edge by the light of a lantern. "See to it they're all sharpened by the end of the day."

"Aye, Captain," Rory replied with an eager nod.

Will glanced over at where another young man was polishing helmets inside the armory. "Ye help him, Fergus … or he'll never get it done in time." He paused then. "Ye don't want to be locked in here catching up on yer chores tomorrow … and miss my wedding."

"Are ye giving us the day off then?" Rory asked hopefully.

Will snorted. "No, lad. I want yer arse up there guarding the walls." Rory's face fell at this news, and Will added. "Don't worry, ye'll all see the ceremony, at least … and ye won't go hungry. I'll make sure someone brings food up to ye."

Both Rory and Fife grinned.

"Now stop flapping yer tongue and get to work." Will pushed a whetstone at Rory. "Those blades won't sharpen themselves."

"Aye, Captain."

Exiting the armory, Will pulled up the collar of his fur mantle against the stinging wind. It was mid-afternoon, and the sky was the color of slate. The weather had been bitterly cold of late, and since they planned to have the ceremony on the steps of the chapel, he hoped it would warm up a little.

But no matter the weather, this time tomorrow, he and Eilidh would be wed.

A slow smile curved Will's mouth at the thought.

God's bones, he loved that lass. The past few days had crept by with agonizing slowness.

Yet now it was almost upon them.

He and Eilidh hadn't lain together again, deciding to wait until their wedding night to do so. It had seemed a noble idea at the time, but days with his intended—walking, conversing, and planning their future together—had frustrated him no end.

Will was impatient by nature, as was Eilidh, yet they'd both waited, and he was glad of it.

Still smiling, Will set off across the wind-swept bailey toward the keep. He had a meeting with Niel now; the clan-chief would be awaiting him in his solar.

However, he'd only gotten halfway across the wide, cobbled space when the thunder of hoof-beats made him draw to a halt.

An instant later, a jet-black courser barreled into the bailey.

Will's breathing caught when he recognized Tavish's haughty face. His brother's dark hair streamed behind him as he drew up his horse. Robina followed her husband into the yard. Spying Will, she grinned.

The Gunn clan-chief's gaze settled upon Will, and his mouth quirked. "Good afternoon, little brother."

Will stared back at him, stunned. What was Tavish doing here? He'd sent word to Farr Castle to Alex. The Gunn firstborn and his wife, Jaimee, had arrived earlier that day. However, he hadn't bothered sending an invitation to Castle Gunn. The memory of the scorn on Tavish's face the last time they'd seen each other had prevented him. He didn't want to sour his wedding day, looking toward the gates and wondering why Tavish hadn't come.

But here he was.

Seeing Will's confusion, Tavish inclined his head. "Lady Eilidh sent Robina a missive ... requesting our presence at Castle Varrich on the Twenty-fifth day of November ... and here we are." His brother's smile widened then. "Ye didn't think I'd miss yer wedding day, did ye?"

"Ye look like a fairytale princess, lass." Beth had tears in her eyes as she stepped back to admire Eilidh. She'd spent an age twisting her sister's long hair up into an elaborate style that exposed her slender neck. It took her a while to get it just right.

Eilidh swallowed to ease the sudden tightness in her throat. "Och, Beth ... ye exaggerate."

"No, she doesn't." A few feet away, Neave brushed away tears, even as she smiled, while next to her, Jean was discreetly dabbing at her cheeks. "Ye truly are a vision."

"Ye are," Jean agreed huskily. "The beauty ye have within glows like a beacon, Eilidh. That, matched with yer loveliness ... makes ye outshine the sun."

"Thank ye, Jeanie." Eilidh grinned back, smoothing her hands upon the skirts of her velvet, fur-lined gown. It was deep purple, the same hue as the pansies Beth had woven through her hair. She moved to Jean then and wrapped her in a tight hug.

Her sister's arms went about her, squeezing hard, before she pulled away. Jean's grey-green eyes glittered. "There now ... I don't want to crush yer dress or mess up yer hair."

"Ye'd better not," Beth warned. "I'm not sure I can achieve that style twice."

Eilidh swallowed, attempting to dislodge the lump of emotion that threatened to choke her. Her gaze traveled about her, taking in her sisters' faces. All of them had earned hard-won happiness, and now so had she.

But as much as she adored Beth, Neave, and Jean, there was someone else she wished were here right now: Ava.

She wanted them to meet her. Initially, she'd kept her friendship with the miller's daughter secret. Yet in the days leading up to the wedding, she'd told all her sisters about Ava. She didn't need to keep secrets any longer.

Eilidh had been down to the mill two days prior, to invite her friend in person.

Ava was delighted by the news that Eilidh and Will were getting married—and she'd promised to attend the ceremony and the banquet that would follow.

"I couldn't have wished for better sisters," Eilidh announced then, her voice roughening. "I'm glad ye are all here ... I wouldn't want to wed without ye at my side."

Beth brushed away a tear of her own. "And ye won't need to."

"Are we ready to go then?"

A gruff male voice intruded, and Eilidh turned to see her father standing in the doorway to the women's solar.

George Munro's bearded face creased into a wide smile as his gaze alighted upon her. "God's rood, lass ... ye are a sight fit to make the angels weep."

Eilidh grinned, warmth suffusing her breast. No, she couldn't have gotten married without her sisters at her side, and nor could she without her father. Growing up, he'd been a steady presence in her life—a mighty oak. These days, signs of age were upon him: his face bore more lines than it had when she'd moved with her sisters to Varrich, and his hair was more silver than brown. Nonetheless, the Munro clan-chief was still as hale as she remembered.

"Aye, Da," she replied, crossing to him. She then linked her arm through his and squeezed tight. "Lead the way."

Eilidh leaned forward, taking a sip from the pewter goblet that her husband held to her lips. Likewise, Will bowed his head and drank from the one she presented him.

Cheers lifted the roof around them, the roar booming off the stone walls and drowning out the music of the piper and harpist playing in the gallery opposite.

Raising her head, Eilidh stared into Will's eyes and grinned.

He favored her with a slow, intimate smile in return.

Eilidh's breathing quickened as she anticipated the wedding night that would follow. They'd not lain together since the eve they'd confessed their love for each other—and need ignited low in her belly as their stare drew out.

Today was perfect. A day she'd remember until she drew her last breath.

Father Lucas had wed them on the steps to Varrich's chapel, binding a length of Mackay plaid around their joined hands. Eilidh barely remembered the words he'd spoken, for she'd been too intent on the man standing next to her. And then, after they'd repeated their vows, Will pulled her into his arms for a passionate kiss that had his brothers hooting and whistling.

Father Lucas hadn't looked impressed by the din they'd made, but Eilidh didn't care. She'd been pleased—and relieved—to see Tavish and Robina amongst the well-wishers. Robina hadn't replied to the missive she'd sent in secret, and she'd worried Tavish wouldn't attend. But he had, and when Tavish and Will hugged after the ceremony, she'd marked the gleam in her husband's eye.

It meant a lot to him, as she knew it would.

Finally breaking eye contact with Eilidh now, Will started to dish up food onto the trencher they would both eat from.

Beth had outdone herself with this feast. The table upon the dais groaned under the weight of dishes: spit-roasted pork stuffed with walnuts and apples, pies, boar stew, and platters of fried pike.

Will took a little bit of everything for them to try, while Eilidh shifted her attention to the crowded hall beneath them. Long trestle tables lined the rectangular space. It was a rare thing to see Mackays and Gunns sitting, elbow-to-elbow, drinking and breaking bread together—and she took the scene in, a smile lingering upon her lips.

However, as her gaze continued to travel up and down the long tables, her smile faded.

Where is Ava?

She'd looked for her friend as her father led her through the crowd up to the chapel steps but hadn't seen her. Ava wasn't present in the great hall either.

A shadow dimmed Eilidh's happiness for a few moments, like a cloud passing over the face of the sun. It meant a lot to her that Ava be here on this day.

But she hadn't come as she'd promised. *I hope she is all right.*

Worry crept in then, whispering in her ear. *Maybe she doesn't want me as a friend.* Ava had appeared to let the matter drop once they'd left the market that day—but their 'argument' had preyed on Eilidh's mind ever since. She didn't want Ava to think her controlling or overbearing, but perhaps she did.

"What is it, Eilidh?" She glanced back at Will to see that he'd finished serving them, and was now observing her, a crease forming between his dark eyebrows. "Ye look worried."

"My friend ... Ava ... isn't here," she murmured, feeling a trifle foolish. "Ye know ... the miller's daughter I told ye about."

Will nodded, his gaze shifting out to the hall, where men were starting to sing, holding their tankards aloft. "Perhaps she was too busy in the end."

"Aye, maybe."

Will glanced back at Eilidh, his mouth lifting at the corners. "Fret not, my love … we shall pay her a visit tomorrow."

Eilidh nodded, a little of the tension ebbing out of her shoulders. He was likely right. Ava's life wasn't an easy one; there were just the two of them running the mill, and her father relied heavily on her. She might not have been able to get away for the afternoon. "I'd like that." Indeed, she wanted him to meet her best friend too—and she knew Ava would be curious to meet the man she'd heard so much about over the past months.

They began their meal then, savoring the beautifully prepared food, as ale, mead, and wine flowed around them.

The clan-chief's table upon the dais was a busy one. Eilidh and Will sat in the middle of it, flanked to the left by the Mackays, and the Gunns to the right.

Surveying those seated at her table, Eilidh realized just what an important day this was: one that signified not just the union between a man and woman, but also a burgeoning alliance between the Mackays and the Gunns.

Aye, Tavish and Niel had barely spoken all day, yet today was another step toward peace between their clans.

Laughter drew her attention then. Will was teasing Tavish about something while Alex looked on, a smile curving his lips.

Eilidh's mouth curved to see the three of them together. The Gunns had been through much over the past years—but now that Roy Gunn was dead, they could finally heal the lingering rifts between the surviving brothers. Over the past days, Will had told Eilidh more about his father. She'd shuddered as he described a cruel, ruthless man fueled by hatred. George Gunn had wished to poison all his sons with his own bitterness, yet he'd failed.

Drunken shouts intruded then, splintering the laughter and lively conversation within the hall.

Eilidh cut her gaze away from her husband and his brothers to see a Gunn warrior, one of the clan-chief's escort, lunge at a Mackay across a table.

Fists flew, as did platters of food and tankards. The music screeched to a halt, and both Tavish and Niel rose to their feet.

The Gunn clan-chief was scowling. "Evan ... Blair," he called to his brothers who were seated at a table just beneath the dais. "Deal with him."

Favoring him with a nod, the two big men heaved themselves off their bench seats and approached the table where the Gunn warrior had just slugged his opponent in the face.

They hauled him off and dragged him, cursing, out of the great hall.

The Mackay warrior, one of Niel's men-at-arms, shook his head to clear it, wiping away the blood that trickled from one of his nostrils.

"What was that about, Fergus?" Niel didn't look any more impressed than Tavish.

"I told him his mother was a dirty whore," the warrior muttered, his voice echoing across the now silent hall. He then glanced at the other Mackay men seated around him, flashing them a smirk. "Can't take a bit of teasing ... isn't that right, lads?"

The warriors cheered, banging their tankards on the table in solidarity.

Niel's mouth thinned. He then looked at where two of his chieftains, John and Robin, had stood up, awaiting his command. Meeting John's eye, the clan-chief nodded, a silent message passing between them. "Put him in the stocks," he ordered, his voice chill. "Let's see how pleased he is with himself after a night out in the cold."

Fergus's face went slack, and he started to protest.

However, John and Robin had reached him by then. Grabbing him by the arms, the two chieftains 'escorted' the man out of the hall.

And when the warrior's drunken protests had faded, Niel's gaze swept over his muttering men. "Silence!" His voice cracked like a whip across the hall, and the cavernous space fell quiet. "Drink flows at weddings," he continued roughly. "And it loosens tongues ... but that doesn't give any of ye leave to forget that the Gunns were invited here as our *friends*. The next man who loses control of his tongue ... or his fists, will feel my wrath."

The Mackay warriors shifted uncomfortably in their seats at this threat. Next to Eilidh, Will watched Niel, a smile lifting the corners of his mouth. Eilidh saw the respect in her husband's eyes—as she did on Tavish's face.

The Gunn clan-chief rose to his feet before his gaze speared Niel's. "Well said, Mackay." He moved across the dais then toward the man he'd long considered an enemy. "Let this be a new start."

The two men clasped arms, and cheers erupted within the great hall of Castle Varrich, echoing high into the rafters.

Eilidh cheered alongside everyone else, warmth suffusing her chest. Aye, this peace between the Mackays and the Gunns was new—but this moment proved to them all that it could last.

Reaching under the table, Eilidh's hand rested upon Will's thigh, and although his gaze never left Niel's face, his hand found hers and squeezed tight.

33

VISITING AVA

"THE MILL IS just upriver."

"I know the place ... I used to work the fields opposite." Will glanced Eilidh's way as they crossed the bridge. "Sometimes, I'd see a lass washing clothes in the river."

Eilidh smiled. "Aye ... that's my friend Ava."

Will nodded.

"I know Cormac has been busy of late," Eilidh murmured, slipping her arm through his. "Perhaps he couldn't spare Ava ... even for a few hours."

Or maybe she's tired of my overbearing ways.

Will favored her with a soft smile. "Aye ... I'm sure there's an explanation, lass." He gave Eilidh's arm a gentle squeeze then. "It's good to get outdoors ... after all that food I consumed yesterday. I swear yer sister's fine cooking will make me fat."

Eilidh snorted, casting an eye down his lean body. There wasn't an ounce of fat on the man. However, she appreciated him changing the subject.

Indeed, she too was enjoying the walk—despite the grey sky and biting wind.

The day before had been magical. And after a passionate wedding night—in which she and Will had slept little—she'd left the castle feeling as if she were floating three feet above the ground.

Earlier, she'd thought Will would need reminding of his promise to visit Ava, yet he hadn't. They'd broken their fast together in his tower, seated at a table near the glowing hearth, before he'd met her eye and winked. "I hope ye have a heavy fur cloak handy, lass … it's a chilly morning for a walk into Tongue."

Eilidh carried a basket looped over her free arm. It contained left-over walnut bread from the banquet, as well as some cakes studded with tart plums. Ava hadn't been able to attend the celebrations, but she didn't want her to miss out entirely.

A narrow path cut through a copse of trees and skirted behind the kirkyard outside Tongue village.

"Looks like there was a recent burial," Will said. "Look." He pointed to the southern edge of the kirkyard, to where a mound of freshly turned soil sat before a wooden cross.

Eilidh's brow furrowed, unease skating down her spine. "I wonder who it was." She'd lived here long enough to develop a kinship with the people of Tongue. She'd gotten to know many of them, and it worried her that there had been a death in the village.

The path led them away from the kirkyard and back to the northern banks of the river. Up ahead, Eilidh spied the wooden outline of the mill. The great wheel was slowly turning, the creak of iron carrying through the damp air.

As they neared the structure, a man stepped out of the doorway.

Squat, with thinning brown hair, he scowled at the man and woman approaching.

Eilidh's grip on her husband's arm tightened.

"That's not the miller," she whispered.

"I know," Will murmured back. He then raised a hand to greet the man. "Good morning."

"Aye," the individual grunted, still eyeing them. "What's yer business here then?"

"Where's Cormac?" Eilidh asked, ignoring the question.

The man pulled a face, folding brawny arms across his broad chest. "Dead. His heart stopped the day before yesterday … we buried him this morning."

Cold washed over Eilidh. The grave they'd just seen— it belonged to him.

"I'm his brother, Lewis," the man went on. "The mill's mine now."

Eilidh's pulse quickened. *Lewis Bain.* Ava had told Eilidh a few tales about her grasping uncle. The brothers had been estranged, although Lewis had always coveted the mill for himself.

And now he had his wish.

"Where's Ava?" she asked. No wonder the lass hadn't attended the wedding. She only wished her friend had sent word.

Lewis Bain's thick lips compressed. "She's busy."

Eilidh drew herself up. "That may be so … but I wish to see her nonetheless."

Bain spat on the ground between them. "The slattern is scrubbing floors. Ye'll have to wait till she's done."

Will drew back his cloak, his hand resting upon the hilt of the dirk at his hip. "We'll see her now."

Bain's gaze narrowed as he took Will's measure.

Eilidh was about to inform the man that she was the clan-chief's sister-by-marriage, and Will the Captain of the Varrich Guard, when the new miller stepped backward, shouting over his shoulder. "Ava! Get out here!"

Eilidh gritted her teeth at his tone. She'd heard folk shout at disobedient dogs with more respect.

Moments later, Ava appeared, wiping wet hands upon a dirty apron. Her fingers were swollen and sore, and her eyes red-rimmed from weeping. Halting in the doorway, she squinted shortsightedly before her lips parted. "Eilidh!" Ava hurried out, giving her uncle a wide berth. "I missed yer wedding … I'm so sorry."

"This is Eilidh Munro?" Bain asked. His expression slackened a little; suddenly, he didn't look so sure of himself.

"It's Eilidh Gunn now," Will replied. His tone was casual, yet there was no mistaking the steel—the warning—just beneath.

Bain's throat bobbed.

"Don't worry about the wedding." Eilidh stepped forward, pulling her friend into a hug. "I'm so sorry about yer Da."

Ava hugged her back, her hold tight. "It was so sudden," she murmured. "One moment, he was hauling a sack of oat husks, the next, he keeled over."

"Ye should have helped him more, lazy wench," Lewis Bain drawled from behind them. "My brother's early death was no doubt due to having such a useless daughter." He grinned then. "Fear not, Lady Eilidh. I'll make sure she works hard from now on."

Eilidh's chin kicked up. "Ye shall do no such thing!"

"Eilidh," Ava gasped, drawing back, her blue eyes snapping wide. Clearly, she was afraid of her uncle. But Eilidh wasn't.

"Ava isn't yer slave," she pointed out, meeting the miller's gaze. "Ye have no right to treat her so. By rights, this is *her* mill, not yers."

Bain snorted. "The lass is as blind as a mole ... and she lacks the brawn to run this place."

Both of those observations were true enough, yet Ava flinched, all the same. The scorn in her uncle's voice wasn't tempered.

Eilidh turned to her friend, catching her hand and squeezing hard. "Ye can't stay here."

Ava stared back at her, tears welling in her eyes. The hopelessness Eilidh saw there made her chest ache. "Where else would I go?" she whispered.

"Ye've kept my niece away from her chores long enough," Bain growled then, his patience growing thin. "Ava ... get back inside."

Ava didn't move.

"Now!"

Swallowing, Ava wrested her hand from Eilidh's and moved to comply. However, Will's voice halted her. "Stop, lass ... ye aren't going back to work there. Not today. Not ever."

Eilidh's breathing caught. Her husband's handsome face was set in a hard mask, his grey eyes flinty, as he focused on the miller. "Ye shall have to get yerself someone else to order around, Bain … Ava is moving to Castle Varrich."

The miller's face turned red, his bullish jaw tightening. "Says who?"

Will's hand moved back to his dirk, and this time his fingers closed around the bone hilt. "William Gunn … Captain of the Varrich Guard." Will shifted his attention to Eilidh then, his expression softening. "There's plenty of space in our tower … Ava can have the first-floor chamber."

Loosing the breath she'd been holding, Eilidh nodded, joy quickening in her breast. It was a generous offer, a wonderful one. Her husband might be a little rough around the edges, but he was big-hearted. She'd recognized that in him, right from the start.

She then glanced over at Ava, flashing her a wide smile. Yet her friend wore a poleaxed expression; Ava was clearly finding it hard to take all this in. However, she'd realize it was all real soon enough.

"Go and fetch what belongings ye wish to bring to Varrich, Ava," Will said then, his mouth quirking into a smile. "Ye shall return with us now."

As Ava went to collect her things, Eilidh reached out and squeezed Will's hand. "Thank ye," she whispered.

"Is that all ye have?" Eilidh inclined her head, viewing the single large bag that Ava carried over her shoulder.

Her friend nodded, glancing behind her at the shadowed doorway of the mill. Inside, Lewis Bain had gone back to work, and they could hear him muttering curses under his breath. "I don't have many kirtles," Ava admitted, her cheeks pinkening. "And there are but a handful of keepsakes … and some figurines made of rosewood that Da whittled for me." She cast another glance over her shoulder, her face tensing. "I wish I could say I'm sad about leaving … but I'm not. Now Da's gone, there's nothing here for me any longer."

Eilidh nodded. Lewis Bain was a vile individual. Ava couldn't remain with him. Indeed, she need never give her uncle a moment's thought again.

Excitement danced within Eilidh at the thought of having Ava come to live with them, at being able to free her from a life of drudgery. She knew Ava didn't appreciate others interfering in her affairs, yet in this case, it was necessary. Even so, she was pleased it was Will who'd made the offer—rather than her. She was still wary of overstepping.

"Come, Ava." She linked an arm through her friend's, steering her away from the mill toward where Will stood a few yards away, waiting for them. "I can't wait to show ye yer new home."

34

THE WHOLE WORLD COULD BURN

THE AROMA OF freshly baked griddle cake drifted through the tower, making Eilidh's belly growl. It was Yuletide, and she'd deliberately not eaten anything at dawn—for the Yule banquet at noon would be a feast indeed.

And now, midday was almost upon them.

She watched as Ava poured hot honey syrup over the cooled cake. "Lord, that looks delicious," she murmured. "I could dive in right now."

Ava straightened up and flashed her a grin. "I could too ... but we must stop ourselves. This is for the clan-chief's table." Wiping her sticky hands on a damp cloth, Ava's brow wrinkled. "Do ye think it's time yet?"

Eilidh crossed to the window and rolled up the heavy sacking. Icy air gusted in, yet she braved it, sticking her head out to peer up at the sky. It was cloudy and cold enough to freeze the breath. Snow lay frozen upon the ground, and the peaks of Ben Loyal and Ben Hope glistened white this morning. However, she could see the sun's weak glow directly overhead. "Aye, nearly."

Turning, Eilidh cast her eye over Ava. A month had passed since she'd come to live with them, and already the lass was blossoming. The pretty blue kirtle she wore today revealed that her tall, bony frame had filled out a little, and there was a healthy glow to her cheeks. Eilidh had wound her friend's long golden hair into an elaborate braid earlier, while Ava had pinned Eilidh's brown locks high on her head, in a style more befitting a wedded woman.

They'd fallen into a domestic routine of late. Ava helped Eilidh keep the tower clean and tidy and had taught her how to prepare some of Will's favorite dishes. To Beth's chagrin, Eilidh had never been an able cook, and her sister's attempts to teach her had nearly always ended in them arguing.

But Eilidh's relationship with Ava was different; they weren't sisters for one, and Ava wasn't half as bossy as Beth.

Seeing the expectant look on Ava's face, Eilidh grinned. "Go on then … take the cake over to the great hall and find yerself a seat at a table. Will should be here soon, and we shall follow."

Ava didn't need to be told twice. Whipping off her apron, she picked up the bowl the cake sat in and moved toward the stairs. "See ye shortly then."

Listening to the soft scuff of Ava's footsteps as she carefully descended the stone steps, Eilidh smiled once more.

Her new life was a simple one, yet she'd never been happier. This tower was more cramped and draftier than her accommodation inside the keep, but she didn't miss her old room. She no longer had a lady's maid. Clara served Beth, as now that her sister was pregnant with her second bairn, the maid who aided her would soon need more assistance.

Eilidh turned then, her gaze traveling around the circular chamber. She and Ava had worked hard to turn what had initially been an austere space into a home. Bunches of drying herbs hung from the rafters, and colorful cushions sat upon a long wooden bench seat along one wall. Above the hearth hung Eilidh's finished tapestry, showing the view from Varrich looking north. A heavy curtain created a partition between the living space and the large bed where she and Will slept.

On the floor below, the small chamber that had once been a storeroom had been scrubbed clean so that Ava could make it her home. She was delighted to have a space of her own, and when Eilidh visited it a few days after she'd moved in, she was impressed by how homely she'd made it, with sheepskins on the floor and woolen hangings upon the walls to keep the cold at bay.

Taking off her apron, Eilidh glanced down at her kirtle. It was the color of rich plum and lined with fur, with a daring neckline—a dress she kept for special occasions. However, a heavy gold-plated chain fastened low around her hips would make it even prettier; perhaps she'd dig it out of her trunk.

"Ye look lovely, my sweet."

Eilidh turned to see Will emerge from the stairwell. He'd come straight from a watch on the walls, and his cheeks were slightly flushed from cold, his dark hair flowing loose, cascading over the fur mantle that emphasized the breadth of his shoulders. He halted on the top step, his gaze raking her head to foot in a long, hot look that made her breathing quicken.

"Thank ye, mo chridhe," she replied, her lips curving. "Ava's gone across to the keep … shall we join her?"

Will's mouth quirked in that sensual smile she knew well. "Not just yet, my bonnie wife. First … I'd like a Yuletide kiss."

Eilidh's own smile widened. "Take one, then."

Three long strides brought him from the stairwell to where Eilidh stood. He then gathered her in his arms, his mouth claiming hers. Arms linking around his neck, Eilidh parted her lips under his, welcoming his tongue. The kiss quickly turned hungry, possessive, and when Eilidh pressed her body up against his and wiggled her hips, Will groaned low in his throat.

"Ye want to start something, lass?" he growled against her mouth.

Eilidh rolled her hips once more. "Aye," she breathed.

"What about the Yuletide feast?"

"It hasn't begun yet … and no one will care if we're late."

Eilidh slid her hands under his cloak, exploring the hard columns of muscle on either side of his spine that tapered down to his tight buttocks. She squeezed him there too, boldly.

The past weeks had taught her that she had quite an appetite for her husband. The more she had of Will Gunn, the more she wanted.

Aye, earlier, she had been hungry for Yuletide treats—but now she yearned for something else.

One small hand slid over his hip and across to where an impressive erection already tented his braies.

Smiling against his mouth, Eilidh gave his rod a long, firm stroke through the material, from root to tip.

Will groaned. "Very well, wife … we're going to be late."

Drawing her with him, he moved back to the bench seat and lowered himself onto it. He then pulled her astride him.

Eilidh brought her mouth down hard on his, kissing him wildly.

Will responded in kind, holding her fast against him as their tongues dueled. Then, when they were both breathless, his mouth left hers, trailing a sensual path down her jaw and throat. He pushed down her kirtle off her shoulders, exposing her breasts to him. Despite the roaring hearth a few feet away, cold air prickled her naked skin. Yet Eilidh didn't care.

And when he started to suckle her with achingly slow determination, her groans filled the chamber.

Will knew just how to touch her, how to render her molten and wanting in his arms. Was it any wonder her belly fluttered with excitement every evening as bedtime approached?

He drew back then before raising his hands and rolling her swollen nipples between his fingers and thumbs. And when he pinched them, Eilidh writhed against him, demanding more.

Will's hands left her breasts, and he hiked up the skirts of her kirtle and lèine. His hands slid over the naked skin beneath, his fingertips leaving a trail of fire in their wake.

Eilidh's breathing now came in short, needy pants. Reaching down, she freed his rod from his braies, fisting the rock-hard length while his hands slid to the apex of her thighs, spreading her for him.

He lifted her up, the head of his shaft nudging her entrance, and then she sank down upon him—in one smooth movement.

Eilidh gasped.

This position took him deep, and the walls of her core tightened around him.

Will let out a low groan, his head falling back to rest against the wall. "God's blood, woman … ye feel incredible. Whenever I'm inside ye, the whole world could burn."

Eilidh gave an answering moan. She knew what he meant. Their coupling was so intense at times that it left them both reeling afterward. She lost herself in Will in those moments, and it was both exhilarating and terrifying.

She rode him slowly, rocking back and forth. Will aided her by gripping hold of her hips and guiding her up and down his shaft.

And despite that the fire inside their tower barely took the chill off the air this morning, sweat beaded across Eilidh's skin in a fine dew, heat enveloping her.

Will whispered encouragement to her before he shifted her hips in a slow circle.

Hot pleasure rippled out from her lower belly, and Eilidh arched against him, crying out as she peaked. Trembling, she collapsed against him, yet Will continued to move her up and down his rod, his hips lifting off the bench seat as he thrust into her.

Eilidh was lost. She buried her head in his neck, eyes closing. The walls of her core clenched around him, the intensity of her climax robbing her of breath.

"Eilidh, love!" Will's hoarse shout echoed around the tower chamber, and then wet heat spread through her loins as he spilled deep inside her.

They clung together for a long while afterward, hearts thundering, breathing labored.

Eilidh couldn't move; the torpor that flooded her body made her limbs feel as if they were made of congealed porridge. Will's arms tightened around her, and he whispered yet another endearment in her ear.

Smiling, Eilidh raised her face from where it was still buried in the crook of his neck, her hand lifting to his cheek. "We could forfeit the Yuletide banquet altogether?" she murmured. "Our bed is but a few feet away."

Will's lips curved. "Ye are a wicked woman, Eilidh Gunn … but I fear someone would come looking for us." He paused then, his cheek dimpling as the smile widened. "Besides … I don't want to miss yer sister's cooking."

Eilidh snorted. "What's wrong with mine?"

"Nothing, mo ghràdh … under Ava's guidance, ye no longer burn our suppers." His grey eyes glinted now, for he enjoyed teasing her about her attempts in the kitchen. It was true: she was improving, yet she'd never be able to cook like Beth.

Eilidh pulled a face. "Knave!"

His laughter, warm as mulled wine, rolled over her. "Aye, guilty as charged." Reaching up, he stroked her cheek. "But I'm *yer* knave."

Their gazes fused, the moment drawing out, before the corners of Eilidh's mouth lifted into a smile.

"Ye certainly are." She lowered her head, her lips brushing across his. "Now, and forever, William Gunn."

Epilogue

A PENNY FOR YER THOUGHTS

Six months later ...

THE SECOND SON to the Mackay clan-chief was born on a glorious morning toward the end of June. The lad's squalls reverberated off the walls of the birthing chamber, announcing his arrival into the world.

Standing back from the bed, next to her husband, Eilidh looked on as Tess the healer wrapped the bairn in tight swaddling and handed him over to Beth. Propped up on a nest of pillows, her cheeks flushed and damp with sweat—her sister looked exhausted. Yet this birth had been easier and much shorter than her first.

Aye, Beth was tired, yet there was no denying the joy upon her face or the fierceness in her gaze as it settled upon the mewling bundle in her arms.

Eilidh's breathing quickened at that expression—one that warned she'd claw out the heart of anyone who tried to come between her and her bairn. She wondered then if she, too, would feel that way when she gave birth. Hand straying to her belly, which had just started to swell, Eilidh felt a fluttering sensation.

She smiled. Aye, she was already bonded to the life she and Will had created. Glancing across to the doorway, her gaze alighted on where Jean stood with Robin. They both were grinning, and like Eilidh, Jean's hand rested upon her own belly. They were almost the same way along—and the healers assured them the bairns would be born around a week after Samhuinn.

"Ye did well, my love." Niel lowered himself onto the bed next to his wife, his gaze shining. He stroked Beth's cheek tenderly before his gaze dropped to his son's red, crumpled face. "Just look at him."

Beth's smile widened. "What will we call the lad? Ye were so certain we were having a daughter."

Indeed, Niel had announced at the noon meal just two days previous that the daughter Beth carried would be named Elizabeth, after his cherished wife.

Niel's mouth quirked. "John William Mackay," he replied without hesitation. The clan-chief glanced up then, his attention shifting to where John and Neave sat upon the window seat. "I named my firstborn after my father ... but I want to name my second son after two men I'd trust with my life. My cousin and" —Niel glanced over at Will then— "my friend."

John's mouth stretched into a wide smile, even as his single blue eye gleamed with emotion. "An honor indeed, thank ye, Niel."

"Aye," Will agreed before clearing his throat. Glancing up at her husband's proud profile, Eilidh saw the surprise etched upon his face. Despite his friendship with the clan-chief, he hadn't expected such a gesture. "It is."

Eilidh stepped out of the keep and raised her face to the sun. The warmth of it was a caress, and she sighed. The air was sweet with the scent of summer. Opening her eyes, she surveyed the bailey, which was busy as usual: the farrier was shoeing a horse, lads pushed wheelbarrows of muck out of the stables, and a group of Will's men were practicing with wooden broadswords, their grunts and the slap of wood ringing through the wide space.

"What glorious weather," she breathed, glancing her husband's way. "When John gets older, we shall be able to tell him he was born on the bonniest day of summer."

Next to her, Will laughed. "Aye ... too nice for working." He looked down at her then, their gazes fusing. "It's not every day someone names a bairn after me. I feel like celebrating. Do ye fancy a ride along the kyle ... we can get Ava to pack us some food, if ye like?"

Eilidh smiled up at him, happiness constricting her chest. She loved that idea. As always, life at Varrich had been busy of late. Niel had taken on ten new men-at-arms, and Will had spent the last few weeks training them. He left their tower at dawn most days, returning briefly for the noon meal before other tasks and meetings with Niel took up his afternoons.

It would be a treat, indeed, to have him to herself for today.

"Aye," she replied. "Ava and I baked some blackcurrant tarts earlier ... and we can bring fresh bread, boiled eggs, and butter."

Will flashed her a grin. "Very well ... I shall ready our horses while ye ready our feast."

A warm wind gusted in from the south, bringing with it the briny scent of salt water and the sharp tang of seaweed.

Seated upon a blanket upon the shingle shore, Eilidh folded her legs under her and leaned forward, pouring ale into cups. She then passed Will one. After their meal, he'd stretched out onto his side, propping himself up on an elbow. His courser, Dusk, and her garron, Gypsie, cropped at grass a few yards back from the shore.

High-pitched screeches caught Eilidh's attention then, and she glanced up, spying a pair of goshawks wheeling across the swathe of unbroken blue sky above.

"Whenever I see goshawks, I'm reminded of Castle Gunn," Will murmured. Eilidh glanced his way to see he, too, was watching the birds of prey. "My sister-by-marriage loves her goshawks."

There was a wistfulness in his voice that made Eilidh tense. "Do ye miss yer home, Will?" she asked. She knew what it felt like to leave one's birthplace behind and settle elsewhere; it wasn't something most Highlanders were comfortable with. She'd missed Foulis Castle fiercely for the first year of her residence at Varrich. Yet these days, she felt settled here.

"Not really," he admitted, lowering his gaze from the sky and focusing on her. "I no longer belong there … and home is where ye are, lass … ye know that."

Warmth suffused Eilidh's chest, her mood lightening once more. It was a foolish fear really, although ever since her womb had quickened, her emotions had been on a wild swing. She was more sensitive than usual.

Just yesterday, she'd dissolved in floods of tears when she'd burned the morning bannock.

Will had eaten it anyway and pronounced it delicious. She'd loved him for that.

"Ye enjoy captaining the Varrich Guard then?"

He nodded. "They weren't keen to have a Gunn lead them … but they trust me now." Will pulled a wry face then. "Well, most of them anyway."

Eilidh smiled. Indeed, the respect he'd earned was hard-won. Nonetheless, like the clan-chief, Will was a natural leader. He was fair, yet not a man to cross.

"Well, Rory has certainly taken to ye," she observed, her smile widening. "The lad follows ye about like a shadow."

Will snorted. "It's not me it's taken with … but Ava."

Eilidh arched an eyebrow. "Really?"

"Aye, he keeps asking me about her … and I caught him watching her yesterday when she was drawing water from the well. I'd say he's smitten."

Eilidh grinned. "Well, that's fine news indeed, for Ava has mentioned him twice this week." She paused then to take a sip of ale. "I'm glad … Ava has been through much. Rory's a good lad."

They fell into companionable silence then, enjoying the caress of the warm wind on their faces and the peace of the kyle shore. A few furlongs behind them, cottars worked the fields. One of them hummed a jaunty tune.

Glancing back at the workers, Eilidh thought back over the past four seasons and all the changes they'd brought.

This time last year, Will had toiled amongst those men, his ankles shackled in irons. Last June, they'd exchanged their first words, when the wind caught her shawl and carried it across the fields, straight into his arms.

It had been destiny—even if she'd noticed him months before that.

"Ye wear a mysterious smile, my love," Will said, drawing her out of her reverie. "A penny for yer thoughts."

Eilidh shifted her attention back to her husband, her gaze drinking in his slightly hawkish features, sensual mouth, and storm-grey eyes that were now watching her with rapt attention. "I was just reflecting on how curious life can be," she murmured. "Ye can never predict the twists and turns of fate, can ye?"

Will's mouth curved into a smile. "No."

"A few years ago, I believed I'd live within easy reach of Foulis Castle, if not within its walls, for the rest of my days. But instead, Beth accepted Niel Mackay's offer of marriage and brought all of us north with her." Eilidh picked up a sun-warmed pebble then, rolling it between her fingers. "I watched each of my sisters find love ... and wondered what my future held. I could have never predicted ye."

"I remember the first time I saw ye," Will replied, pushing himself up and setting aside his cup so he could reach out and take her hand. "Ye were walking into Tongue with yer sisters. I looked up from my toil and spied ye, and it was as if someone had just punched the air from my lungs." He paused, and when he continued, his voice turned husky. "I thought ye bonnie then ... yet ye have never looked lovelier than ye do today, Eilidh." His hand shifted to the gentle swell of her belly, resting there. A moment later, his eyes widened. "I felt something ... a kick against my palm."

"Aye, he's a wriggler."

Will inclined his head. "Who's to say we'll have a lad?"

Eilidh grinned. "So Niel isn't the only one who longs for a daughter?"

Will's gaze softened, his free hand cupping her face. "No ... I grew up being pummeled by my elder brothers; I would have liked to have a sister to protect instead. I wouldn't mind a brood of daughters ... like yer father was blessed with."

Eilidh laughed, even though his words made joy squeeze at her ribcage. "I'm not sure he always found it a blessing," she admitted with a rueful smile. "Especially when we fought like cats." She sobered then, covering his hand that cupped her belly with hers. "But whether this bairn is a lad or a lass, they will be loved, and that's what matters."

The End

FROM THE AUTHOR

I hope you enjoyed the fourth, and final, installment in the COURAGEOUS HIGHLAND HEARTS series.

I admit I do love those Gunn brothers. I had so much fun writing Alex and Tavish's stories in the previous series—and Will's tale was no different. I adore his resilience, and his arrogance, and enjoyed seeing how he changes throughout the story. Eilidh, too, has quite a character arc. She starts out as a girlish, romantic dreamer but ends up being a woman to be reckoned with.

Sisterly bonds are central to this story (and the whole series), but Eilidh's friendship with Ava was also a special one. When creating Ava's character, I wanted to explore what it would be like for someone with terrible eyesight to live back in the 15th Century. I'm seriously shortsighted (-7.00 in both eyes), and without my contact lenses, I'd view life as a blur. Eilidh and Ava have very different upbringings, but their friendship transcends social class.

This was another slow-burn romance (HIGHLANDER TEMPTED was one of those too!). Sometimes it takes a lot of water under the bridge before my couple gets together—but I love the chemistry in slow-burn romances, and when Eilidh and Will finally get together, it's volcanic. I hope you'll agree, it was worth the wait!

Eilidh and Will's wedding took place on November 25, which has special significance for me—for it's the date this author married her editor!

Jayne x

HISTORICAL NOTES

Like HIGHLANDER HEALED, I don't have lengthy historical notes for this book. However, there are some details you might find interesting, as I certainly did!

Unlike Niel Mackay and John Mackay of Aberach—my previous two heroes who were actual historical figures—William Gunn, like Robin Mackay, is entirely fictional. There aren't any real battles or historical events in this story either, although the tension between the Mackays and the Sutherlands did exist during this period.

Robert Sutherland was the Sutherland clan-chief at the time. As stated in the novel, he sided with the Neilson-Mackays and fought alongside them against the Mackays at the Battle of Drumnacoub in 1433. Sutherland was sore about the defeat and blamed John Mackay for it.

However, I've taken some liberty with history in my story. The battle at Lochnaver was entirely fictional, although Niel Mackay did gift that land to John Mackay in thanks for his loyalty while Niel was incarcerated at Bass Rock.

The seat of the Sutherland clan was Dunrobin Castle, which features briefly in this story. The castle visible today looks very different to how it would have appeared in the Medieval period. The current castle was likely built on the site of an early medieval fort. The earliest part of the building dates from around 1275. Overlooking Dornoch Firth, Dunrobin Castle is thought to be named after Robert Sutherland, 6th Earl of Sutherland, himself.

Most of this novel takes place at Castle Varrich. This fortress was the seat of the Mackays. Built out of sandstone, the castle perches upon a high point of rock, overlooking both the Kyle of Tongue and the village of

Tongue. The castle's precise origins and age are unknown, although some historians believe it is over a thousand years old, and the medieval castle may have been built atop a Norse fort. The original castle had two floors, plus an attic. The ruin is located around one hour's walk away from the village of Tongue. It has views of the mountains Ben Hope and Ben Loyal.

During the novel, we take a brief trip to Castle Gunn, a real location. The fortress, also known as Gunn's Castle and Clyth Castle, is situated on a rock above the sea, eight miles southwest of Wick, Caithness. It was once a splendid and strong castle. Sadly, virtually nothing remains of it these days.

I hope you have enjoyed my notes—brief as they are! I really enjoyed researching the history and landscape of this wild and beautiful corner of Scotland.

COURAGEOUS HIGHLAND HEARTS CHARACTER GLOSSARY

The Mackay clan

The Mackays of Varrich
Beth Mackay (neè Munro—Niel's wife)
Niel Mackay (Mackay clan-chief)
Angus Mackay (Beth and Niel's son)

The Mackays of Farr
Connor Mackay (Mackay chieftain—laird of Farr Castle), married to Keira (they have three children: Rose, Rory, and Quinn)
Morgan Mackay (Connor's brother), married to Maggie (they have one daughter, Tara)
Jaimee Mackay (Connor's sister), married to Alexander Gunn (they have two children, Anice and Aodhan)
Kennan Mackay (Connor Mackay's cousin), married to Cait (they have two sons, Blake and Logan)

The Mackays of Loch Stach
Hugh Mackay (Mackay chieftain—laird of Loch Stach)

The Mackays of Aberach
John Mackay (Mackay chieftain—laird of Achness—Mackay clan-chief's cousin)
Neave Mackay (John's wife)
Lyla Mackay (John and Neave's daughter)

The Mackays of Melness
Robin Mackay (Mackay chieftain—laird of Melness broch)
Jean Mackay (Robin's wife)
Grace Mackay (Robin Mackay's daughter)

The Mackays of Balnakeil
Breac Mackay (Mackay chieftain—laird of Balnakeil broch)
Janneth Mackay (Breac's wife)

The Mackays of Dun Ugadale
Iver Mackay (Mackay chieftain—laird of Dun Ugadale)
Lennox, Kerr, and Brodie (Iver's younger brothers)

The Gunn clan
Tavish Gunn (clan-chief)
Robina (Tavish's wife)
Knox, Mungo, Laurie, and Finn (Tavish and Robina's sons)
Roy, Blair, Evan, and William Gunn (Tavish's younger brothers)

The Munro clan
George Munro (Munro clan-chief)
Laila Munro (the clan-chief's wife)
Fionn Munro (the clan-chief's son)
Eilidh (pronounced Ay-lee) Munro (the clan-chief's daughter)

The Sutherland clan
Robert Sutherland (Sutherland clan-chief)

Other characters
Ewan Reay (Captain of the Varrich Guard)
Ava Bain (the miller's daughter in Tongue)
Cormac Bain (the miller)
Lewis Bain (the miller's brother)

ABOUT THE AUTHOR

Multi-award-winning author Jayne Castel writes epic Historical and Fantasy Romance. Her vibrant characters, richly researched historical settings, and action-packed adventure romance transport readers to forgotten times and imaginary worlds.

Jayne is the author of a number of best-selling series. In love with all things Scottish, she writes romances set in both Dark Ages and Medieval Scotland.

When she's not writing, Jayne is reading (and re-reading) her favorite authors, cooking Italian feasts, and going on long walks with her husband. She lives in New Zealand's beautiful South Island.

Connect with Jayne online:
www.jaynecastel.com
www.facebook.com/JayneCastelRomance
https://www.instagram.com/jaynecastelauthor/
Email: contact@jaynecastel.com